Anteater

James Rosenthal

ISBN: 0998334901
ISBN-13: 978-0998334905

To Chell

Chapter 1

The grizzled old fox looked out over the desert valley, a paw at his brow to shield his eyes from the setting sun. Jess stayed back a dozen meters from the ledge on which her trainer stood, shivering as she leaned against their buggy. The once scorching sands had already relinquished their heat to the night sky. Despite his age and circulation issues, her mentor didn't appear to be the least bit chilly. He stood rigid with eyes fixed—on what, Jess could not say.

A rapping from the other side of the buggy drew her attention to the anteater drumming his paws on the steel hood. Ray, her brother, was only a year older than her but already at least a dozen centimeters taller. For an anteater his age his muscles were impressively toned, the fruits of many hours of rigorous training, but Jess knew he was still not nearly as strong as his smug demeanor would suggest. The hair on his back grew wild and unkempt, enough so to make Jess wonder whether he would actually make good on his promise to get it trimmed upon graduation.

"Hey, quiet!" she said, trying to her voice down. "Enough with the drumming."

"Really, Jess?" he said. "Is the noise that bothersome? I think Mast is too old to care."

"He can still hear you. He's sharper than he looks."

"I know. I didn't say he couldn't hear. I said he doesn't care."

"Are you serious, Ray?" asked Jess. "We crossed the salt pan into hostile territory. For all we know, there could be a pack or two in earshot right now. You really think Mast wouldn't be the least bit concerned about you telegraphing our location?"

Ray raised his eyebrows and then tapped on the buggy again. He raised his finger to do it a second time, but Jess glared at him until he withdrew it. Still, his challenging look never left his face.

"Mast isn't afraid of a few wolves. He knows that if they try to attack us, we'll kick their asses. That's why we came here in the first place, isn't it?"

Jess took too long to respond, and Ray gave her a smirk.

"Figures," he said. "And I thought you were as excited to come here as I was. Haven't we been training for this trip for years? Aren't you tired of only beating up bums who think they can try their luck at a sparring tournament?"

"We've had plenty of worthy opponents," said Jess. "What about all those veteran soldiers? What about Edward's former operatives?"

"Please, you know we surpassed all of them long ago. The only one left in the Fox Nation who's any match for us is that old timer over there."

The 'old timer' had not moved from his spot. Not even a twitch of the ear betrayed him, until suddenly he extended a finger toward the horizon.

"There," he said.

"Where?" Jess and her brother walked over to him.

"Out over yonder," said the fox. "There's a pack of wolves heading due south."

Ray squinted. "I don't see anything."

"And they don't see you either—which is how it's going to stay until precisely the moment we decide to engage them—if we decide to engage them."

"Why wouldn't we engage them? That's why we're here."

Mast sighed. "Fret not, child. You'll wet your fists with wolf blood before our stay is up. However, I might advise you to pick a weaker pack than this one. They travel the Highway of Fangs, a road with access to the best hunting grounds reserved only for the strongest packs. If that pack down there were anything but the best, insulted alpha packs would have wiped them out long ago."

"Come on, Mast," said Ray. "We can take them."

"Have it your way. I'll be keeping a close eye on you in case anything should go awry. I'll leave you with that, along with my warning not to underestimate them."

"We understand," said Jess. "There's an entire pack of them. It won't be the same as fighting one on one."

"It's more than that," said Mast. "You haven't faced opponents as savage as these."

Ray paused. "They're just wolves. They're pre-ops."

"Oh, so you have a chat with the sheep collecting your garbage and you think you understand pre-ops? Wolves are nothing like anything you've seen before.

"Let me make it simple for you. On the top of the ladder, you've got us, the formal operationals. The Quaternity. The big four. Monkeys, foxes, bears, and anteaters. Capable of creative thinking and abstract reasoning. The founders and leaders of the civilized world. They'll tell you that we're the next rung down from the gods, but don't let that go to your head. You cut us open and we'll bleed and die just like the rest of them.

"After that come of the concrete operationals. Not much to worry about here. Still smart enough to use proper grammar, but you probably wouldn't hire them to be research scientists.

"And finally, you have the pre-operationals. Barely a step above the wild animals. They can talk, and they can use things that better people have made, but that's it. Most are docile; wolves are not. Most have integrated themselves into our society; the wolves have not. Most understand the consequences of attacking a formal; the wolves do not. And conversely, the thing most formals don't understand about pre-ops is that they're more than just a dumbed down version of ourselves. When our ancestors developed the capacity for art and mathematics, they had to make a trade-off. To create space for their more highly-evolved attributes, they gave up certain amounts of intuition, connection to nature, and primal drive. The wolves haven't separated themselves from these things yet, and if you meet one in battle, you will come face to face with a ferocity the likes of which you've never seen."

Jess waited until their master gave her a nod before she spoke. "If what you say is true, how should we fight them?"

"I'm not saying don't use your brain," said Mast. "It's the best asset you have, and if you can trick them or fake them out, you should. Your technique will serve you well, but there will come a time when the only option is to fight ferocity with ferocity. We suppress our primal selves in our day to day lives, but buried down somewhere we have that savage animal drive too, just like the wolves do.

"Your grandfather understood that better than anyone. Everyone knows that Anton mastered the Temple's martial arts, and I've told you how he also learned the brawling discipline of the ancient Arnold the Ogre King. What I haven't told you yet is that he spent years studying the fighting styles of pre-ops too. He understood when to enter the battlefield calm and collected and when to let the adrenaline flow freely. I imagine he was half a wolf himself the day of his escape, when he struck down a hundred monkey priests and countless bear traitors. He taught me to learn from my enemies, and you would be wise to do the same."

The fox went back over to the buggy and grabbed the edge by the steel frame.

"Enough talk," he said. "If you still want to intercept that pack, we need to get moving."

The sun had long since disappeared by the time they had piled into the car, driven down the mountain, and found a suitable location to make their challenge. A glow in the west was all that remained to light their makeshift arena. The Highway of Fangs, little more than a dirt road, cut through an uneven field of boulders, each tall enough to hide someone.

Mast gave them a short lecture about facing their enemies in the dark of the night, and elaborated on the merits of learning to trust their other senses and their intuition. Next, he gave them a final time check, estimating that they had about five minutes before the arrival of the wolves. Finally, he left them with his assurance that he wouldn't be far and that he would monitor the situation and come to their aid if need be. With that, he jumped back into the buggy and disappearing into the darkness.

Then the Anteaters were alone. They stood, side by side, staring down the Highway of Fangs as the last hints of sunlight disappeared. They waited in silence for the first few minutes, listening for the first signs of their approaching attackers. Jess's heart started to race, and the familiar sensation she often had before a sparring match began to creep over her body.

"I thought they'd be here by now," Ray finally said.

"They'll be here soon," said Jess. "We just need to listen."

"I don't hear anything. Maybe they stopped to rest."

"Or maybe they're all around us already."

"I doubt it. I wouldn't give them that much credit. If Mast wanted us to fight animals, why didn't he just have us fight hippos or lions? We could have just gone to the zoo."

"They're not animals, they're wolves."

"Sure," said Ray. "We'll see if you feel the same way after the fight. That is, if they ever show up."

A vicious snarl broke through the quiet. Something burst out from behind one of the nearest boulders and lunged at them. Even in the dim light, Jess could make out the outline of a wolf.

As startled as he was, Ray collected himself in time to swing his foot in an arc, striking the wolf across the forehead for an instant knockout. As soon as he had, another wolf charged at them from the shadows, and then another, and another.

The ensuing fight was a blur in Jess's mind. In her prior duels, she had meticulously chosen every strike, every block, and every counter to masterfully undo her opponent. Not here. Here, when faced with a sea of claws and teeth, the drive to fight and survive took over. Her body moved on its own, carrying out the techniques she had committed to muscle memory, executing them with a frenzy she had not known herself to possess.

When she could feel herself breathe again, she stood beside a pile of battered wolves. Ray stood next to a pile of his own. His body had become a mess of bruises and claw marks, but he had a huge grin plastered across his face.

"How was that for battle experience?" he said. "We showed them!"

"You die now!" came another yell from the dark. A final wolf leapt out at them, his teeth homing in on Ray's neck.

"Ray! Look out!"

Jess jumped in between them, and her fist struck hard against the wolf's temple. She felt something beneath her knuckles shift as the wolf fell to the ground like a ragdoll.

"Holy shit!" said Ray, clutching his neck. "That was close. Are you all right, Jess?"

"Yes, I'm fine." She wasn't looking at the other anteater. Her eye was on the wolf, who wasn't moving.

"Jess?"

She turned back to her brother and threw her arms around him.

She buried her face into his shoulder, squeezing tight as she did.

"Hey, I'm here, Jess," he said. "Everything's going to be fine."

"I know," she said. "I know."

She broke the embrace and they stood face to face for a moment.

"We did great," said Ray. "Now come on, we need to find Mast before more wolves show up."

"You got it," said Jess. "Let's get the hell out of here."

Chapter 2

"If you will, look up at the night sky. Can you make out those tiny lights above? Can you see any of those little specks in the distance? They say each speck consists of a million million suns like our own, each with its own planets. Just think. There are countless worlds out there in the deep reaches of space, countless worlds just waiting for someone to explore them."

At first she humored him and looked up. True, she could see the specks, but she failed to see what looked so interesting about them. They were just dots, nothing more. She felt a chuckle build in her belly, but she managed to contain it.

He turned to her. "Well? What do you think?"

"I'm sorry," she said. "I'm just a little distracted right now."

"Distracted? With what?"

"I was thinking about that training exercise three years ago. Do you remember when Mast took us to fight the wolves?"

"Of course I remember," he said. "Why is that on your mind now?"

"I don't know," she said. She took in a moment to breathe in the stillness of the night. "What were you doing just now anyway? Were you rehearsing a speech?"

"No, I was just talking about the night sky."

"Ray, no one talks like that."

"Well, excuse me," said Ray. "I just can't help but feel poetic when I look at something this beautiful."

"What's so beautiful about a bunch of dots?"

"The beauty is in knowing they're more than just dots. Each one—"

"Yeah, yeah, each one contains millions of worlds just like our own. So what? You want to go explore them all?"

"Wish I could. Unfortunately, they say it would take several million years just to reach the closest one, so I think we're stuck on Earth for now."

"So why bother looking at them?"

He sighed. "Jess, you're no fun."

"No," said Jess, "staring at the sky is no fun."

"Whatever," said Ray. "I don't know why I bother showing you anything cool. Come on, we should get moving if we want to catch the show."

"I'm all ready to go," she said. "You're the one who brought me out here."

"Did you feed the rabbit already?"

"Yes! You're the one who wanted a pet, and somehow I always wind up being the one who has to feed her."

"All right, calm down. I'll go get the lights. Meet me by the car."

As he shuffled back towards the house, Jess stood under the sky for a moment longer. Sure, it wasn't much to look at, but there was something to be said for the peace and tranquility. She took a deep breath, finding that she enjoyed the warm summer breeze on her skin, the massage of grass beneath her feet, the gentle buzz of insects in the trees and bushes. Her stomach growled. She should have eaten a bigger dinner. Perhaps there would be concessions at the show.

The light in the front window went out, and she walked back around the lawn and onto the driveway. An involuntary smile cracked across her face as she laid eyes on her baby. Her baby boasted a perfect coat of red, complete with a black racing stripe down the center. She ran her hand over the finish, admiring its smooth feel.

She heard the front door slam and the screen door rattle. The wooden planks of the porch creaked as a shadow moved closer.

"Are we taking the new car?" asked Ray. "We can take the beater instead if you'd rather not get this one all dusty."

"No, let's take it," said Jess. "It's no good just sitting in the driveway."

Ray nodded. "An inaugural drive it is."

He tossed her the keys and she unlocked the doors with a click of a button. She sat down on the leather seat, turned the ignition, and let the motor hum to life.

Ray jumped into the passenger seat. "Hey, don't leave without me."

"I wish."

She shifted into gear and fed the engine some power. The car responded with a whispered purr and shot forward, down the driveway and off into the night.

Jess smirked. "Best fifty thousand I've ever spent."

"The promotion sure has its perks."

"We'll have to think of a name for him. Something ending in 'mobile' I think."

"The Eatermobile?"

"No, that's stupid."

There are nights when a town is hopping, nights when everyone makes plans to go out and the streets come alive with laughs and muffled music. Tonight was not one of those nights. Half of the houses they passed had already gone dark, and even the downtown avenue met them with an almost eerie silence, without so much as a homeless dog strolling the sidewalks. Nights like these were the ones Jess loved, and if she couldn't spend them at home, then catching a movie was the next best thing.

"What's playing at the drive-in tonight?" she asked.

"Just the new Mr. Explorer flick."

"Oh barf."

"What? You love Mr. Explorer."

"Maybe when I was a kid. Are you sure there's nothing else playing?"

"Do you feel like waiting two hours for the next show?"

"No."

"That's what I thought," said Ray. "Besides, we should be supporting domestic cinema, not to mention this film stars one of our own."

"Supporting domestic cinema would be easier if our country knew how to make movies. I don't think our society would collapse if I caught a screening of High Mountain Pass."

"Good movie."

"I thought so. Does it really matter that it's from the East?"

Ray sighed. "I just thought this would be fun. We've been training hard all week and this outing sounded like a nice break. Would you rather just go back home?"

She shook her head. "No, let's go see it."

The top edge of the giant screen loomed over the fence as they neared the lot. Brake lights flared ahead, but the line wasn't nearly as long as it usually was. She reasoned the movie had its mediocre reviews to thank for that.

Jess paid the attendant at the gate and then wheeled around to find a good spot, being careful not to kick up dust from the gravel surface. Plenty of space was still open, so she snagged a spot right in the middle.

"Perfect," said Ray. "We're right on time too."

"I suddenly feel really tired," said Jess. "What a week. So much training."

"I hear you. The training was great and all, but it's no substitute for real battle experience."

"Is that all you think about?" she asked. "You must be at least a little wiped out. The exhaustion just hit me. I may doze off."

"If you do, I'll give you a kick."

"If you do, I'll kick you back. Leave me be."

A knock on the driver side window made her jump. Someone was there, holding a small barrel in both hands. She rolled down the window.

"Hello," the stranger said. "I was just wondering if I could bring you anything before our feature—"

She paused when she got a better look at her customers.

"I'm sorry," she said. "We currently don't have any ants or termites."

"Are you serious?" asked Jess.

"If you want, I could check the storage unit again," she said. "Maybe I could find something for you and your boyfriend."

Jess scowled. "For your information, he's my brother."

With only an uncomfortable nod, the vendor turned around and left. Jess rolled the window back up.

"Charming as always," said Ray.

"Shut up." She punched him in the shoulder.

"Ow! You said you wouldn't do that unless I did it first."

"That was regarding kicking, dummy. I reserve the right to punch at will."

The floodlights dimmed, and the screen flickered to life. Much to her dismay, Jess found herself unable to nod off. It made no sense; she was certainly tired enough, her leather seat was comfy as it could be, and the movie was as devoid of content as they come.

The airplane on the big screen cruised at high altitude with the hero gazing out over the frozen landscape.

"Are you sure you're up for this, Mr. Explorer? Your landing window is only ten meters wide, and you'll be jumping right into enemy fire. It's not too late to turn back. No one asked you to do this."

Mr. Explorer turned to the crew chief, a serious glare plastered across his face. A rush of air blew in from the open cargo bay door, and his smooth fur blew in the breeze.

"No one asked me to do this, but I'm the only one who can," he said. "They may not say it, but everyone is counting on me. Kristen is counting on me."

He reached into his belt and pulled out a locket with a picture of his sweetheart. There was a close-up on Mr. Explorer's face as he gazed longingly at the image. Then the locket slammed shut and his eyes shot back up.

"Let's do this."

And with that, Mr. Explorer took a deep breath and leapt out the hatch. As the plane disappeared behind him and he dove toward the frozen landscape below, all Jess could think of was the quality of his thermals. He must have been freezing.

The first Mr. Explorer film had been all right. It was cheesy, yes, but charmingly so. It featured Mr. Explorer traveling east to infiltrate a shrine, which turned out to be a cover for an enemy training station. The baddies were planning an invasion, and it was up to him to save the day. The film boasted only low-budget special effects, but with a competent director it added up into an honest worthwhile movie.

The second had been a lazy carbon copy of the first, and Jess didn't even remember what the third had been about. The latest installment had thus far proved to be the worst of the bunch. Mr. Explorer's newest mission was to investigate some northern research lab, which, of course, turned out to be no ordinary research lab. Even that much was all well and good, but the pacing was all wrong and the writing was just ridiculous.

Juan was a decent actor, or at least he did the best he could with his terrible lines. The guy who played the villain, however, was awful. He was some Tromian actor, which made sense, considering the setting, but this 'actor' had no idea how to act. What made things even worse was knowing that someone had approved this footage.

Their hero on the big screen had made it safely to the ground.

"Not so fast, Mr. Explorer."

Mr. Explorer spun around.

"Boss Evil. I thought I might find you here."

"And I was hoping you would pay me a visit." Boss Evil waved his hand and a dozen thugs appeared behind him. "I'm afraid your days of adventuring are over."

"I don't think so," said Mr. Explorer. "I'm not going down without a fight."

"Fool!" Boss Evil pointed a finger at his adversary. "Dispose of him."

With that, a wide grin spread out over Boss Evil's face, exposing his shiny white teeth. Finally, he leaned back and laughed maniacally.

Jess could only shake her head in disbelief. How could any movie do something like this and take itself seriously? In the real world, there were only two kinds of villains: those who believed they did good, and those who didn't care. No one actually liked being evil for the sake of being evil.

Now the screen was ablaze with another fight scene. Jess yawned; after years of real combat training, everything here looked so fake. Her brother somehow seemed into it, but that was his problem.

She heard something else behind the punches and explosions on the big screen. It sounded like some sort of beeping and it didn't sound like it was part of the movie. Was the noise coming from her car?

She cracked the door open and poked her head outside.

"Jess? What are you doing?"

"Shhh!"

Her ears perked; it was louder now. She stepped out of the car and stood still, listening.

"Come on, Jess, you're going to miss the movie."

Ignoring him, she lowered herself to the ground and took a peek under the car. Something was there. A large, metallic bump protruded from under the fuel tank, with a tiny red light flashing with every beep.

She could not say when the jolt of terror hit her.

"Ray! Get out of the car!"

"What?"

She lunged into the driver side, grabbed him by the wrist, and yanked him out of the car. Ray nearly fell over, his knee scraping the gravel as he struggled to find his feet. Jess kept running, brother in tow.

"Jess, what's going on?"

Jess didn't answer. She pushed him to the ground and then dove beside him, covering her head.

The explosion shook the lot, short-circuiting the projector and shattering the windows of the nearby cars. Jess could see the burst of orange through her squeezed eyelids, and she could feel the surge of heat on her skin. Something grazed her shoulder—glass maybe, but she could tell the cut was superficial.

She looked up, trying to find her bearings through her blurred eyes and ringing ears. The lot had become a chaotic mess of screams and car alarms. Some patrons huddled behind their wheels, some stepped out for a closer look, and some ran. Yet one in particular caught her eye; on the far corner of the lot, a bear scaled the fence.

"Jess? Jess?" Her brother shook her shoulder. "Are you all right?"

"I'm fine." She pointed at the bear making his getaway. "There. It was him."

Ray followed her finger. "I see him."

"Let's go."

She jumped to her feet, fighting off a wave of dizziness. She took off across the lot, vaulting over the hood of a minivan, Ray following close behind. An overweight customer teetered in their way, but Jess ducked around him.

Jess leapt onto the fence, clasped the top in her hands, and hoisted herself up. She paused for a moment on her perch, scanning the block. Several streetlights had burnt out, but something still moved through the shadows. The bear hadn't gotten far.

"This way."

She hopped down onto the grass, and Ray touched ground beside her.

"See if you can get him to turn right at the next block," he said. "I'm going to circle around and cut him off."

Ray shot off in one direction while Jess sprinted after the target. He was fast for a bear, maybe even faster than Jess. She blitzed over the grass, road, and back onto the sidewalk, keeping him in sight.

She couldn't tell if she was gaining on him, and the next corner was coming up fast. Jess veered to the left, running out onto the road, hoping to persuade him to take a right turn. Sure enough, the bear noticed her and disappeared around the upcoming corner.

A jarring honk blared through the night. Jess saw the headlights and only had an instant to dive back onto the sidewalk before a truck sped through the intersection. The truck shouldn't have taken Jess so long to notice; she was still disoriented from the blast.

Jess needed a moment to recover, during which the bear gained some ground. She bolted after him again, faster than before. After a minute, he ran beneath a streetlight. She got a better look at his belt and from what she could tell, he was unarmed.

A shadow swept in from the right. Ray landed a perfect tackle, driving his shoulder into the bear's side and knocking him from his feet. They rolled over the grass and onto the road, coming to a stop with Ray's knee over his foe's chest. Her brother looked up at her and gave her a grin.

Had he not been so cocky, Ray might have seen the bear's fist coming at him. The bear knocked Ray to the side and shoved him away. He stood up to face Jess, looking as though he was unsure whether to run or fight.

As if to give him an answer, Jess launched her fist into his face, striking him across the cheek and sending him staggering backwards. He recovered much faster than she thought he would, throwing a punch of his own back at her. Too late to dodge, Jess took the hit in the shoulder, absorbing the blow.

She fell back against a parked car, setting off its alarm. Pushing back against it, Jess launched herself into the air and at her foe. She spun around, bringing her leg in an arc and delivering a brutal blow to his head.

The bear fell to his knees, and tried to step back to his feet, but Ray was there as soon as he did. He took the bear by his arm and flung him to the ground, this time not letting go. Ray twisted the bear's wrist with one hand, and with the other, he grabbed him by the shoulder.

"You're not going anywhere," he said.

Finally, Jess caught her breath and got a better look at their foe. He was taller than either of the siblings, but still about average for a bear. He didn't appear particularly muscular, but it was hard to tell through all of the thick fur.

"Hey! What's going on over there?"

Two fox cops had left their vehicle and were heading over with flashlights. Jess waved them over.

"It's him," she said. "The one who bombed our car."

One of the officers shot Ray a look, and Ray let go and stepped off. The cop reached for his handcuffs and then paused and looked at his partner.

"What are you waiting for?" asked Ray. "Arrest him."

"I don't think so," said the bear.

He pushed himself to his knees and then lifted himself to his feet. He reached for something from his belt; Jess prepared to lunge at him, but it was only a badge.

"You can't arrest me," said the bear. "I'm a Council agent. I answer to them."

The cop studied the badge, nodded, and loosened his grip on the handcuffs.

"We're sorry to bother you, Sir—"

"Not so fast," said Ray. He whipped out a badge of his own, and his sister did the same. "I'm Anteater Ray and this is my sister, Anteater Jess. We're Presidential agents. Proceed with the arrest."

The other cop walked over for a closer look at their badges. He turned to his partner.

"These check out."

The first cop let out an exasperated sigh and reached for the handcuffs again.

"Sorry, buddy." He fastened the bear's wrists behind his back. "I'll have to ask you to come with us."

As the police secured the bear, Ray and Jess put their badges away and turned to each other.

"What screwed up councillor would choose that guy as an agent?" asked Ray.

"I don't know," said Jess, "but that councillor will have to answer to our boss."

Their suspect restrained, the cops began to lead the bear back to their cruiser. Before he disappeared into the back seat, the bear turned to the siblings and flashed a malicious smile.

"This isn't over, Anteaters," he said. "I'll be seeing you again."

In that moment, Jess found she couldn't turn away from the bear's menacing grin. Something about him unsettled her. There was something about the way he bared his shiny white teeth, something about the sparkle in his eyes, that seemed almost unreal.

And that was when the bear reeled back and laughed.

Chapter 3

They made their way down the hall, but the secretary stopped them before they could reach the door.

"Species, family name, given name." He pointed to a form on his desk.

"Come on, Stewart." said Ray. "You know who we are."

"Species, family name, given name."

"What is this, a library?"

"What's that supposed to mean?" asked Jess.

"We've never had to sign in here before," said Ray. "Edward told us to be here at this time, so here we are."

"The president will be ready to see you shortly," said Stewart. "Now if you would like to see him, I suggest you sign in and wait."

"I just told you that he instructed us to be here now."

The secretary removed his glasses. "And sir, I just told you that he's busy."

"Sorry for the trouble, Stewart." Jess took the pen and signed 'Anteater Lee Jessica.' "We'll be happy to wait."

"Thank you, Jess. As I said, he'll see you in a minute. The president is having a very important meeting with the councillor from the Second Province."

"I appreciate it," said Jess. "We'll be here."

Ray signed his name as well, and the Anteaters stepped towards the window as an intern carrying a heap of files ran past them. They leaned back against the wall and listened to the building, abuzz with ringing phones, footsteps, and occasional shouting. Jess stared down at the rug while Ray peeked out the window to the garden and street below. He turned to her.

"So, an unscheduled meeting with a councillor."

"What about it?"

"You don't suppose this councillor is the same one who hired that bear? Edward might be in there doling out some pain."

"Maybe," said Jess. "But did he say the Second Province? Aren't they the ones who elected the horse as their new councillor?"

"Oh, that's right," said Ray. "What was her name? I don't remember."

"Me neither. Would that even make sense? Why would she want us dead?"

"I don't know."

Jess thought back to the other night, remembering the bear's grin and laugh. He did not have the manner of a lackey on someone's errand; this bear enjoyed the spectacle all too much.

The door swung open and a flaxen brown mare walked out. She was an older horse, with bags under her eyes and strands of hair breaking loose from her combed mane. As soon as she was out the door, her eyes fell on the Anteaters.

"And who might you two be?"

Jess stood up straight and Ray did the same. He started to extend his hand for a handshake, but his sister gave him a hard nudge.

"I'm Anteater Jess, and this is my brother, Anteater Ray." She extended her left foot towards the councillor and tapped the floor twice.

The horse stared at the Anteater's foot for a second, and then extended her front hoof and did the same. "You're the first Anteaters I've seen in here."

Ray followed suit with the foot gesture. "We're here to see the president."

"So you're the old friends he was planning to meet with? I see how our president spends his time. I, however, have none. Good day to you."

She walked down the hall and disappeared into the crowd of staffers.

"Stewart!" A voice blasted from the open door. "She's gone! Are the Anteaters here yet?"

"Yes, they are," said the secretary. "You do know you can use the phone."

"Well, what are you waiting for? Send them in!"

Stewart gave the Anteaters a reluctant nod, and the Anteaters walked into the office, letting the door close behind them. They found themselves in a spacious room with a large rug sprawled across the floor. The rug boasted the presidential coat of arms against a background of Fox Nation blue. The vast wall window opposite them offered an impressive view of the city and allowed the rays of the sun to pour in across the rug and mahogany desk.

Behind that desk sat a large and burly Fox. He was nearly as tall as the Anteaters, and he was quite a bit thicker in most places. His wavy hair parted down the middle of his head, allowing them to see his grin. Someone might mistake his look for that of a sleazy politician, but the Anteaters, who had known him long before his debut in politics, knew better.

Edward stood up and motioned for them to come closer. "Come on in, Anteaters," he said. "How do you like the new office? Quite an upgrade, isn't it?"

"It's very nice, Mr. President," said Jess.

"Hey, none of that 'Mr. President' garbage with me." He shook a finger at them. "With the two of you I'm Edward, or Uncle Edward if you're feeling sentimental. I have to put up with all this protocol nonsense from my staff and the media. I sure as hell don't need it from you two."

"Our apologies," said Ray, "Uncle Edward."

Edward chuckled. "Now that's what I like to hear. Please, sit down."

"That horse you were talking to," said Jess, "who was she?"

"The latest pain in my ass," said Edward. "That was Councillor Helen from the Second Province. I'm sorry to have kept you two waiting on account of her. She barged in and demanded a meeting, even though I insisted I was booked. She wouldn't listen, as if were against her principles to show courtesy to a formal like me. For goodness' sake, there's nothing empowering about poor manners."

"Was it she?" asked Ray. "Was she the one who hired that bear?"

"What? No, she was only here to spew the same Horseshoe crap she always does." Edward chuckled again. "That's a funny way you phrased that, Ray. It sounds like you're suggesting someone *hired* that bear to kill off my agents. The Council is not some circle of feudal lords scheming to murder each other to win the crown. They'll steal my office through slander, not assassination. If things were that bad here in the Fox Nation, we might as well give up and go back to the Monkeys."

"I know, but all the same, which one hired the guy who attacked us?"

"You're lucky my position allows me access to such information," said Edward. "It was Fox Tammy—I'm sorry, *Councillor* Tammy."

Ray nodded. "I've heard that name."

"I'm sure you've heard me rant about her if you haven't already seen her on the news. She's the councillor from the Tenth Province, a staunch Developmentalist credited with most of the recent economic reforms. She always runs a strong campaign; it's fair to say she's my biggest political rival. Hell, everyone expected the Council to appoint her as the next president, but as you can see, that's not how it turned out. I guess there's still enough fear of another Monkey invasion that they decided an old soldier like me was more fit for the job."

"So she has a reason to dislike you."

"Again, I doubt she had anything to do with the attack."

"You think the bear acted on his own?"

"I agree with Edward," said Jess. "That bear wanted to be there. He was the one who wanted us dead."

"How could you tell?"

"He just gave me this feeling."

"He's a Council agent," said Ray. "Are you suggesting he goes around offing people on the side? That wouldn't be very good for his career."

"I'm sure Tammy will take some heat when this reaches the press," said Edward. "Or so I can hope. Anyway, before you speculate any more, how about I read you his files? We do keep information about our agents."

"Oh right," said Ray. "That makes sense."

Edward reached into his file cabinet and pulled out and opened a thin folder. "There's not as much as I'd like, but it's something. His name is Bear Theo, but it seems he sometimes just goes as 'the Bear.' Real creative, I know. It doesn't say anything about his parents, but it does say he was born here in the Fox Nation. He spent some of his childhood across the channel in the Bear Nation, training to fight alongside their warriors, but later returned to the mainland. Believe it or not, he's an alumnus of your own Alma Mater, the Beni Academy for Non-Foxes."

"No kidding," said Ray. "I don't remember seeing him there. So then he's rich, unless he was there on a scholarship."

"No scholarship listed here."

"Edward, we didn't make any enemies at the Academy," said Jess. "I don't see why he'd want us dead."

"Well, I was never one to avoid the obvious, so I may as well just say it. He's a bear, and you two are anteaters."

"So what?" asked Ray. "He's some specist jerk who wants to finish the genocide?"

"It could be that simple. Of course, that wouldn't explain why he picked the two hardest targets in the country." Edward paused. "By the way, I probably should have asked this first, but are you doing all right? I can only imagine how scary that bombing was."

"I'm fine," said Jess. "I'm more upset about the car than anything else."

"I don't blame you," said Edward. "Let me know if the insurance company tries to monk out on you, and I'll see to it that you get your money back."

"I appreciate it."

"I have to say, I'm really impressed with both of you. Less than a month on the job and you've already managed to exploit the one technical difference between a Council agent and a Presidential agent—you put a Council agent behind bars."

"So what are we going to do about the Bear?" asked Ray.

"He's in the hands of the police now. They're still investigating the crime scene, but they'll contact me as soon as they know anything. Tammy might try to bail him out, either that or she'll shred all his employment documents."

"So there's nothing we can do?"

"You're just going to have to sit tight and let the police do their jobs. It all works out, though, because I have a different task for you."

The siblings exchanged a glance.

"What sort of task?" asked Jess.

"Tell me, have you ever dealt with wolves?"

"Just once," said Ray. "Mast took us on a trip across the pan to train. He identified a rogue pack and then had us challenge them."

"I didn't realize your mentor had such a dangerous take on training."

"It wasn't that bad. Wolves are fierce, but they know nothing about fighting technique. Mast just wanted to make sure we had some real battle experience every once in a while."

"Well then, this next mission shouldn't give you any trouble." Edward pulled a different file from his cabinet. "We have a situation along the southern border. All the information you need is there, but I'll give you the gist of it now. A pack of wolves braved the salt and traveled up here to cause trouble."

"What sort of trouble?"

"It seems they've taken to eating my citizens," said Edward. "They've only hunted other pre-ops so far, just two pigs and a sheep, but there's no saying who'll be next. Wolves don't discriminate based on intelligence, so long as you're made of meat."

"So our job is to stop them?" asked Jess.

"In a nutshell, yes. Sending in an Army unit would be expensive and might spread panic. Why do that when I have the two of you? They've been spotted hiding out near the cliffs south of Marshton. Take the pack leader alive, same with the rest if possible."

"Are they armed?"

"Read the file," said Edward. "Everything you need to know is in there. Most wolves can't afford guns, but wear your liquid body armor just to be safe."

Ray nodded. "We'll get it done."

"I'm sure you will," said Edward. "Godspeed, Anteaters."

Chapter 4

The black had become a dark blue, the dark blue had become a pale blue, and the pale blue had become a blur of reds, pinks, oranges, and yellows. At any one instant, the sky was static, unchanging, just a picture frozen in the heavens above. Yet the sky did change, although no observer could perceive this change, even if she were to do nothing but watch the sky for hours.

And Sky had done just that.

Sunrise grew nearer, and Sky lay awake in her bed, watching the daybreak through her window. Her memory told her that she hadn't fallen asleep all night, but it hadn't felt like she'd been awake ten hours either. It felt like it had been four, or maybe five. Perhaps she had drifted in and out of a shallow slumber, with nothing to distinguish the waking moments.

But now she had some continuity. Now she had the sunrise. Sky held still, anticipating the moment the sun would slip over the horizon. In that instant, and only in that one instant, Sky would perceive the change. The sun only moved the tiniest bit at a time, but only the tiniest bit would be necessary for the sun to flood the world with its overpowering light.

She waited a minute, and then another, but still there was no sun. The distant glow grew brighter, but did not reveal its source. More important matters began to nag at her mind. Master Nyah would arrive soon, and Sky would do well to be ready.

She pulled the blankets aside and sat up. She didn't feel tired, but the light from the window suddenly got to her and she had to turn away. She felt a chill and wrapped her arms around her sides. It would be warmer soon.

Sky made her way over to the refrigerator. She knew she should eat breakfast and she had some bananas leftover from the day before, yet all she did was stare at the little white door handle. Breakfast wasn't happening.

She eyed the razor on the counter. Sky had forgotten to put it away the night before, but perhaps she could do with a morning touch up. She grabbed the blade and went over to the mirror, scanning herself for any unwanted stubble. She ran her other hand down her side and then over her legs, but she had done a flawless job the other night. Other than the ceremonial patch left atop the crown of her head, there was not a hair to be found.

There was nothing to do but wait. Sky sat back down on the bed, twitching her tail as she did. After a moment, she reached back and took hold of her tail, bringing it around for a closer look. She flipped it back and forth within her fingers, almost chuckling at how silly it looked. She thought back to when she was a child, to when she would stage puppet shows for her family and use her tail to operate the third puppet.

Still holding her tail, Sky turned back to the window. There was still no sun, yet it was even brighter than before. It could be any moment now. She would witness the change take place.

There was a harsh knock on the door and Sky immediately let go of her tail and stood up. She walked over and opened it to find the face of an elderly monkey staring back at her. Sky bowed.

"Good morning, Master Nyah."

"Good morning, Sky," said Master Nyah. "It is time."

Sky nodded. "I'm ready."

"Leave everything behind," said her master. "You will not need your belt or your thermals."

"I understand."

As Master Nyah turned around to leave, Sky noticed a thin strip of yellow across the walls and doorframe. She stole a glance back to see that the sun had risen; she had missed it. There was nothing to do now but follow her master.

Nyah awaited her by the front door of the lodge.

"Hurry along now," she said. "If you arrive too late, the initiator will not proceed with the ceremony."

"We're not going to be late, are we?"

"Never has a pupil of mine been late to her own initiation. I don't intend to sully that record."

Nyah stepped out the door and Sky followed. It was even chillier outside, but the rays of the sun felt warm, hot even, against her bare skin. The morning had the makings of another beautiful day in Bear country. The priests back home had told her stories of the endless rains of the big island, but Sky's own visit had been everything to the contrary. All she could see were picturesque grassy hills spotted with bushes and trees. The only clouds were the ones far off on the horizon.

As they hiked through the fields, Sky found herself staring at the tattoo on her master's right hip. It was a simple design, three lines forming an upward pointing arrow.

"Sky, we need not walk in silence," said Nyah. "You can talk to me."

"Forgive me, I'm just a little—" Sky paused. She did not want to say she was nervous. "Preoccupied."

"Understandable," said Nyah. "Would it ease your mind to discuss the ritual?"

"We've already been over it a dozen times. Is there anything you haven't already told me?"

Nyah shook her head. "Your part will be quite simple. It's the initiator who will do all of the talking, and he'll tell you what to do. Just let him perform the ceremony, and you will walk away with your mark of honor."

"And what if he deems me unworthy?" asked Sky. "What if he gives me a mark of disgrace? It will all be for nothing. The initiator will see into my spirit. If there is any fear in me, he will know."

"Sky, you've completed your training. You've done the difficult part. All that remains now is to focus on what you have learned."

"I will."

"Listen to your old master," said Nyah. "I have no doubt that you will pass this final trial. You are one of the finest students I have ever had the privilege to instruct."

"And what about Soy?"

"Don't worry about Soy. This is about you, only you."

The unmistakable array of stones took form in the distance; the Ancient Circle had come into view.

Master Nyah stopped. "This is as far as I go."

Sky nodded. "I'm ready."

"It will go just as we practiced," said Nyah. "Remember that you're allowed to talk to the initiator. Ask him a question if you must, though I wouldn't advise interrupting him."

"I know," said Sky. "I think I'd prefer to stay quiet."

Nyah gave her a smile and put her hand on Sky's shoulder. "May the Celestial Monkeys watch over you, Sky. I'll be back at the lodge when you're finished. Don't keep the initiator waiting."

With that, they parted ways. Sky continued forward with a moderate pace, not too slow as to make her late, yet not too quick as to begin the ritual earlier than she had to. She did this even as she knew it wouldn't make a difference; the ceremony would begin when the shadows reached their mark, whether she was early or right on time.

She couldn't see the initiator yet, but she could see a cloud of smoke rising from the center. There was a flicker of orange between the pillars, a flicker that disappeared and reappeared as though a distant someone had walked by.

In spite of herself, Sky's mind turned back to the ritual and the verdict. Anxious thoughts exploded in her mind before she had a chance to snuff them out. Why would anyone base such a crucial decision on whether or not one felt fear? If the Gods really had contrived this ceremony, the Gods had a sadistic sense of humor. No, she told herself, the Gods were not sadistic. They were fair and kind, mysterious, but fair and kind.

It wasn't the pain she feared. She could handle pain. They had trained her to handle pain. What really bore into her head was the thought of losing everything, the thought of never becoming a priest, all because of some spark of fear she couldn't extinguish. The thought of that fear undermining her would itself become a fear, until that spark was no longer a spark but a blaze, a self-fulfilling prophecy that would brand her with a mark of disgrace. Who thought of such trials?

Sky stopped and took a deep breath, fighting to come back to her training. She closed her eyes and exhaled, clearing her mind and calming her heart. The corrosive thoughts quieted until all she heard was the breeze. Her focus was her own. The slip up had never happened. Sky opened her eyes and continued.

One step after the other, she made her way to the Ancient Circle. A blazing bonfire roared in the center, coughing smoke up into the heavens. Beside the fire stood a wooden stump with a sharpened saber resting against its side. Beside the stump stood the initiator.

The initiator was older priest, not nearly as old as Master Nyah, but at least old enough to be Sky's father. He was one of the biggest monkeys Sky had ever seen, with an enormous belly hanging over his feet and thick, fat arms at his sides. The initiator looked at Sky but said nothing. He was waiting, thought Sky, waiting for the sun to align itself between the stone pillars.

And then he spoke.

"Not even stone is eternal." His deep voice boomed in Sky's ears. "Not even stone can withstand the trials of time without crumbling to dust and floating away with the breeze. Yet the Ancient Circle lives on forever. Its primordial pillars have endured all, be it wind or rain or the fires of mortals. The Celestial Monkeys built the Ancient Circle, and in doing so, they blessed it with eternity. Now the Ancient Circle beckons you, Sky, just as the Celestial Monkeys beckon you to enter their service."

He picked up the saber with one hand, and with the other, a stick from the fire. He turned back to Sky.

"Step into the circle."

Sky did as she was told. She now stood face to face with the initiator, close enough to the bonfire to feel its searing heat.

"The Celestial Monkeys made the world as it is now," said the initiator. "They gave the gift of life to many, the gift of wits to some, but only to us did they give the gift of their likeness. A blessed few advance further still to take the image of the Celestial Monkeys and pledge to serve them for life. That is why you are here."

The priest pressed the flat end of the saber on Sky's shoulder and ran it down the side of her arm.

"Though we shave our hair, we cannot stop our hair from growing back. Though we devote our lives to serving the Celestial Monkeys, we cannot stop ourselves from yearning for earthly joys. The Celestial Monkeys do not ask us to stop doing either of these things. They only ask that we continue doing that which is within our power."

The initiator turned to the cutting block.

"However, the Celestial Monkeys do ask that we leave behind a symbol of our worldly attachment. We our born with our tails, and those of us who choose to enter a life of service must separate from them. Our tails do not grow back, as this is a sacrifice that cannot be undone."

He turned back to Sky.

"Sky, you have trained in our sacred martial arts. You have studied the history of our people and the teachings of the Celestial Monkeys. Your master has deemed you worthy of the priesthood. All that remains is this final sacrifice."

He paused for a moment, the wrinkles on his face shimmering in the raw heat of the blaze.

"As you undertake this sacrifice, I will judge your spirit and bestow upon you my mark. Be it a mark of honor, you will become a servant of the Celestial Monkeys, and a warrior, teacher, and leader of your people. Be it a mark of disgrace, you will become a servant of the Celestial Monkeys, and nothing more. Whichever mark it be, to run from your vow carries the punishment of death. Do you, Sky, offer this final sacrifice and swear to serve the Celestial Monkeys in whichever way they see fit?"

"I swear."

The initiator pointed the saber at the wooden block.

"Proceed."

As Sky turned her back to the block and laid her tail across it, she heard a faint rumbling sound. At first she figured it was only the bonfire, but then she heard it again, louder, deep and echoing. She looked up to see that the clouds in the distance had grown darker, and flashes of white danced between the shadows. The initiator looked up as well.

"Thunder on the morning of an initiation," he said. "A bad omen."

"An omen?" asked Sky. "What do you mean? Can we still go on?"

"You have already sworn your oath," said the initiator. "We cannot stop the ceremony now."

He turned back to the wooden block and slowly raised the saber. In that moment, the thoughts broke back into Sky's mind. What did he mean about it being a bad omen? Why would he even say anything if it was already too late to turn back? How could he expect her to be calm about the trial after knowing something like this?

Sky closed her eyes and took another deep breath. The thoughts were gone, locked somewhere far away from her conscious mind. As she opened her eyes again, the blade fell.

She heard the chop, but felt nothing. Then the pain hit her, a searing, throbbing, unfathomable pain, far worse than she had foreseen. She shut the pain out, locking it away with the anxious thoughts in the back of her head. The pain hammered behind the locked door, begging to be let back it, but Sky wouldn't let it. The worst was over, she told herself.

The initiator applied the torch to the wound, cauterizing the stump and twisting Sky's world with a whole new kind of pain. This was not another clean, precise pain, but one where each cell screamed in agony as it turned to charcoal. The worst was over, she told herself, the worst was over. No, the worst was not over. Sky had never feared the pain. Sky feared the judgment, and that was yet to come. The unwanted thoughts had returned.

Sky tried to take another deep breath, but it turned out shaky. The trauma had weakened her, and weakened her ability to control her focus. Her grip on her mind loosened, and one by one the thoughts slipped back through the door. She was shaking visibly by the time the initiator stepped around to look at her.

The initiator stared into her eyes, and somehow, the shaking was gone. The thoughts were gone. The pain was still there, but it didn't bother her. By some miracle, her mind filled with complete clarity.

"Turn around."

Again, Sky did as she was told. The initiator held the saber to her hip and whipped it up and down. The motions had been so swift that it took Sky a moment to realize that the priest had made three slashes in her skin, although she could not say whether or not they converged to form an arrow. Finally, the initiator extinguished his flaming branch, crumbled a chunk of charcoal from the tip, and rubbed it over the cuts.

"It is finished."

Sky turned to him once more.

"I have seen your truth and given you your mark," said the initiator. "May the blessings of the Celestial Monkeys be upon you,

Friar Sky. You are the newest priest of our sacred order."

Chapter 5

A pair of wolf ears perked at something, and a dark wolf snout poked out of the mouth of the cave. Something, be it the wind, the moon, or the night itself, made him open his mouth to respond.

"ARROOOOOOO!"

"My goodness," said Jess. "They're not even trying to stay hidden."

"What do you see?" asked Ray.

"What do you think? There's a wolf down there, in the cave across the valley." She adjusted the binoculars.

"Is he alone?"

"No, there's at least one other wolf in there with him. Someone else is coming out now."

The other, larger wolf pounced over and smacked the first one in the snout before grabbing him by the neck and dragging him back into the cave.

"At least one them has some concept of discretion," said Jess.

"So is this the group then? Have we found our pack?"

"It would be quite the coincidence otherwise."

"Let me see."

"Here." She handed him the binoculars.

Even without the binoculars, in the dark of the night she could see the mouth of the cave, glimmering from the reflection of a campfire hidden within. A waxing moon presided over the night, revealing the entire landscape to the Anteaters on their perch on the hill. Behind them she could see the town, still aglow with the lights of residents finishing their dinners and settling down. Ahead were more hills and spires, gradually giving way to cliffs, and finally, the salt flats.

With the breeze, the temperature was perfect. It was one of those summer nights in which Jess might have favored a neighborhood walk had it not been for the mission. Although both siblings wore full sets of liquids, neither had bothered with thermals.

"I bet the wolf was howling at the moon," said Ray. "You know they can't help it."

"Oh?"

"It's true what they say, pre-ops can really be slaves to their primal instincts. In some aspects, they're still more animal than person."

"We're all still animals."

"Biologically, maybe." He put down the binoculars. "What do you think? Hit them now before they have a chance to raid the town again?"

"We'd best wait," said Jess. "They might have the advantage in their cavern. We should engage them in the open field."

"I'm sure we could take them anywhere."

"Yes, I know, but we're not taking chances."

"As you say. So we follow them when they emerge."

"Keep your eyes out."

They didn't have to wait long. After a few minutes, one of the wolves climbed back up to the mouth of the cave. The glow of red from behind faded away, and one by one his pack flocked to his side until there were at least twenty visible. They all looked up towards the moon, but this time there were no howls.

The leader turned and said something to his pack before leaping from the ledge and racing down the mountainside, his fellow wolves close behind. They moved silently and gracefully through the night, like a school of fish swimming beneath an ocean of moonlight. The pack took advantage of every crevice or bush in their path, meandering between patches of cover as they negotiated the landscape.

"This is it," said Ray. "Let's go."

"Just be sure to wait for my signal to strike."

The Anteaters slid down the gravelly slope near the peak of the hill, and continued running down the grassy side. As the town and salt flats vanished beneath the hills, the Anteaters disappeared beneath the trees, moving to intercept the pack. Near the bottom they caught sight of the rear guard jumping through the bushes, and the siblings followed close behind.

They trailed the pack around the outer corner of the cliffs to see the town once more take shape as a collection of lights in the distance. Some of the lights were already disappearing from sight; the townspeople were going to bed.

The landscape changed from stones and shrubs to deeper soil and tall leafy trees. Some of the nicer houses dotted the outskirts of city. These were spacious homes with vast yards overlooking the cliffs or the salt pan. For whatever reason, the wolves avoided these houses and continued on toward the center.

They snuck deeper into town via the untrimmed hedges beside the road. In the cover of darkness, the wolves were only shadows behind the twigs and leaves. At the end of the bushes, they came upon an apartment complex, and a lone pig sitting out and chewing a corn husk. The wolves all came to a crouch behind their leader, some already salivating as they eyed the boar. The Anteaters took cover about twenty meters back, ready to make their strike if the need arose. Hearing them speak, Jess leaned forward to make out their words.

"No street lights," said one of them. "No one see us take him."

"Wait," said the other.

"Why we wait? We miss chance."

The leader simply held up his hand, and his pack stood down. For a moment, they all lay in wait belly down in the tall grass. Then a beam of light appeared around the corner of the building.

A fox carrying a flashlight stepped into view. He was short, even for a fox, but he wore a full set of liquids and he carried a flintlock on his belt. The pig took notice and waved him over.

"Hello, officer."

"Good evening," said the fox. "What are you doing out here so late?"

"I no sleep," said the pig. "I come out here to enjoy night and eat corn."

"I don't mean to bother you, but you should be careful," said the fox. "There have been rumors of wolf sightings recently. From what I hear, they prefer to hunt at night."

"There no wolves here. I eat in peace."

"Well, if that's what you want to do, I can't stop you. It's no crime to sit out here and enjoy a beautiful night. Just keep a lookout, and if there's trouble, holler."

"All right, officer."

"Take care."

The fox continued on his patrol, and once again the beam of light weaved back and forth with his footsteps. After a minute, the light had faded away, and the pig remained with his late night snack.

"He gone now," said one of the wolves. "Time to kill pig."

"No," said the leader. "We leave. We look somewhere else."

"Why leave? Border guard gone."

"Too risky. We find another target. Stay quiet and follow me."

Before anyone could voice a word of protest, the leader took off back the way they had come. Jess motioned for Ray to stay down, and they ducked beneath the plants as the wolves ran by.

After a hundred meters of backtracking, the wolf in front swung a left turn and brought them around a small fenced community. The white fence proved terrible cover and the Anteaters had no trouble seeing the line of shadows. They wouldn't get a better chance than this. She gave Ray the signal.

Increasing their pace, the wolves dove into the ditch at the other side and lay flat. The leader sniffed the air and looked from side to side.

He turned to his pack. "We must turn back. Hunt tomorrow."

None of the wolves responded with growls or scoffs. They glanced from side to side, their noses twitching in the dark. A twig snapped several meters away, and all heads turned.

"Hear that?"

As the leader peered up for a closer look, two shadows burst out from between the trees. One of the figures bolted into his point guard, striking hard at the face and slamming him into the ground. The other figure sprinted around the side, taking out another wolf who had drifted too far from the group.

In the moonlight, one could clearly see that the two attackers wore liquids, but they were no species the wolf had ever seen before. They were too big to be foxes, but too small to be bears. It took him a moment to notice their long noses, and another moment to process what he saw. Could the attackers be anteaters? He never thought he would see one for himself. He bared his teeth and pounced on the closer anteater, but his target was gone before he landed and he wound up with a mouthful of grass and dirt.

Dizzy from the miss, he stood back up, hearing snarls and whimpers from behind. He turned around to see half his pack lying unconscious before him, and no sign of the anteaters. He turned around again to see a fist flying at him. He never remembered falling to the ground.

He opened his eyes to see one of the anteaters standing over him. He struggled, but his hands wouldn't move. Someone had bound them.

"Are you the leader?" the anteater asked.

He managed to nod. "Yes. I am."

The anteater turned to his companion. "Good work, Jess. We got him."

Chapter 6

A snarl sounded through the bars. The guard responded with a kick to the door.

"Shut up in there!"

"You no bring enough food," said the wolf in the cell.

"You had your meal an hour ago," said the guard. "That's it until tomorrow."

"Your food bad, not filling for wolf."

"I suppose you want more pig? I may not be one of those Horseshoe nuts, but I have no sympathy for anyone who kills my countrymen. It's kangaroo meat and filler for the rest of your days."

"I eat bad meat, yes, but please, feed my pack good meat. They deserve good meat."

The guard put his face up to the bars and glared at the furry figure in the shadows. "What they deserve is a whole lot worse than what they got."

The wolf lunged forward and snapped, his jaw pressed against the edge of the bars. The guard recoiled, almost tripping over his own feet as he stumbled backwards. He caught his balance, glanced left and right, and then glared at the wolf again.

"Mindless savage."

The door at the end of the hall swung open. The guard turned to see two anteaters walk through.

"Here to check on your prisoners?" he asked.

A large fox followed them.

"Mr. President! I wasn't expecting—"

"At ease, my good man," said Edward. "I'm just here to make a last minute visit with the prisoner. I didn't bother to notify the warden."

"It's an honor to have you, Sir. You didn't have to come all the way down here."

"No, but I wanted to. I ordered the capture of these wolves, so they're my prisoners. It makes sense that I take the time to talk to them in person."

"You'd like to question them yourself?"

"Just point out the leader."

The guard stepped back and pointed to the cell. Edward stepped up to the barred doorway and the Anteaters followed close behind. The cell lacked windows, but even without natural light, Edward could sense the griminess of the space. A ball of grungy fur inhaled and exhaled in the corner.

"So you're the leader of our little excursion," said Edward. "Do you have a name?"

A pair of eyes appeared in the darkness. "My name Wolf Bob. I lead pack from Wolf lands."

"Hello Bob, my name's Edward. I'm here to have a little chat."

"You want to let me go?"

"No."

"Then why you come here?"

"I told you, to have a chat. I want to know how and why you found your way into the Fox Nation."

"Why you care?"

"Maybe I'm just curious."

"Fine, I tell you. For longtime, I know Warlord of the Wolves. He and I good friends. One day, he become angry at me, and banish me. My pack good wolves, very loyal. They stay with me even though banished. I reward them for loyalty. I promise them we travel across Great Salt Pan and feast on pig and sheep from Fox Nation."

"So that's the only reason you came here?" asked Edward. "To eat our people?"

"Yes."

"There are plenty of animals around here. You see cows and deer all over the place. Why not just eat those?"

"Pig and sheep taste better than cow and deer."

"Maybe they do, but one of those cases is murder and the other isn't."

Bob bared his teeth. "Big, ugly fox don't get so big without eating many berries. You be mad too if I tell you to eat blueberries but not strawberries."

"I might, but if strawberries starting talking and showing signs of self-awareness, I sure as hell wouldn't eat them anymore."

"Then I think you get very hungry."

Edward turned to the Anteaters. "We're done here. I didn't come all this way to teach Ethics 101 to a damn pre-op."

"Right behind you," said Ray.

Edward walked back down the hallway and opened the door, motioning for the Anteaters to walk out first.

"Go on ahead," said Edward. "I'll meet you outside."

The guard peered back at him.

"What should I do about these wolves?"

"Listen to the warden," said Edward. "She'll tell you what to do."

He turned and walked out the door, making his way into the nicer parts of the prison. He walked through the fox wing and down the main stairwell, waving to the guard who buzzed him out. The Anteaters awaited him on the other side of a gate of barbed wire fence.

It was a warm day, not a hot day, but a warm day. A strong breeze swept through the chain fence, making the air seem much cooler than it was. A quiet street and empty field lay opposite the prison. The only sound came from a whirring generator somewhere within the concrete walls. Edward stepped through the final gate to meet his agents, who both eyed him and awaited directions.

Parked on the curb was a black limousine, gleaming in the midday sunlight. Edward walked over to it, opened the side door, and turned to the Anteaters.

"Let's go for a ride."

"Where are we going?" asked Ray.

"Back to my office. We have a few things to discuss."

The Anteaters piled into the car and plopped down onto the leather seats. The barrier between the air-conditioned compartment and the outside was tangible, and was a relief after feeling the limo's red hot exterior. Edward hopped in after them and slammed the door behind them.

"Take us home."

He barely had time to sit down before the car lurched forward. They sat for a moment, watching the fields roll by through the tinted windows. Edward opened the side compartment and turned to Jess.

"Can I offer you a beverage? Non-alcoholic, of course. We can't show up to work tipsy. I've got some ant extract here."

"I'm fine," said Jess.

"Come on," said Ray. "Don't make me ask for some by myself."

"Just go ahead, I really don't think Edward cares."

Edward popped open a can and passed it to Ray. "Here, I insist. Just don't ask me join you. No offense, but it's not really my thing."

"Thanks." Ray took a sip.

"So what about the wolves?" asked Jess. "Do you think the pack leader is telling the truth?"

"I don't see why not," said Edward. "He and his pack were bound to get caught. It was really stupid of them to relocate up here, but I reason he's stupid enough to do it and not smart enough to lie about it."

"You don't think they were a scouting party for something worse?"

"I doubt it."

"So it's finished then," said Ray. "We have the pack behind bars. There's nothing more we can do about it."

"Oh no, we're going to do something about it." Edward sighed. "I really thought I was done dealing with wolves. After I left the Army, I didn't think they'd give me any more trouble, but here we are."

"Wolves are vicious and they never listen to reason. They'll always be trouble."

"But they shouldn't have to be. Sure, they like to prey on civilians, but they live on the other side of the Great Salt Pan. Left to their own devices, the Wolves would never be able to make the crossing. They don't know how to make buggies. They only have them because they buy them from vendors, and they only have the money to do so because our own citizens hire them as mercenaries. It's not just private security for merchants either. Our people don't feel safe traveling to or through the Monkey Nation, and more often than you'd think, they'll hire a pack of wolves to keep them safe for the journey. As crazy as it is, as long as everyone sees the Monkeys as a threat, the Wolves will also be an issue."

There was a long silence. Jess eyed her brother, then turned to look out at the passing buildings. Edward had dropped quite a mouthful, and she wasn't sure if he was looking for a suggestion to solve such a problem. Ray took a lengthy sip of his drink, but the silence persisted until after he had finished the gulp.

"So what's the solution then?" asked Ray. "Raise an army and march east to defeat the Monkeys for good?"

"You think that would make the region safer? No, the answer is just the opposite. The world won't be safe until there is peace, and I'm not the fox to bring about that peace."

The limo coasted through green lights, making good time through the downtown morning traffic. It swung a turn onto a fenced off block, speeding past a field of freshly cut grass on the other side. The car took another turn, disappearing off the street and into an underground parking garage. Orange lights and shadows raced across their faces as the limo sped deeper into the compound. After passing a handful of other cars, the limo skidded to a stop at a lone space in the back.

"Everyone out," said Edward.

He slid the door open, jumped out, and held the door for the Anteaters. Jess's footsteps echoed as she touched the cool pavement. The vast complex met her with an unsettling silence.

"It's so quiet here."

"Only my senior staff get to use this parking garage, and only I get to use the secret elevator."

"Secret elevator?"

"Well, it can't be that big a secret," said Edward. "The builders know about it, the past presidents know about it, and I imagine by now someone other than my driver has seen me slip in, but I'm the only one who gets to use it. Follow me."

Edward walked up to the wall and lifted a metal panel to reveal a digital touchpad. He tapped in a few buttons, and the display beeped happily in response. With a hiss of compressed air, the concrete wall sunk back and slid to the side to reveal the open doors of an otherwise normal elevator.

Without a word, the fox walked in and motioned for the Anteaters to follow. As soon as they stepped in, the doors closed behind them and they felt the familiar subtle rising sensation. They heard a 'ding' and the doors opened again to reveal the president's office.

"Isn't it great?" said Edward. "Whenever I don't feel like going through that gauntlet downstairs, I can sneak right up here. They won't even know I'm in the office."

The president stepped out first and walked over to his chair. Jess followed close behind, but Ray stepped out slowly, still marveling at the elevator. He jumped as the doors slammed shut and a bookcase shot up from the floor to fill the space.

"Careful there," said Edward. "If you want to read my copy of *Postbellum Statutes and Ordinances of the Border Provinces*, you might want to watch your fingers."

"All of this just to avoid seeing your staff?" asked Ray. "What if they have something important to talk to you about?"

"You think those buzzards have anything important to discuss with me? I doubt it. Their only concerns are petty things, such as running the country. I jest, of course. There's plenty I need to go over with them, but right now, my time is yours."

Jess sat down opposite the desk and her brother sat beside her.

"How have things been going for you?" she asked.

"Lousy," said Edward. "I really shouldn't be giving my staff a hard time; they're just trying to help. The Council, on the other hand, is driving me insane."

"Have they?"

"It's not even the Developmentalist Party. It's Helen and her Horseshoe Party fanaticism. Here, take a look at this."

Edward pulled a remote control from his desk and switched on a TV screen in the back of the room. The siblings craned their heads to take a look.

"This footage is from the most recent Council session."

A fuzzy image appeared on the screen, an image of nine foxes and a horse sitting on one side of a long bench, and Edward sitting opposite them. A small audience of mostly foxes surrounded the central table. After a few seconds, the image came into focus and the garbled sounds turned coherent.

"With their monopoly, Ramirez International sets the prices high enough as it is." Edward's distinct voice boomed through the TV speakers. "If we pass this tariff, we'll only make everything more expensive for our own citizens—and our military. I won't stand by and watch us succumb to a Monkey invasion because we couldn't afford liquids for our soldiers."

"The Army has no shortage of supplies," said one of the other foxes. "The tariff would bring in more than enough to fix the healthcare deficit, and there are other ways to obtain germanium. We haven't provided enough incentives to domestic entrepreneurs."

"We all know why those incentives don't work—"

Edward hit the fast forward button. "Hold on. It's a bit later on. Ah! Here we go." He hit play again.

"That sums up the provisions of the proposed Kraphton School Fund Bill." The Edward on the screen looked up at the Council. "Before we take a vote, would anyone like to offer any final comments?"

"Mr. President, I have something I'd like to say," said the horse.

"The Council recognizes Councillor Helen from the Second Province," said Edward. "Proceed."

"Thank you, Mr. President," said Helen. "With the Council's permission, I ask that we would delay a vote on this bill until we can make proper revisions."

Hushed murmurs floated among the audience.

"Madam Councillor, you'll have to elaborate," said Edward. "What is wrong with the bill as it is?"

"The Kraphton Bill proposes many beneficial educational programs, but these programs only benefit foxes."

"I would be inclined to disagree," said Edward. "The bill's benefits apply to all formals, and it even extends some opportunities to pre-ops and concretes."

"Then I too must disagree," said Helen. "The bill does not provide for horse students, all of whom require special equipment or assistance to write or otherwise participate in normal school activities."

Edward sighed. "We've been over this issue before. Special provisions would cost us money, much more than the funds we've already allocated to this project."

"Then we should rethink the budget. We would do just that if the changes concerned the well-being of foxes."

"This is not the time for such accusations. The Council values all of its citizens."

"Is that so?" asked Helen. "Then what do you have to say about the ongoing discrimination against horses in our society? Recent studies have shown horses to be just as intelligent as foxes, monkeys, bears, or anteaters. Our only crime was being born without opposable digits. It shames me we haven't made the same strides as our neighbors in the Bear Nation—they even elected a horse as their Chancellor over one of their own."

"Madam Councillor, this is not the Bear Nation."

"No, but we could be better than the Bear Nation if it weren't for this injustice. As of today, only three provinces allow horses to run for a seat on the Council, and in four, including your own, Mr. President, horses aren't even guaranteed the right to vote."

"Those matters are under the jurisdiction of the governors of said provinces," said Edward. "What would have me do?"

"I'll tell you what you should do. Draft a new amendment. Recognize horses as formals."

Once again, the audience erupted with murmurs, this time much louder than before.

"Horses as formals?" asked Edward. "Do you understand what you're asking? Our nation didn't create these categories. You're talking about an institution that has been around for thousands of years."

"Do you need to call up the Monkeys and ask their permission first?" asked Helen. "As a hero who has led armies against our old oppressors, Mr. President, are you really such a stickler for their ancient traditions? Maybe we should have opened this Council session with a prayer to the Celestial Monkeys. Is this the freedom that Anton and Julia fought for?"

"Enough of this," said Edward. "I move for a vote to end the discussion here and proceed with the decision."

"I second that," said one of the foxes.

"Thank you, Councillor Tammy. All in favor?"

The foxes raised their hands.

"The vote is ten to one. We will proceed with the vote over the Kraphton School Fund Bill. All in favor?"

The foxes raised their hands.

"Again, the vote is ten to one. The bill passes, pending my signature."

With a click, the screen went black.

"You see what's I'm dealing with?" asked Edward.

"Horses as formals?" asked Ray.

Edward nodded. "The Horseshoe Party was so much easier to ignore before they squeezed one of their own onto the Council. Now I have to hear everything: horses joining the other four species as formals, equal protection under the law for pre-ops, recognition of tromians and their designation as concretes."

"Tromians? Really?"

"Yes, didn't you hear? Helen threw in with the Tromian immigrants to secure her election. Sure, it got her the Council seat, but as far as getting her bills passed, she screwed herself over. Now if we recognize horses as formals, we might have to acknowledge tromians as citizens. If we acknowledge tromians as citizens, we'll have to rewrite our Deist constitution. If we're no longer a Deist state, then we may as well go back to worshipping the Celestial Monkeys. No one would stand for it."

"You're worried these proposals will pass?"

"No, not at all. Her province loves her, but Helen is alone on the Council. Without the support of the other councillors, she's just an annoyance, but quite an annoyance at that." Edward sat back and shook his head. "The craziest part is that I agree with most of what she says. Give the horses their rights, separate church and state—such things could do no harm. So why not go for it? Because I'm a Defender. The people elected me for my ability to kill monkeys, and it's not my place to give them any other sort of president."

The Anteaters sat in silence. Edward leaned forward again.

"Dammit, listen to me jabber. We have missions to discuss and all I can do is talk your ears off about my own problems. My apologies."

"It's fine," said Jess. "I asked."

"You asked how I was doing. You didn't ask for my life story."

"I don't mind."

Ray shot her a look—raised eyebrows that said 'of course you mind'. She glared back without turning her head.

"Is that so?" asked Edward. "Well then, you're a kind young lady."

Ray raised his eyebrows again, and Jess had to resist giving him a kick.

"Moving on," said Edward. "We have three orders of business

to discuss and we may as well start with the fun one. I have a very important mission for the two of you."

"Concerning invaders?" asked Ray.

"No, this mission is more important than that." Edward grinned. "Are you ready for this? Anteater Juan is throwing me a fundraiser next month, and I'd like for the two of you to attend. So how about it? How would you like to meet Mr. Explorer himself?"

"Are you serious?"

"Dead serious. I have two open spots at the head table."

"That's very generous of you," said Jess. "We appreciate it."

"Don't thank me too much. I have a selfish motive in inviting you: the more I can impress Juan, the more he'll donate to my campaign."

"You think he'll like you more if we're there?" asked Ray.

"Of course! He'll be thrilled to learn that I employ two anteaters as my personal agents. Hell, he'll just be thrilled not to be the only anteater at the party. Talk to him a bit, maybe tell him a few stories of your old man and me back in the days of the campaign. He'll be delighted."

"I think we could do that."

"Very good. I'll send you the details later. For now, just get excited." He cleared his throat. "Now for the next matter. Please don't hate me."

"What for?"

"Councillor Tammy worked out a deal for her agent," he said. "They released Bear Theo from prison."

"What? How?" asked Ray. "He blew up our car. He tried to kill us."

"That's just it," said Edward. "The police reviewed the footage from the surveillance cameras and saw someone sneak under your car during the film. The image was too fuzzy for an identification, but the culprit clearly wasn't a bear. It was a dog."

"A dog?" asked Jess. "That doesn't make sense. Look, maybe he didn't plant the charges himself, but that bear had something to do with the attempt. He may have paid someone to do the job for him. I know he's guilty."

"Listen, I believe you, but everything the police had was circumstantial, and they had little stomach to argue with a councillor. They had to cut him loose."

"So he's out there right now."

"Do your best not to worry about the Bear. I have a team of investigators looking into him. They'll uncover the connection and get him back behind bars."

"Put us on that team," said Ray. "We'll help put him away."

"No," said Edward. "I can't spare the two of you at the moment. I have another task for you."

Jess and Ray shared a quick glance.

"That brings us to our final order of business. We're going to do something about the Wolves."

"What did you have in mind?" asked Ray.

"When the people elected a former general as their president, they did so in the hopes that I'd keep our borders safe. That being said, if I were to raise an army and march it into the Wolf lands without a good reason, they would think twice before electing me again. That's why I'd rather keep this between the three of us for now. That's why I'm sending the two of you."

"You're sending us to fight the Wolves?"

"No, I'm sending you to spy on the Wolves. They appear to be a threat, but we know very little of what goes on beyond the salt pan. We can only scrape together rumors from merchants and pilgrims. I want you two to be my eyes. Travel to the Wolf lands, infiltrate their ranks, assess the threat, and say the word if I should mobilize the army and crush them."

"At the risk of pointing out the obvious," said Jess, "wouldn't we stand out?"

"Not this time," said Edward. "I've procured some invaluable items for your mission. In addition to the standard supplies, food and whatnot, I managed to get a buggy just like the ones the Wolves ride around on—and two full sets of Wolf liquid body armor."

"Wolf liquids?"

"Obsolete pieces of junk. These liquids are massive and bulky. It will be a pain just to move around while wearing them, and don't expect any ventilation, because they cover your entire body. On the plus side, they cover your entire body."

"They won't be able to tell we're anteaters," said Ray. "They'll think we're two of their own."

"Precisely. You should be able to fall in with a pack and learn what the Warlord has planned."

"Could they sniff us out?"

"That would be a concern if you were foxes, but few wolves have ever encountered an anteater before—and with any luck, the liquids still smell of their previous owners."

"Hold on," said Jess. "There's more to fitting in than looking and smelling like them. We don't know how to interact as part of a pack."

"Normally I'd agree with you, Jess. If this mission concerned the Monkeys, I wouldn't even consider an operation like this one. But these are pre-ops, so I trust you can fool them."

"It should be easy," said Ray. "We just have to act half as smart as usual."

"Yeah," said Jess. "Or maybe two thirds, in your case."

"You will need some preparation," said Edward. "I'll get you in touch with Dr. Wilson, a good friend of mine and a leading expert in pre-operational psychology, with a focus on wolf pack behavior. She'll give you a crash course on the dos and don'ts south of the salt."

"Crash course? As in a few days?"

"That should suffice; your time is valuable. It's a simple mission. You'll have a camera in case you see anything worth documenting and you'll have an electronic flare in case there's trouble. I'll have a regiment or two on standby, ready to deploy within minutes of seeing that blip on their radar."

Ray nodded. "Sounds good."

Edward passed them a folder from his file cabinet. "Everything you need to know is in there. This shouldn't be a problem for either of you. You'll do great."

"Thanks."

"I mean it," said Edward. "I couldn't ask for better agents. Your father would be proud of you. And not that I'd know, but your grandfather would be proud of you too."

Jess smiled. "I'm sure he is."

Chapter 7

It was a cloudy day, so breezy and autumnal that it was almost disorienting to see the trees still bearing green. It had been warm and sunny while the Bear had been in prison, warm enough to nearly cook him alive in his greenhouse of a cell. Now that he was free, the dull, chilly days had taken over. Such was his luck.

The Bear stood on the balcony, looking over his estate and watching the wind blow ripples through the fields. He reached into his belt and pulled out one of his favorite Tromian cigars, turning to block the wind so he could light it. He took a deep inhale and let his eyes and mind wander off into the distance.

A sleek black limousine winding up his driveway brought his trance to an end.

"Dammit." He dropped the cigar and smothered it with his foot.

The Bear stepped back into the room and slid the door shut behind him. He raced down the stairs and across the hall to his living room.

"I need you all out of here," he said. "She's coming."

No one seemed to notice him. His guests were four dogs, three on the couch and one on the rug. The one with the center seat was the only female of the bunch, with pristine white fur and a copper necklace. To her left was a dark brown dog, his arm straddled behind the lady's seat but not quite touching her neck. To her right was a messy light brown pooch, also leaning as close as he could to her. The black furred dog sat on the floor, directly in front of the lady.

A half-eaten pizza atop a greasy box lay spread out across the table. Several open beer bottles accompanied the meal, including one on its side, contributing drop by drop to a puddle on the floor.

"You remember those days," said the dark brown one. "No goalie could stop me. I could make a shot from halfway across the rink."

"Oh come on," said the lady. "I made more goals than you did and you know it."

The scruffy one laughed. "That's right, Brad. And now all you do is stuff your face with donuts all day."

"Shut up, Fuzz."

"Aw," said the lady. She reached over and rubbed Brad's belly. "That's all right. He's so cute with his little gut."

Brad's face lit up with a dumb smile, while Fuzz glared. The Bear stepped forward, shoving the coffee table aside.

"Did any of you hear what I just said? Tammy will be here any second!"

Brad looked up. "Who?"

"Our councillor!"

"Oh, Fox Tammy," said Brad. "Yeah, I know her."

"She's heading up the driveway as we speak," said the Bear. "She'll want to talk to me, so I need the four of you to clear out. Clean up this mess while you're at it."

"Wait a minute," said Fuzz. "Do you want us to clean or do you want us to leave?"

A harsh knock on the front door rang through the house.

"Theo!" A sharp voice pierced the glass. "Open up! I know you're in there!"

The Bear cringed. Brad raised a confused eyebrow.

"Aren't you going to answer that?"

Without acknowledging the question, the Bear walked over to the door, reluctant to look at the distorted brown image through the glass. He took a breath through clenched teeth, turned the handle, and pulled it open.

A middle aged fox stared back at him through thick glasses. As soon as she saw him, she wiggled her nose and grimaced.

"Ugh. You reek. I told you not to smoke those disgusting cigars before our meetings."

"Forgive me, Madam Councillor. I didn't know we'd be meeting."

"Spare me the 'Madam Councillor' bullshit." She shoved her way past him. "I need a drink. Whiskey will do."

"Hold on—will you wait?"

The Bear kicked the door shut and tried to catch up to her, but Tammy had already made it to the living room. The four dogs met her with unblinking stares. She turned back to the Bear.

"Who are these lovely individuals?"

Brad waved. "Hi, I'm Brad."

"These are a few of my friends," said the Bear. "They were just about to leave."

"Nonsense, I wouldn't dream of it," said Tammy. "You haven't even introduced us yet."

Brad looked from side to side. "Well, I'm Brad."

"Yes, dearie, you said that already."

"This is Fuzz, this is Larry, and this is Sonya. We call ourselves the Dog Quartet."

"Oh? Do you sing?"

Brad tilted his head. "No. Why would we?"

Tammy cracked a smile. "No reason. Just a hunch. So if you don't sing, what do you do?"

"Well," said Fuzz, "we're all demolitions experts. Brad here helped the Bear by planting that bomb on the Anteaters' car."

She turned to the Bear with raised eyebrows. "Isn't that interesting? So Theo here enlisted you in his noble cause."

"Tammy, could you please just—"

"Don't interrupt, Theo. It's rude." She turned back to the dogs. "Please, go on."

"We knew the Bear from school," said Brad. "We used to be friends with the Anteaters, too. We have a lot of useful information about them."

"Oh really?" said Tammy. "I wasn't aware the prestigious Beni Academy admitted pre-ops."

Brad glared. "Hey! Dogs aren't pre-ops."

"No, of course not. So let me guess: smashball scholarship?"

Brad paused, and then lowered his head and nodded.

"All four of you?"

The others nodded as well.

"Well, this has been a nice chat," said the Bear. "Tammy, don't we have business to discuss?"

"Yes, I suppose we do."

"You heard her. Dogs, get out of here."

"Oh, let them stay and enjoy their meal. We can have our talk in the kitchen. You were about to get me that drink anyway."

She left the room without waiting for a response, leaving the Bear to stumble after her. He raced down the hallway, following her shadow as she flipped on every light switch in her path.

"I don't know how you keep it so dark in here," she said as she entered the kitchen.

The Bear stopped under the doorframe. "Was that really necessary back there?"

"If it sheds any light on your recent idiocy, then yes, it was. I'd say it was quite enlightening. Wouldn't you agree, Theo?"

"Stop calling me that."

"I'm not going to call you 'the Bear'. That's just obnoxious. Your choices are 'Theo' or 'Bear Theo'."

"I told you, my choice is—"

"Why are you standing there instead of getting my whiskey?"

The Bear sighed, walked over to the liquor cabinet, and grabbed the nearest bottle.

"The good stuff. None of that knockoff pisswater."

"Yes, I know," said the Bear. "It's in the back. I have to move the other bottles first."

"Then get on with it."

The Bear put a few of them on the counter, reached deep in the back to retrieve the tall brown bottle, and put the others back. He got out a glass, threw in a handful of ice, and filled it halfway with the whiskey.

"Here you go," he said. "This is Oaken Barrel. Even better than Vince Andrews."

Tammy's expression finally softened as she took a sip.

"You're lucky your whiskey is smoother than you are. Care to join me?"

"I'll pass. I never drink after smoking."

"Suit yourself. To business then."

He nodded. "To business."

"I don't even know where to start," said Tammy. "What the hell were you thinking?"

"Just listen—"

"You've been telling me all about this other grand plan you have, and then the next thing I know, I'm bailing you out of jail for something entirely different. Why do I have to bail you out, you ask? Because you decided to bomb the Anteaters in the middle of a drive-in movie!"

"I thought it might be simpler. I figured it was worth a try."

"Well, guess what? It didn't work! And then like a moron, you fled. No one would have suspected you. All you had to do was stand there. You could have even run out the exit like a normal person, but no, you had to leap the fence and give them the perfect reason to suspect you."

"I didn't expect them to get out of the car," said the Bear. "I panicked."

"At least you had the sense not to plant the bomb yourself. Then again, you entrusted that task to a bunch of idiot concretes, one of whom volunteered this incriminating information to the first person who walked through the door!"

"Fuzz knows I work for you."

"That's a funny way to put it," said Tammy. "You're lucky the police don't have a case against you. If they did, things would be a whole lot worse for both of us."

"So what do I owe you?"

"For starters, from now on you do nothing, NOTHING, without running it by me first. Understand?"

He nodded.

"Good. And secondly, half a million. Right now."

"That much?"

"It's damage control. You weren't convicted, but rumors are bound to spread and it's a big country."

The Bear sighed. "I'll transfer the money right after you leave."

"This little payment is just in regards to your mishap. If you want to continue your stint as my agent, I'll need another thirty by the end of next month."

"Thirty million? Why? You already got elected."

"My province wants to keep me as councillor. I have no concerns there. However, if I want to be president I need the votes of the other councillors, which means I need people I trust in those seats. This money is for their campaigns."

"I wasn't planning to sponsor the entire Developmentalist

Party."

"And I wasn't planning for the Council to elect that brute Edward. Don't act like this payment will even make a dent in your account."

The Bear looked down and dragged his hand over his face. "Fine. Take what you want. Just keep me as your agent long enough to complete my plan."

"Your real plan? The one not involving car bombs?"

"Yes, that one."

Tammy gave her glass a swirl and took another sip. "It turns out we may have complications with that plan as well."

"What do you mean?"

"I just got word of a rogue pack of wolves terrorizing the border. Edward shut it down right away, but he has every reason to be wary of the Wolves, and his agents might see the attack coming."

"Dammit," said the Bear. "No. No, it will still work. We'll have surprise and numbers on our side. I've already made contact with the Wolf Warlord."

"Listen, Theo," said Tammy. "You seem really set on this, but does it have to be wolves? Hire a few of the Disgraced. You could get a team a hundredth of the size and for a quarter of the price."

"I'm not a fan of monkeys."

"None of us are, but these ones hate the Temple even more than we do, and they get results. Those two anteaters of yours would disappear without a sound."

"Maybe they would, but I'm going to stick with wolves. It will be easier to get them to do what I want. It's all part of the plan."

Tammy sighed. "Whatever. It's your money. Provide my funds and stay out of trouble, and I'll keep my paws off your stupid plans. But if they catch you for real, I won't be there to protect you."

"I know," said the Bear. "They'll never know I was involved."

"Good. Actually, have that thirty million in my account before you head south. I'd rather not take my chances."

"I will, don't worry."

"So it's settled."

Tammy took another sip that soon turned to a gulp.

"More?" asked the Bear.

"No," she said. "I'm just finishing it up so I can get out of here." She paused and looked the Bear in the eye. "You're sure going through a lot of trouble to get this done. What do you have against these two anteaters anyway? What did they do to you?"

"It wasn't anything they did," said the Bear. "Our family history goes back a long way."

"So it's a species thing. I should have guessed."

"No, it's more complicated than that."

"Don't bother. I don't want to hear it."

"Fine. Then you won't."

"What about those dogs? They said they used to be friends with the Anteaters. They must have had a reason to join up with you."

"The Dogs used to be on the school smashball team with them. Brad's little cousin got badly injured in one of the games, and Brad blames the Anteaters. It's a sad story."

"Tearjerker." Tammy downed the rest of her drink and left the glass on the counter. "I should be going. I enjoy our little talks, but I have other things to attend to. Thanks for the whiskey."

The Bear took the cup and rinsed it out in the sink.

"Don't worry about the money. You'll have it soon enough."

No reply. He turned around and Fox Tammy was gone. He finished cleaning the glass, put it away, and hit the lights.

The Bear walked back into the living room to see that the Dogs hadn't moved, although there seemed to be an additional bottle of beer on the table.

"Have you seen Tammy?" he asked.

"Yeah," said Brad. "She came through here a second ago. She just left. Weren't you with her?"

"I was."

"Huh," said Brad. He turned back to Sonya. "Hey Sonya, would you like to go out with me? On a date?"

Sonya smiled. "Sure!"

Fuzz's jaw dropped, but no sound came out. Another dumb grin lit Brad's face. "Wow, I didn't think that would be so easy!"

Chapter 8

Majestic cliffs and rocky spires shot up into the sky, dancing among the swirling clouds. Smaller hills surrounded the cliffs, stretching from one end of the sky to the other. Trees covered the hills, painting the landscape a deep green. Little by little, the cliffs and hills shrank away until only a blur in the distance remained. Then the blur was gone. Then there was only white.

Jess floored the accelerator, kicking the buggy into full gear. The hardy vehicle motored along the salt, its sizable tires and shock absorbers easily accommodating the endlessly flat expanse. The sun-cooked ground crunched as the buggy roared overhead, adding to the untold labyrinth of spider web cracks in the salty floor. North, south, east, and west had no mark on the Great Salt Pan; only the sun served to distinguish one horizon from the other.

Ray leaned back in the passenger seat, doing the best he could to stay under the shade of the tarp. The buggy sported an open frame exterior without glass or anything else to ward off the hot air. He had rigged the tarp to the top of the frame, tying it down to each corner with a length of twine. The back left corner kept coming undone, forcing Ray to reach back and refasten it every ten minutes.

The supplies sat in the back crate, two thick straps securing them in place. The bulky wolf liquids demanded a duffel of their own, stretching at the sides and pushing at the buckles. A few spare power cells lined the center of the crate, rattling as the frame shook back and forth. A metal bin lay opposite the duffel, holding food, water, and other goods.

After fixing the tarp for the twentieth time, Ray lifted up the strap enough to pull a bottle from the supply bin. He popped the lid and took a long drink before extending it to Jess.

"Water?"

"Thanks."

She took a sip and handed it back to her brother.

"Want me to take a turn at the wheel?"

"I'm fine."

"Are you sure? You've been at it for a while."

"I'm sure. It's not like there's anything to run into."

"Good point. We could just tie down the pedal and both take a nap."

"How about we don't."

Ray shrugged and tossed the canteen back into the crate. He reclined in his seat and closed his eyes, feeling the rhythm of the hull as they rolled along. After adjusting several times, he drifted off to sleep.

Late afternoon clouds crept in, gradually extinguishing the blue and reducing the sun to a glowing silhouette. Jess had been too hasty in her previous judgment; *now* there was nothing but white. She couldn't tell where the salt ended and the clouds began. The balmy summer warmth had become a sickening muggy heat, one she felt despite the gusty air whipping at her face.

Something ahead protruded from the salt. Jess squinted, trying to sense of how large and how far away it was. It was white, but not the pure, untouched white of the salt. This was a darker white, the color of cream—or bone.

"Ray? Do you see that?"

No answer from her brother.

Jess glared at him. "Ray?"

Still no answer. Ray's eyes stayed shut and his head bobbed up and down with the motion of the car.

She gave him a punch to the shoulder. "Ray!"

"Ow! Why'd you do that?"

"To wake you up."

"Couldn't you see I was sleeping?"

"I couldn't wake you up if you weren't. Besides, you'll want to see this."

"See what?"

Jess pointed to the distant oddity, which grew bigger by the second. "What do you think? The only thing that isn't salt."

Ray rubbed his eyes. "What is that? It looks like a skeleton."

"That's what I thought."

"Do you think it could be a wolf? They say that when wolves become too sick to go on, sometimes they leave their packs and wander into the salt pan to die. It's because the salt preserves their bodies—for a time."

"That's not a wolf, dummy. A dying wolf could never make it this far north. No one could, not without water or a vehicle."

"Hey, cut me some slack. How do you expect me to know how far from the border we are?"

Jess scowled. "You've been here with me the whole time!"

"I've been sleeping," said Ray. "I have no idea how far you've driven."

"You think you've been napping for two days straight?"

"I wouldn't put it past myself." He paused. "You're right, though. That can't be a wolf. It's much too big."

The buggy passed within fifty meters of the bones, close enough to validate Ray's observation. Each of the ribs hanging from the behemoth's spine was almost as tall as Ray himself. The massive eye holes on the skull met them with an eerie stare as they drove by.

"Want to get out and take a look?" asked Ray.

"I'd rather pass."

"All right then."

"Could it be an elephant?" asked Jess. "Maybe the wolves were hunting them. This one might have separated from the herd and found its way up here. An elephant might be able to make the journey."

"I don't see any leg bones," said Ray. "Also, it's too big. I think that's a whale."

"A whale?"

"You know, an extinct large aquatic mammal—"

"I know what a whale is. They were related to dolphins. But really, do you suppose it swam here?"

"I'm serious. They say the Great Salt Pan used to be a sea, one of the largest in the world. Everything here was underwater back when this whale died. They say the sea got cut off from the world ocean and dried up, leaving only the salt behind."

"Who are they?"

"They who?"

"You said *they* say these things about the salt pan."

"Oh. You know, scientists, archeologists, historians and such. Didn't you pay attention in school?"

"Better than you did."

"Well, our classes never taught us the interesting stuff anyway. There were many books I read besides our textbooks."

"You mean instead of? You didn't even unwrap your textbooks."

The skeleton became smaller as the buggy moved on. Ray watched as it disappeared behind the horizon, and eventually Jess took a peek as well, but it was already gone.

"Eyes on the road," said Ray.

"What's there for me to hit?"

"Maybe that lake."

Jess looked ahead. "What lake? I see only white."

"To our left. If you look closely, you can make out a shimmer."

"That? I thought that was just a mirage."

As they neared the anomaly, Jess saw that the mirage was in fact a lake. With nothing but white sky to reflect, it had blended in perfectly with the salt; only the wind's ripple gave it away. In the dimming light, Jess found herself surprised that Ray had noticed it in the first place.

"Stop the car," said Ray. "I want a closer look at the water."

"Could you not? We're in a hurry."

"Not really. We have all month to get this mission done. Besides, Mast never let us see the saline lakes."

"Because we had work to do then, just like we do now."

"Whatever. I'm getting out of the car either way, so you may as well stop."

He undid his seatbelt and jumped up onto the seat, holding a side of the doorframe in either hand.

"Ray, come on. Don't do it."

"Your call. You're the one who'll have to drive back for me."

Just as Ray prepared to jump, Jess slammed on the brakes. He left the doorframe off balance, but still managed to regain his stability midair. He landed into a somersault, spinning off his excess momentum, but Jess could tell his landing wasn't perfect. He had made the initial touchdown with bump rather than a swoosh.

She brought the buggy to a halt, turned off the motor, and ran to her brother. Ray hopped up and down as though his feet touched hot coals, clutching his shoulder as he did.

"Are you all right?"

"I'm fine," he said. "It's just a scrape."

"You're jumping around like you're in pain—or like you have to go to the bathroom."

"Have you ever had salt in a wound? Literally?"

Jess sighed. "You're an idiot. This wouldn't have happened if you hadn't jumped from the buggy."

"You're the one who slammed the brakes on me."

"You told me to stop!"

"I told you stop before I jumped, not while I jump. Lucky for me, I was able to take the hit in the shoulder."

"And now you have a scraped shoulder. Let me see it."

Jess yanked his hands from the wound and took a closer look. The cut was no longer than a finger, but seeing the salt particles ingrained in his flesh made her cringe.

"The shoulder is where you want to go down," said Ray. "Better the shoulder than the neck or chest. It can take more punishment. If your enemy is bound to land a strike, make sure it's in the shoulder."

"You don't need to repeat Mast's lessons for me," said Jess. "And you'd better get a bandage on this scrape."

"Maybe after my swim."

"Your what?"

"You heard me."

Ray ran off to the lake and Jess ran after him. Before she could catch him, he threw his belt onto the salt shore and waded out into the water.

"It's sort of warm," he said. "Still cooler than the air, though. Quite refreshing, actually."

"Ray, come back here."

He waded deeper into the murky water, and finally pushed off and began to float on his back.

"This is incredible! Look how easily I float!"

"I'm serious, get out of there. That water is poisonous. There's more than just salt in there."

"Do you see me drinking it?"

"You have an open wound. The toxins will find their way into your system."

"The cut is already as salty as it's going to get."

"There's more than just salt—"

"Yes, I heard you the first time."

Jess sighed. "We're falling behind schedule."

"Aha! I got you."

"Got me?"

Ray fumbled for the bottom with his feet and stood up to face her. "First you say you're worried about poison, now you say you're worried about wasting time. Well, which is it? You're just making excuses."

"Excuses? For what?"

"For being no fun."

"I'm fun!"

Ray whipped his hand through the water, splashing her with a giant wave. A dripping Jess glared back at him.

"So you're fun?" he asked. "Prove it."

Jess reached down and grabbed a handful of salt from the crumbly ground. She packed it in her hands like a snowball and chucked it at her brother. Ray leaned out of the way and let the saltball plop into the lake behind him.

"Missed me!"

She reached down again, this time not bothering to form a perfect sphere. Her claws dug beneath the cracks and ripped up a solid chunk of salt, which she flung at Ray. He dove backwards to let the salt fly over his head, and he proceeded to paddle on his back as before.

"Missed me again!"

Jess grabbed a third handful, but didn't throw it. Instead, she took off her own belt and sprinted out into the lake, splashing through the warm water as she closed in on him. Hearing the commotion, Ray looked up, but it was too late. Jess tackled him, grabbed him in a headlock, and rubbed the slab of salt into his scalp.

"All right! You got me!" Ray pushed himself free. "You win. You're plenty fun."

Jess took a step back. "I didn't get any in your eyes, did I?"

"No, I'm fine."

She looked down at herself. "Wonderful, now we're both

covered in salt. You realize we won't be showering for an entire month, and wearing that armor all day will just make things grimier."

"It's too late now." Ray reclined on the surface once again. "You might as well just enjoy it."

Jess sighed and turned back towards the shore, but then she stopped. She ran her hand through the water; it felt cool compared to the humid breeze, yet still warm enough to feel strangely relaxing. Somehow, it felt thicker than normal water as well. In her own shadow, she could see the unappealing murky depths, but everything else was the same white as the salt and sky, an infinite expanse of pristine.

She knelt down, finally letting her own buoyancy lift her feet from the bottom. She leaned onto her back as Ray had done, and kicked some distance between herself and the shore. Then she stopped. There was nothing left to do but float.

She stared at the sky, finding not a single break in the clouds. At first she worried the water would splash up onto her eyes, but the salinity held true and kept her amply afloat. There was nothing to hear but the breeze and the gentle waves, and soon, even these sounds faded away. Basking in the silence, Jess let her eyes close as she drifted through the ivory abyss.

Jess had not fallen asleep. Her mind had wandered somewhere far away, but she had not fallen asleep. Even still, she realized she had lost track of time when she noticed the darkening clouds.

"Hey Jess!"

Her head shot up. Ray stood over by the buggy with an unloaded crate and a sheet over the ground.

"Good, you're awake," he said. "I thought you might want some dinner."

"Dinner?" She felt for the bottom, finding it much shallower than expected. As Ray opened a can of preserved ants, she made her way to dry land to meet him.

"I hope you're hungry after your little snooze," said Ray. "For someone who's so concerned with the dangers of salt water, you're quite daring to take a nap right in the middle of it."

"I wasn't sleeping," said Jess. "I was just resting."

"Right, resting. Don't worry, I kept an eye on you. I would have jumped in to save you had you gone belly-down." He plopped half the can onto a tin plate and handed it to Jess. "Here you go."

"Yuck," she said, taking the tin. "Thanks, but still, yuck. I hate these."

"We have some termites too, if you'd prefer those."

"Doubt it. If it's in a can, it's gross." She slurped up a few slimy insects and resisted making a face.

"I took a look around the shore a few minutes ago. I thought there might be brine flies—you sometimes see those around salt water—but I couldn't find any. Guess no vegetation grows here, so there's nothing for them to eat."

"I'm not surprised." Jess looked back at the lake. "This place is about as dead as a place can be."

"It could be a lot worse for us," said Ray. "Braving the salt used to mean something back before they had buggies. Trekking on foot lends itself to exhaustion or injury, and some people would simply go mad after a day or two. Now you just drive across."

"The crossing is still no picnic."

Ray pointed at the sheet. "It looks like a picnic to me."

"You know what I mean. I could do without the heat."

"There's a chance it will get cold at night, but with this cloud coverage I doubt it. We should camp here until morning."

"We could put in another hour behind the wheel."

"Maybe, but it's getting dark. We'd be better off just setting up the tent and getting some rest. How about I build a fire?"

"How about you don't. Anyone nearby will see the flame."

"Who would be there to see it? The whale skeleton? You said it yourself—there won't be any wolves this far north."

"Let's not take chances."

"Fine," said Ray. "We'll skip the fire, but I'm setting up the tent. I doubt it will rain, but with these clouds, who can say?"

He finished his can of ants and tossed it into a plastic bag. He walked over to the supply crate and pulled the tent loose from the rest of the luggage.

"We should go over some of the things Dr. Wilson talked about," said Jess. "Just so we'll be prepared when we arrive."

Ray tossed the tent on the ground and began to take out the stakes. "All right. Like what?"

"Just a few basic things about their customs and behaviors. Enough so we won't stand out too much in a pack."

"Sure. I'll quiz you first. In what type of duel is it expected of the victor to kill his or her opponent?"

"Hold on," said Jess. "We should practice talking like wolves too."

"What do you mean?"

"You know how pre-ops talk. Use poor grammar and such. They might notice if we speak differently, so we'd better to get into the habit now."

"If wolves don't understand correct grammar to begin with, how will they tell?"

"Let's just play it safe. Give it a try."

"Fine," said Ray. "Now answer question. Which type duel make wolf kill opponent?"

"Duel between two wolf in same pack," said Jess. "Duel between two wolf from different pack good for settle dispute between pack, but wolf no need kill opponent. If dispute between two wolf of same clan, it bring discord into pack to have both live."

Ray grimaced. "Jess, talking like this sounds awful."

"Talking like this *sound* awful," said Jess. "No conjugate verb."

"I wasn't even—"

"I know you not. Just do, all right?"

"Fine," said Ray. "Now you ask me question."

"Tell me about pack structure. Who in charge of pack?"

"Easy. Pack leader in charge of pack."

"Tell more. Who in charge if pack lose leader?"

"No one. If pack lose leader, wolves join other pack. If one wolf strong enough, that wolf start new pack."

Jess nodded. "My turn."

"Who do pack take order from?"

"Most pack take order from strongest pack. Leader is Warlord. Some rogue pack too, take order from no one. Question for you now. How do people hire wolf as mercenary?"

"If you need one pack, you find one pack and pay. If you need more than one pack, you go to Warlord. Warlord arrange for many pack."

Ray threw the rainproof sheet over the finished tent. It wasn't exactly a camper's palace, but it had more than enough space to sleep two anteaters comfortably.

"Tent done," he said. "It soon get pitch black. If you want stay outside, we need flashlight."

"No light," said Jess. "Someone see."

"Whatever you say. Then we go to bed now. Wake up with light."

Jess stashed her plate in the trunk, not sparing any of their precious fresh water to rinse it off. Ray had rolled out two sleeping bags, but she doubted she'd need hers. Nightfall had done little to dispel the muggy heat, but if the clouds cleared and the temperature dropped, she could always awaken and slip inside where it was warm. Ray zipped up the door behind them and turned to his side, facing away from her.

She lay atop her sleeping bag, watching the dim glow through the fabric fade until it was dark. No light from the moon or galaxies made it through the clouds, and no nearby cities turned the clouds a dull purple with their lights. She brought her hand in front of her face and found that she could not see her fingers. Nothing but black.

Sleep did not come easily. It was much earlier than she was used to going to bed, but Jess doubted the hour was to blame. Her thoughts turned to the bear they had fought at the drive-in movie. He hadn't been a particularly strong opponent, but somehow his cruel grin and maniacal laugh stuck in her mind.

She could hear Ray breathing, but his breaths weren't the smooth, rhythmic inhales and exhales of slumber. They were disjointed enough to suggest he hadn't found sleep either.

"Ray? You awake?"

There was a rustle as though he had rolled around.

"Yeah. You?"

"Obviously. I can't sleep. I keep thinking about the Bear."

"Don't worry about Bear, he lousy fighter."

"Ray, you can cut that out now. You don't have to talk like that."

"Well, forgive me," he said. "You were the one who made us do it in the first place."

"I know, but now I just want to talk. Yes, I know he wasn't the best fighter, but there was something else about him that bothers me."

"What bothers me is that he didn't try to face us in a fair fight," said Ray. "He tried to blow us up without us ever even knowing who he was. All my battle training is useless against such a cowardly move."

"You should have spent more time honing your instincts," said Jess. "Mine saved our lives, and they will again if need be. That's not what concerns me."

"Then what is?"

"Believe it or not, he reminded me of the bad guy in that cheesy movie."

"Hey, that movie was pretty good, and I never got to watch the end of it."

"No, it was awful, but that's beside the point. This bear seemed to enjoy what he was doing. He liked acting like he was evil."

"Are you saying he's a movie villain?"

"No. I don't know. Maybe that's not it."

There was silence for a time, enough to suggest the conversation had ended for the night. Then Jess turned to Ray once more.

"Do you ever think about Dad?"

"All the time," he said. "I think about Mom sometimes too."

"Let's not talk about her," said Jess. "I do think about Dad all the time though. Do you remember the day we heard the news that he died?"

"I'll remember it for the rest of my life," said Ray. "Edward took leave from the division just to come home and tell us in person. He told us they had found his body, but no one knew how it happened. They suspected Monkey spies."

"But it wasn't Monkey spies," said Jess. "We both know who killed him."

Ray said nothing.

"We're descendants of Anton," said Jess. "We will never be safe from Lazarus."

"Anton will protect us."

"If he's even still alive."

"Well, maybe Lazarus is dead too. And if he isn't dead, but Anton is, then your big brother will protect you."

Jess scowled, although she knew Ray could not see her face. "Hey! I'm only a year younger than you."

"And don't you forget it."

There was silence again, and this time, the silence seemed there to stay. Jess rolled over again, finally finding herself comfortable. As she drifted towards the edge of sleep, she thought she heard Ray's voice, although it might have just been a dream.

"Anton isn't dead. He can't be."

Chapter 9

Two dozen, no, three dozen wolves stood in a circle, each reeling back as though ready to pounce into the center. Behind them, a handful of buggies lay scattered across the sand, no logic or reason behind their parking arrangement. Although she couldn't hear it, Jess could see their jaws clench and snap as they growled and barked at one another. Despite their fierce displays, no one stepped into the center of the ring. These wolves were just blowing off steam; the fight was only a fight of snarls.

"What do you see?" asked Ray.

"Wolves."

"I know that. How many are there?"

"At least thirty."

"Do they have liquids or weapons?"

"I don't see any, but they might have them in their buggies."

"Do they—"

"Here, just look yourself."

She shoved the binoculars in Ray's face. He took hold of them in his gloves and lifted them up to the eyeholes in his liquids. He adjusted them and stared for a moment.

"Yeah, that's a pack of wolves all right."

"No, really?"

"What do you think?" asked Ray. "Is this the one? Should we go make contact?"

"You reckon we'll find a better one?"

"I don't know. Maybe."

"What's wrong with this one?"

"Nothing as far as I can tell, but it might be a rogue pack, which we don't want. We want a pack in contact with the Warlord."

"Ray, we're not going to be able to tell whether or not it's rogue from here. The only way to know is to join them and listen in on what they have to say. If they are on their own, we can always sneak away again."

"So that's a yes?"

"Yes, that's a yes."

Jess turned the ignition and the buggy responded. She hit the accelerator and they sped down the hill in a cloud of dust. She weaved around patches of dry grass towards the gathering in the distance.

They had made it out of the salt pan on the third day, out of the salt pan and into the desert. The sun was just as hot, the air just as dry, and while the salt stuck to itself, dust found its way everywhere.

She noted it wasn't as dead and sterile as the salt pan. What little water to be found was safe enough to drink, and a few yellow shrubs had found enough moisture to take root. Still, the desert seemed a sorry place to make a home for oneself. The Wolves only lived in such a place because it was the only land the old empire hadn't deemed worth holding.

The dirt had appeared on the horizon early that morning, and as soon as they had crossed it, Jess had made them get out and put on the liquids. Each had plopped to the sand as the Anteaters yanked them from their bindings. Donning the liquids had proved quite a challenge; each leg and arm took a minute to fit and strap into place and they had to help one another buckle up the back. The headpiece covered all but the eyes; only a thin filter covered the mouth.

Their utility as armor was questionable at best. The files insisted that they were in fact composed of dilatant particles, but then again, cornstarch and water was a dilatant too. She was used to lightweight, high-concentration germanium polymer dilatant liquid body armor. These liquids were brown and bulky, not thin and clear and barely noticeable like the ones she normally wore. Jess couldn't extend her arms all the way out or bring them all the way back in around her chest. She could only turn her head a few degrees to either side, and her legs were stiff and sluggish. The thought crossed her mind that perhaps these liquids wouldn't even harden to stop a musket ball, in which case, she may as well be wearing an oversized sack of potatoes. On top of everything else, they smelled. At first, they carried an unsavory aroma she guessed to be wolf, but soon the stench of her own sweat and grime replaced the old one. She could only hope she wouldn't smell too foreign. It was a good thing the filter didn't block water, as Jess found herself indulging in her canteen every chance she got.

Ray seemed even more uncomfortable than she did, but he said nothing, so she did the same. They had gotten back on the buggy, and after a few hours, they had stumbled across the pack.

It was farther away than it appeared, as was everything else in the desert. The motor still drowned the distant barks and snarls.

"You're thinking of your old car, aren't you?" asked Ray.

"What?"

"This buggy isn't as nice as the car the Bear blew up. That's all right, the insurance paid up. We'll get a better one as soon as we're home."

"Oh that," said Jess. "Yeah, the car's a shame. A buggy's better for this sort of driving though. We wouldn't want to ruin a nice car on the sand."

"We never even got to think up a name for the old one. How about we call the new one the 'Antmobile'?"

"We could do better, but we'll keep that in mind until we think of something else."

As they neared the wolves, heads began to poke up and stare at the approaching vehicle. The circle broke as the largest members of the bunch stepped forward, noses twitching at the visitors.

"This is it," said Jess. "Remember our story."

"I will."

"And remember to talk right."

"I will!"

She fought the urge to make another comment. The pack was only fifty meters away and the Anteaters' last chance to speak in private had passed. None of the wolves stepped out of the way of the buggy. Jess coasted to a stop at the foot of a stocky, shaggy wolf.

Jess turned off the motor and stood up from her seat, but the hairy wolf spoke first.

"Are little pups lost? You come long way to find dangerous place. Why you challenge Tusk Pack?"

She had a response prepared, but somehow her words dissolved into her mind before she could speak. Her eyes fell to the sharp teeth and broad shoulders of the pack warriors. In truth, the group they had apprehended a week ago had looked just as menacing, but Jess hadn't noticed then. This time was different.

A taller warrior leaned against the driver side and dug her claws against the steel frame.

"Afraid to talk?" she asked. "You should be. Big liquids no keep you safe here. I rip them off and stab you with dagger."

"We no want fight," said Ray. "We part of other pack, but pack leader die. Now, we no have pack."

"And how that our problem?" asked the stocky wolf.

"It not, but we look for help."

Ray stood from his seat and shifted toward the door, but the wolf stepped over and blocked his way.

"Where you think you going?"

"Let him by," said Jess. "My brother right. We no want harm your pack. I tell you, we lose our pack a week ago."

"Which pack you lose?" asked the she-wolf.

"Razor Pack."

"I never hear of Razor Pack. Must be weak pack. How your leader die?"

"He die in fight against rival pack."

"See? Weak pack." The tall wolf pinched Jess's liquids in the manner one mocks a fat child. "She weak too."

Jess glared and smacked the wolf's paw off her arm. At once, the she-wolf bore her teeth, as did the entire pack. Jess's hand shot for the ignition, her foot ready to slam the buggy into reverse.

"Stop!" said Ray. "No fight! We want to join Tusk Pack!"

"What you say?"

The wolves unclenched their jaws as the largest of their ranks stepped forward. His claws weren't the longest or sharpest, but toned muscles bulged beneath his short fur.

"Marissa, Ralph, step back. Let wolves out of buggy."

The stocky wolf and tall wolf lowered their heads and did as told. The other wolves made room as well, and the biggest extended a paw to the two in the buggy. After exchanging a look, the Anteaters climbed out of the vehicle to face him. Each kept a hand on the frame.

"My name Wolf Ben, leader of Tusk Pack," said the wolf. "You want to join my pack?"

"Yes," said Jess. "My name Wolf Jess, this my brother, Wolf Ray. We need new pack."

Ben chuckled. "Tusk Pack stronger than all other pack. Not all wolf can join."

"We train hard. We know how to fight. We already have buggy and supplies, so we no need take any of yours. We make good warrior for your pack."

"If you so strong, why your last pack lose against enemy?"

"We no fight. Only leader fight, and he die."

"Leader of Razor Pack fool to die in pack duel," said Ben. "He not strong or smart. Anyone good enough to join Tusk Pack never let weak wolf lead them."

"We strong. We prove it."

"Yes, you will, but not here. We find chance soon." He paused. "Why you wear liquids?"

"Rival pack have muskets. They say they hunt and kill all old member of Razor Pack. We keep safe."

"You no need liquids now. No one hurt you when Tusk Pack protect you."

The she-wolf walked up to him. "What you say? You let them join Tusk warriors so easily?"

"For now," said Ben. "No worry, Marissa. We test them when we get chance."

"Tusk Pack no need new warriors. We have enough for job."

"We have enough when pack leader say we have enough. Who is pack leader?"

Marissa growled, running her claws over the back of Ben's neck as she walked away. Unfazed, the leader grinned at the new arrivals.

"Tusk Pack heading out soon. If you want to join, follow along. Warlord have big plans."

Chapter 10

"Attention, attention." The voice blared over the loudspeaker. "We apologize for the delay. We've been monitoring a little bit of inclement weather, and here at Carrie's Ferries the safety of our customers is always our number one priority. However, it looks like our storm won't be heading south anytime soon, so we should begin boarding within the hour. Thank you for your patience."

A few cheers and claps broke out among the crowd, but most of the customers were already too agitated to celebrate. Sky wasn't among the applauding or the agitated.

Everything since the initiation had been a blur. She didn't even remember walking back to the lodge to greet a proud Master Nyah. She had always imagined that if she ever passed the trial, she would spend the following days in utter euphoria. The euphoria never hit her. She was indeed happy, not to mention relieved, but for the most part she still couldn't believe she had really done it, that she had actually become a priest.

The pain in the stub that had once been her tail kept her more occupied than anything else. Enduring an instant of agony was one thing, but suffering a week of extreme discomfort was another trial altogether. The wound demanded constant care, exhausting her supply of bandages and ointment, and it made sitting or lying on her back unpleasant. Only after a week had it finally become manageable.

Above the chatter of the queue, Sky overheard voices, voices that seemed directed at her. She turned to see two bears leaning against the railing and glaring at her and Nyah. They were locals by the looks of it; they carried no luggage for the ferry.

"I don't like the way those bears are looking at us."

Nyah looked over at the locals. "I wouldn't worry about them. They'll look and jeer, but that will be all. The High Priest negotiated the agreement with the Bear Nation years ago. So long as we keep to ourselves, the priesthood has amnesty here."

"I shouldn't need amnesty," said Sky. "I've done nothing wrong. They're looking at me like I'm some sort of war criminal."

"You were born many years after the fall of our empire," said Nyah. "In all likelihood, so were those two. But they've heard the stories. They've grown up to the heroic tales of their parents and grandparents fighting for freedom against the tyrannical Monkeys. To them, you're not Sky, you're simply a monster from an old legend."

"But I don't mean them any harm. None of us do, none of us ever did, but especially not me."

"Sky, everyone has always loved you, but this is your first time traveling beyond your home. You see now that monkeys, especially us priests, are not welcome beyond our borders. I know how much you want to be loved by all, and if anyone deserves to be loved, it is you. But no one can please everyone, whether you be monkey, bear, fox, or even anteater. You serve the Celestial Monkeys now, and theirs is the only approval you need seek."

Sky nodded slowly. Nyah grinned and gave her a playful shove to the shoulder.

"Would it hurt to smile, Sky? This should be a happy time for you."

Sky managed to crack a smile. "It is. It really is. Initiation is all I've thought about for months, but now that it's over, I don't know what to think."

"You'll have plenty to think of soon enough. Perhaps you should devote most of this voyage to solitary meditation."

"Maybe," said Sky. "I should be ready to receive my assignment with a clear head. You wouldn't mind if I kept to myself during the ferry ride? It will only be a few hours."

Nyah paused for a moment, turning to glance out over the ocean. "I was waiting for the right moment to tell you this, but I don't think I'll get another chance."

"Tell me what?"

Nyah turned back to her. "I received a message from the

Temple."

"What did they say?"

"Two things, actually. The first is that they approved my request: I will remain in the Bear Nation."

"You're not coming with me?"

"Hadn't you wondered why I didn't bring my suitcase?"

"Why do you want to stay behind?"

"I'm just getting too old to continue this routine," said Nyah. "I always knew you were to be my last pupil. What better place to live out my days than near the holy grounds of the Ancient Circle?"

"And all that you said about priests not being welcome here?"

"The years have thickened my skin. The sacred monument is more important to me than a kind unkind looks."

"I'm happy for you, Master," said Sky. "But what am I to do now? If you're not going back with me, who will give me my assignment? Will I have to go all the way back to the Temple to receive it?"

"That's the second thing," said Nyah. "They've already approved your first assignment, and they gave me permission to pass it on to you before we part ways."

"Already?"

"Would you like to hear where you're headed?"

Sky nodded.

"Congratulations, Friar Sky," said Nyah. "You have earned yourself a place among the Sand Monoliths."

"Are you serious?"

"I gave you nothing but my highest recommendation. You are to report to Grand Master Shariff to begin your service."

Sky hugged her. "Thank you, Master! Thank you so much!"

Nyah laughed and returned the embrace. "Oh, Sky, how I will miss you. It has been a great pleasure guiding your path, and I know the Celestial Monkeys have big plans for you."

"Attention, passengers!" The loudspeaker blared again. "We are now ready to proceed with boarding. Have your tickets and identification ready."

The two monkeys let go and stood apart for a moment.

"I guess it's time for me to go," said Sky.

Nyah nodded. "Don't keep the Monoliths waiting."

As the line began to inch forward, Sky took her place in the queue and moved along with the stream of bears and foxes. The ferry ahead was quite an impressive ship, a dark red triple decker vessel so large that Sky wondered why the weather had ever been a concern. Her previous ride to the Bear Nation had been as smooth as if it were on solid ground. Perhaps the talk of weather had been a front for something far more dangerous, such as a dolphin pod sighting. She shuddered at the thought and put it out of her mind.

When she reached the ramp, a scruffy bear greeted her with a smile and held out her hand to take her ticket and card.

"How are you today, ma'am?" she asked.

"I'm fine."

She handed back her ID and ticket stub. "Go right on ahead. Head to the main compartment and show them your stub to check your luggage."

After she had checked her bag, Sky headed back out do the deck to overlook the harbor. Try as she may, he couldn't see Master Nyah anywhere. The pier had become crowded, but it would be easy to pick out a monkey, particularly a priest, in the crowd.

After a few shouts from the dock, the ramp retracted and the engines roared to life. The boat began to float away from the harbor, swinging around in a gradual arc until it pointed out into the channel.

Sky could have run around the ship to maintain her line of sight with the crowd, but instead she remained where she stood and let the boat face her to the sea. As the breeze ruffled her tuft of hair, she felt a smile form on her face. Master Nyah was right; she had every reason to be happy. Perhaps the question of her assignment had been the last lingering thread of apprehension.

A distant flash of lightning lit up the clouds along the horizon, and the boom of thunder soon followed. In that moment, she saw the lightning from the morning of the initiation, the lightning that had split the sky right before she had lost her tail.

The initiator had said the storm was a bad omen, and that had terrified Sky. Yet she had completed the initiation and emerged triumphant, so what was there to worry about? She tried to shake the feeling of dread.

Someone tapped on her shoulder. She turned around to see a wide-eyed sheep.

"Sorry to bother," the sheep said. "I notice you in line. You are priest, yes?"

It sounded so weird to hear someone say.

"Yes," said Sky. "I am a priest. What can I do for you?"

"My son very sick," she said. "I take him to see doctor in Bear Nation, but it do no good. He no get better."

"I'm so sorry," said Sky. "Is there anything I can do to help?"

"I pray every night to Celestial Monkeys, but they no hear my prayer. But you are priest. If you pray to Celestial Monkeys, they hear you and make him better."

"Take me to him."

"Follow me."

She followed the sheep to the rows of benches lining the interior of the cabin. It was a quiet day for the ferry and very few pre-ops were aboard. Almost immediately Sky spotted the sheep's son, a little ball of wool curled up in one of the front seats.

Sky put her hand to the tiny lamb's forehead. It felt hot and sweaty, yet she could still make out the faint breath.

"Wake up, Bava. I bring priest. She pray to Celestial Monkeys and make you better."

A weak murmur came from the lamb, but his eyes didn't open.

"Wake up. You feel better soon."

"It's all right," said Sky. "He doesn't have to be awake. I will pray."

She put her hands together and bowed her head.

"Almighty Celestial Monkeys, hear my prayer. I speak to you as your humble servant and ask that you listen. This child before me is very ill, and no earthly remedy can make him well. Only a miracle from you can make him whole again. My heavenly mothers and fathers, I ask that you show him mercy, and let him live."

Sky remained in silence for another moment, letting her mind clear and her soul connect with the beyond. Then she opened her eyes.

The lamb remained curled in a ball, as still as before. Sky listened closer, and then put her palm against the sheep's wooly side; he wasn't breathing.

His mother began to cry, and the cry grew into a wail. Sky wanted to put her hand on the mother's shoulder, wanted to comfort her, but instead she did the opposite. She ran.

Sky raced out of the cabin and around the deck until she found a deserted corner of the ship. When she did, she sat against the wall, covered her eyes, and curled up against her knees.

As she did, the stump of her tail screamed in pain.

Chapter 11

The glow of the morning sky fought its way through the thin fabric of the tent. Little by little, the glow illuminated the huge lump in front of him. The lump stirred and Ray held his breath. Best not to wake his sister and begin the day earlier than they had to.

Jess stopped moving and Ray let out a quiet exhale of relief. Despite how comfortable he was, he just couldn't seem to fall back asleep. Chilly air filled his lungs with every breath, but the rest of his body had stayed warm throughout the frigid night. The heavy liquids had been torture during the day, but at night they proved pleasantly toasty.

His sister stirred again, and this time she came to a stop a bit too deliberate for Ray's taste. She turned her head to him.

"Ray? Are you awake?"

He shut his eyes.

"Ray? Can you hear me?"

She reached over and shook him. He responded with an incoherent grumble.

"Ray, wake up."

She shook him again, this time too hard for him to pretend to sleep through.

"Wha—?"

"Not so loud. The wolves might hear you."

He looked at her and rubbed his eyes.

"What time is it? No one is up yet."

"That's the point. We're going to sneak away to use the

bathroom and get a bite to eat before any of the wolves wake up."

"You go. I'm staying here."

"We're both going. We need stand guard for each other."

"How about we go in ten minutes."

"No, we're going now. We've waited long enough already."

Before Ray could protest again, Jess stood up and dragged him out of his sleeping bag. Holding his wrist in one hand, she unzipped the tent with the other.

"Keep your voice down. We don't want anyone to hear us."

"I heard you the first time."

The sand and sky were a deep blue, but one side of the horizon was much pinker than the other. Not a single cricket disturbed the eerie silence of the morning. He could hear every tiny noise he made, from his breath to his feet sinking into the sand.

He followed Jess around the nearest sand dune, far enough that they were out of sight of the camp. On the other side, a few large shrubs poked out from the cracks between the rocky floor.

"That should do," said Jess. "I'll go first. You keep watch and make sure none of the wolves come over."

"Got it."

She undid her headpiece first, revealing a thick strand of saliva between her mouth and the filter.

"What do you have there?" asked Ray.

"It's nothing," Jess said as she wiped her lips. "Don't you ever drool while you're asleep?"

"Lovely."

"Shut up." She began walking towards the bush. "Don't peek."

"Wasn't going to."

Ray turned around and watched the corner of the dune. He realized even if a wolf did come around the corner to investigate, Jess wouldn't have time to buckle her liquids back up. He would have to stall them.

The wolves hadn't given them much trouble the day before. They had spent most of the daylight driving around, with the leader occasionally stopping to get out and sniff the air. For whom or what the wolf had been looking, Ray couldn't say. He had hoped for some discussion about the Warlord's agenda, but Wolf Ben and the others had remained silent on the matter. Come nightfall, the wolves had turned in without a word, and the Anteaters had done the same.

A series of buckles and snaps echoed from behind the bush. A fully covered Jess stepped out and walked back to join him.

"I'm done," she said. "Now you go."

"I'll be fine."

"Ray, it's going to be a long day. Go now."

"No really, I'm fine. I went twenty minutes ago."

"You what?"

"I woke up and I had to go. I figured it was a good time. It was still dark out and no one else was up."

"Why didn't you wake me and have me stand watch?"

"Because you were sleeping. I thought it would nice of me to leave you alone."

"What if one of the wolves had followed you?"

"No one did. Don't worry about it." Ray reached into his belt and pulled out a can of ants. "Are you hungry?"

Jess paused. He imagined a grimace behind her mask. "Just be careful with those cans," she said. "An empty can of insects would look suspicious."

Ray held out the naked aluminum container. "These are unmarked. So long as we finish them off, no one will know what was inside."

She shrugged. "All right. Fine."

"You don't need to worry so much." Ray popped open the lid. "Will you insist on taking turns behind the bush again?"

"Don't bother."

Facing off into the desert, the Anteaters undid the fronts of their masks and pulled the filters aside. Ray took a scoop of ants and then passed the can to his sister, who endured as many nibbles as she could manage. She offered the can back to Ray.

"I already had plenty," he said. "You finish it."

"Any more of these and I'll puke."

"Really? You're going to make it through the day on two mouthfuls?"

"Just finish them up. Suspicious can, remember?"

Ray downed the rest of the ants and licked out the inside with his long tongue. He tucked the empty can back into his belt and buckled up his headpiece.

"Shall we head back to camp?" asked Jess.

"How about we wait out here for another minute. No one is up yet, and once the day begins, we won't get another chance to really talk to one another."

"All right. What do you want to talk about?"

"I don't know. How are things with you?"

"Ray, you've been here with me this whole time. What do you think?"

"We're traveling with wolves. How are you holding up?"

"They really didn't give us any trouble yesterday. No one seemed interested in talking, but they'll want to talk soon enough. And they had better—we do need information from them."

"True," said Ray. "It shouldn't be too hard to get what we need from them. Did you ever have any pre-op friends?"

"We know all the same people. There's that nice sheep who delivers our newspaper, and that cat I sometimes see stocking the grocery store."

"I remember him. He never said a word to me."

"Me neither. So maybe I wouldn't exactly call either of them my friend. I haven't had a real pre-op friend since I was too young to tell the difference."

"There were the Dogs at the academy."

Jess chuckled. "Dogs are concretes, not pre-ops."

"I know. I just say that to piss off Brad."

"It's about time," said Jess. "We should get a head start on packing our stuff."

He followed her back through the sand and around the dune. At first the camp looked just as quiet as before. Then he noticed the lone wolf sitting outside her tent.

It wasn't one of the wolves he remembered from the day before. The wolf looked up at the Anteaters. Ray's mind raced for an explanation, but the wolf said nothing. She kept her eyes on the siblings, but withheld any remark she might have had.

The Anteaters did the best they could to ignore her. Jess collapsed the tent while Ray stuffed the supplies back into the buggy's crate. When he had finished, he sat in the passenger seat and waited. He couldn't talk to Jess anymore, and the wolf certainly wasn't one for conversation. There was nothing to do but sit and wait.

Ray opened his eyes to incoherent chatter and a bright morning sun. He sat up straight and rubbed his face, trying to adjust to the blurry image in front of him. Most of the wolves were up and about, packing their tents and prepping their buggies. Jess was leaning against the hood of their own buggy.

"What time now?" asked Ray.

"Late enough," said Jess. "I punch you to wake you up."

He spotted the pack leader across the encampment. The wolf seemed intent on checking up on all his soldiers, checking on their supplies and health. Before long, he made his way to the newcomers.

"You find Tusk Pack good, Jess?" he asked.

"I do find it good, thank you Ben."

"You sleep good?"

"Yes, I do."

"Tusk pack keep you safe now. Why you still wear liquids?"

"We never be safe while enemy pack leader alive. He send warrior to sneak after us and kill us. Until he dead, we wear liquids."

"Even while sleep?"

"Yes."

Ben thought for a moment. "I think I know pack that destroy Razor Pack. Black Sun Pack known to destroy a dozen other pack. Wolf Maurice brutal. He think if he kill enough wolf, he become next Warlord. Was it Black Sun Pack?"

Jess nodded.

"No worry," said Ben. "Black Sun Pack no last long. Many other wolf hate them. You get justice soon."

"I hope we do. Black Sun Pack cruel and ruthless. I remember every day how they kill leader."

All the other wolves were awake, and most of them had finished packing their supplies. As they finished, they began to wander around, gravitating towards their leader. Ben walked back to meet them in the center of the camp, and Jess followed. Ray pulled himself from the passenger seat and followed as well, keeping an eye on the nearby wolves on either side. As the group congregated, some of the warriors began to growl.

"Quiet!" said Ben. "No growl now. I need announce plans."

The pack silenced and all eyes went to Ben.

"Very good. We need meet with Warlord as soon we can and Grand Oasis is a few days south."

"Our supply low," said one of the other wolves. "We need food."

"I know," said Ben. "We no travel today. Today we hunt."

Happy shouts and barks rang across the camp.

"Good hunting grounds a hundred kilometers to west. They crowded this time of year, but weak wolves make way for Tusk Pack! I need volunteer to take half of pack when we arrive. Two groups circle around and catch gazelle."

Marissa stepped forward. "I lead second group." She turned to the Anteaters. "But you take new recruits. I no want them slowing me down."

"Thank you, Marissa. I happy to have new warriors in group with me."

"We try not to eat all gazelle before you catch up." Marissa turned and walked back to her buggy.

"We leave now," Ben said to the group. "Follow my buggy. We arrive in a few hours."

The group dispersed and the Anteaters found their way back to their vehicle. On his way, Ray veered one step too close to one of the warriors, who growled until Ray gave him some space. Their own buggy was parked in the far corner of the camp, some distance from the gaggle where everyone else had parked.

"I take turn at wheel?"

"Fat chance," said Jess.

Ray climbed into the passenger seat as his sister revved the engine. She kept it in park as they watched the wolves start up their buggies and drive off into the desert. Finally, making sure to keep track of Ben's buggy and not Marissa's, Jess shifted into gear and sped off after them.

The treacherous desert path proved a greater trial than the salt pan, but the massive tires beneath the frame handled the loose sand and jagged rock. After negotiating several dunes, the procession found its way onto more solid ground, and Ray sat back to watch the rocky hills roll by.

The buggies kept a wide spacing from one another and the poorly muffled engines provided ample noise. Ray felt it safe to venture a few words.

"We could just ask him, you know," he said.

"Ask who what?"

"Ask the pack leader about the Warlord's plans. As soon as we have the information we need, we can make our getaway."

"Wouldn't that sound suspicious? They probably assume we're already up to speed with the plans."

"You think he'd catch on?"

"I don't know, but Edward entrusted us with this mission. We owe it to him to do it right, to get him some high quality photos."

"So we'll tough it out then," said Ray. "We'll follow Tusk Pack right to the Warlord."

"If all goes as planned. Now let's be quiet. I know they can't hear us now, but we shouldn't get smug."

Ray considered responding, but decided against it. He had already violated their early morning assertion that they wouldn't get another chance to speak.

He spent the next few hours admiring the passing landscape. Some of the rocky hills were almost perfectly triangular, enough so to remind him of the Sand Monoliths. For a moment, he wondered if he would get to see the monoliths themselves, but that was ridiculous; the monuments were thousands of kilometers east of the Wolf Lands.

After spending so much time in the salt, Ray found it easy to appreciate the variety of life that had found a home in the sand. There was no shortage of vegetation, and every now and then a frightened hare would jump out from behind the rocks and sprint away. He admired the birds soaring above, that is, until he realized they were probably scavengers. A wolf pack on the move promised an impending kill and an easy meal.

The vultures followed them all the way the hunting grounds. Ray had again considered offering a turn at the wheel, but remembered his sister's insistence of both silence and her uncontested spot in the driver's seat. She had been that way ever since her learner's permit, and Ray found no reason to complain.

The hunting grounds looked no different than any other stretch of the desert, but the wolves knew it when they saw it. When Ray and Jess arrived, all the buggies but only half the pack awaited them.

"Marissa and her group leave already," Ben said as the Anteaters joined the circle. "They chase gazelle into our trap and we kill. They have ten minute start on us, so they ready soon."

"She give signal?" asked one of the pack.

"She give signal when gazelle move, yes." Ben looked up at the two in liquids. "Liquids slow you down. You no want take off?"

"We run fast even with them," said Jess.

"If you sure. Follow me."

The wolves took off at a reasonable jog that wasn't too hard to keep up with. They made their way up the nearest hill, and as they approached the top, the wolves dropped to all fours and crawled to the summit.

"There, I see gazelle." The wolf to Ben's right pointed.

"I see too. There big group, fifteen, maybe twenty."

"They no see us. We kill now."

"No. We wait. Marissa signal soon."

Ray squinted. Where were these gazelle? Sweat dripped in his eyes, sweat he couldn't completely wipe away with his bulky gloves.

"ARRROOOOOOO!"

The howl echoed from the distance and a swarm of shapes burst from the grass below. Now Ray could see the gazelle, but by the time he got his bearings, the pack had already given chase. Ben and the others raced down the side of the hill, howling and snarling, with Jess trying to keep up. The herd of gazelle noticed the oncoming wolves, and served to the right to avoid the pack.

Ray ran down the mountain as fast as he could, conjuring all his focus just to catch himself with each step. The liquids fought him with every leap, always yanking his foot back in the wrong direction as he tried to make solid landing. He soon gave up on running and slid feet first, painlessly down the hillside. The howls grew more and more distant.

As he approached the bottom, his footing gave way beneath him. He struggled to catch himself, but it was no use; he had entered freefall. After the first two bounces, Ray made no further effort to catch himself. The liquids cushioned every blow, and there was something strangely relaxing in letting gravity tumble him to the base.

He landed face-first in the dirt and immediately looked up to make sure no one had seen him fall. There was no one to be seen; even Jess was long gone. Breathing a sigh of relief, he sat up—and felt a familiar tickle on his face. He rubbed his eyes and then brought his hand back for a closer look. Ants!

He had fallen right in the middle of an anthill, one of the biggest he had ever seen. North of the salt, the ants only bothered to carve out tiny tunnels in the dirt, but here they crafted skyscrapers. Ray almost felt guilty for what he was about to do. He looked up again to ensure he was alone, and then tore the filter from his headpiece and ripped open the hill with his sharp claws. The frantic insects poured out in every direction, only to fall victim to Ray's sticky tongue. He ate and ate, slowing down only to breathe. It was heaven. He may not have complained as Jess did at the canned ants, but Ray had been craving fresh food all the same.

"Ray?" The voice called from behind. It was a female voice, but it did not belong to Jess. He froze.

"You all right? You fall behind."

Ever so slowly, he reached for his filter and pressed it back into place. Only then did he turn to face his visitor. It was the wolf they had seen awake at the camp earlier that morning.

"I fine," he said. "I trip on hill, but liquids keep me safe."

She nodded. "You no meet me yet. My name Wolf Sam."

"My name Wolf Ray."

"I know." She walked over to him. "Marissa already make kill before Ben arrive. Enough gazelle for everyone. I stay back to find you."

"Where Jess?"

Sam didn't answer. She just stared at him. When Ray felt another tickle near his eye, he realized why.

"You fall in anthill," she said. "You need be careful."

"Oh, right. I no notice."

He stepped away from the anthill and Sam reached over to brush the ants off him. She paused and gave him a strange look.

"You smell. You smell like, well, odd."

Ray stood still. "How I smell odd?"

"Don't know."

"Maybe I smell like fox? I kill fox last week. I still smell like him."

"You stupid," she said. "Fox very dangerous."

"Fox not dangerous. Fox small, easy to crush."

"Fox smart. They build gun and better liquids. Some know how to fight even better than wolf. If any wolf become a danger to one fox, other foxes always find out and kill wolf. You need no worry about rival wolf pack. If you kill fox, you need worry about other foxes."

"Fox attack me. I need kill him to survive."

"They no care about that. You kill one fox, now they hunt you like we hunt gazelle. My mother tell me smart wolf leave fox alone."

Ray did his best to sound concerned. "I don't know what to do, but it too late now. This explain why I smell like fox."

She shook her head. "You no smell like fox. I never smell anything like this before, but I know it not fox."

There was a long silence. Ray tried to think of another explanation, but nothing came to mind.

"We waste time here," he said. "We go find rest of pack."

Sam waited a moment, and then nodded. She walked alongside him, but said nothing more as she led him back to the other wolves.

The pack encircled three gazelle strewn across the desert floor, each with entrails hanging out of their gaping wounds. Most of the wolves were already neck deep in the carcasses, but a few of them guarded the perimeter, snapping at the bold vultures. Jess sat off to the side, and right in the middle of the scene was Marissa.

"You and your sister useless in hunt," she said with a grin. "Because you no help catch gazelle, you no get to eat anything."

Ben looked up at Ray with a more sympathetic expression, but said nothing. Knowing the headpiece hid his own face, Ray allowed himself a smile.

"That fine," he said. "I no help, now I no eat."

But Marissa did not continue smiling. She looked confused. She glanced at Jess, and then back at Ray again.

And then she glared.

Chapter 12

Brad awoke and sat up in his bed with outstretched arms.

"This is it!" he said aloud. "Today's the day!"

He sprang into the air and landed on his feet. He ran over to the window and looked out over the sandstone buildings and deep blue water.

"Good morning!" he shouted to the world.

The wolves on the street below stared up at him, wondering what his problem was, but Brad didn't care. He closed his eyes and took a deep inhale. The city air carried the scent of rotting meat, but all Brad smelled was the aroma of desert flowers on the summer breeze.

He danced over to his dresser and took out his hairbrush. He studied himself in the mirror, beaming at what a handsome dog he was. All of the girls back at the academy had had eyes for him, even the formals. Since those days he had fallen out of shape, but that didn't matter now. Now he had a date with the only girl who ever mattered to him.

Brushing his hair was usually a task Brad despised, but today it flew by. Even as he yanked the worst knots loose, all he could think of was Sonya. He took a minute to brush his teeth, and then he was out the door.

"Meow!"

Brad stopped. He had only made it two steps when the sound echoed through the stairwell. He turned around, but there was no one there. Only him.

Confused, Brad turned back to the steps. By the time he had reached the bottom, his mind was happily back where it was before: with Sonya.

He found Fuzz and Larry sitting in the common area, nibbling on the bones that remained of their breakfast.

"Good morning Fuzz! Good morning Larry!"

They looked over at him.

"Good morning Brad." Larry's voice was barely loud enough to hear.

"Are you excited for today?" asked Brad.

Larry stood up. Before Brad could ask what he was doing, Larry had left the room.

"What's wrong with him?"

"What do think is wrong with him?" asked Fuzz.

"I don't know. Did a wolf bite him?"

"No, you idiot. He's upset about Sonya."

"Why? What did Sonya do to him?"

"She's going on a date with you," said Fuzz. "Larry is jealous, and if we're being honest, I'm jealous too. Come on, Brad, you know that all three of us have been into her since the academy."

"Huh. Well, I guess I knew that. Still, if you liked her too, why didn't you ask her out?"

"Why didn't you?"

"I did, remember?"

"Yes, but why did you wait until now?"

"I wasn't sure how to ask her back then. Also, I didn't know if she already had a boyfriend."

"Brad, the four of us spent every waking moment together. If she had a boyfriend, we would have seen him."

"Yeah, I know," said Brad. "Anyway, you still didn't answer the question. Why didn't *you* ask her out?"

"Well, I wanted to. I'd love to go on a date with Sonya, but you guys are my friends, and you're more important to me than getting a girlfriend. I know how much you like her, and I wouldn't want to do anything that would hurt our friendship."

"Wait, you didn't ask her because of me?"

"And Larry. The poor guy likes her just as much as we do, but he's so quiet I know he'd never make a move. I wouldn't want to flaunt her in front of him."

"I'm not trying to flaunt her in front of anyone," said Brad. "Fuzz, if you really think me dating Sonya means you, Larry, and I can't be friends, then I'll call off the date."

Fuzz shook his head. "No, don't call it off. Go have fun with her. Just whatever happens, don't forget us, all right?"

"I won't. Now, what do we have for breakfast? I'm starving."

"Meat and more meat," said Fuzz. "I love vacationing with the wolves."

Brad walked over to the icebox and opened the lid for a look. Most of the wolves didn't bother with refrigeration, but the Warlord made an exception for his guest suite. It was a good thing too, as Brad had little appetite for spoiled meat. He dug out a juicy chicken leg.

"Meow!"

There it was again! He looked up, just in time to see a tiny white cat through the window. The cat gave him a playful smirk and then jumped out of view. Brad ran to the window and looked out into the street, but the cat was gone.

"Did you hear that?" he asked.

"Hear what?" asked Fuzz.

"There was a cat outside."

"What? Here?"

"Yeah."

"Did he say anything?"

"It was a she."

"All right. Did she say anything?"

"No, she just meowed at me then ran off."

"Huh," said Fuzz. "I didn't think there would be any cats in Grand Oasis. Wolves tend to eat other pre-ops."

"Maybe this one is better at avoiding them," said Brad. He walked over and sat down at the table.

"What about Sandra?" asked Fuzz.

"Who?"

"Sandra, that bear from the academy. She definitely liked you. You could have dated her."

"Oh, I remember her. She liked me?"

"You couldn't tell? I should have dropped you a few hints. You could have had a formal as a girlfriend."

"Yeah, but she's, well, a bear."

"Come on, Brad. Don't tell me you've never had a thing for a girl of another species."

"Well sure, everyone has. It's just that we'd have to deal with all that garbage from everyone for dating outside our own kind. And we couldn't get married, unless we wanted to take a trip to the Bear Nation."

"It's not that far."

"And we couldn't have kids," said Brad. "I want kids."

Fuzz shrugged. "You know she'd support you with her fancy business degree. I hear she's planning to take over her mother's company."

"I don't think we have to worry about money as long as we're with the Bear. He doesn't even need us for this trip, but he's paying us just to come to the Wolf lands and sit around."

He took the last bite of his chicken and tossed the bone into the trash pile. He stood up from the table and headed to the door.

"Brad?" said Fuzz.

He turned around. "Yeah?"

"There is another reason I never asked Sonya out. I didn't think she'd say yes."

"Why not?"

"I'm not the one she likes. She's clearly into someone else I know."

Brad paused for a moment and then pointed at himself. Fuzz nodded.

"Have fun on your date."

"Thanks. I will."

Stepping out onto the street, Brad couldn't help but wear his big dumb grin. He beamed at the wolves on the street as he passed by, not even noticing them return dirty looks. He would normally have been more careful around wolves, most of whom viewed dogs as their weaker, snobbier relatives, but at the moment he found it hard to care.

Two wolf pups ran out into the street ahead, tackling each other and rolling in the sand. As much as they looked too adorable to be dangerous, Brad gave them space as he walked by. He guessed them to be about three or four years old, but they might have been younger. Dogs grew up more quickly than most species, but he had heard somewhere that wolves aged even more quickly.

Brad imagined two puppies of his own, twin boys perhaps, playing and wrestling with one another. If the plot against the Anteaters were to work, he could finally move on with his life. He could start a family. If he indeed had a future with Sonya, that future could begin right away.

The road came to an end at a grove of palm trees and the crystalline spring behind it. Brad hadn't noticed the stench of the city before, but as he ventured beyond the line of buildings he could indeed smell the purity of the oasis. For all their mental shortcomings, the wolves knew better than to contaminate their own water supply. The rising sun had already done away with the cool morning air, and Brad found himself panting. A slight breeze made its way through the grove, but it was too small to be of any relief. It was only just strong enough to disrupt the glimmering surface of the lake, making it ripple to and fro, winking, inviting Brad in for a dip in the cool water. However, he knew better, so he waited.

"Meow!"

He spun around to see the cat standing a few groves down the shoreline, watching him with a smug grin. As soon as Brad saw her, she turned and pounced away. This time, Brad ran after her.

He raced along the shore, keeping his eye on the blur of white dashing between the trees. There wasn't enough brush near the water to conceal someone her size; she had nowhere to hide. As he closed in on her, Brad caught himself barking.

The cat, only meters away, still had not made any attempt to scamper up one of the palm trees. Brad leapt forward to catch her, but all he got was a mouthful of sand. He spit it out and looked around, but the cat was gone.

"Meow!"

The call came from above. Brad looked up, but as before, none of the trees held a cat.

"Meow!"

He turned around. A few triple story buildings stood on the outskirts of town. From the roof of the closest one, the smirking white cat looked down on him.

"How did you get up there?"

"I climbed," said the cat.

Brad's eyes widened at hearing her speak. "Stupid cat."

"I'm Ling," she said. "We'll see each other again."

With that, she jumped out of view.

There was no way he would catch up with her now. Wiping the sand from his tongue, Brad turned around and began to walk back the way he came. How could she have evaded him so easily? He could see how she might have kept safe from the wolves. He was lucky no one had been around to see him lose it back there. Some of his old friends might have joked that he had acted like a pre-op.

He managed to spit out the last few grains of sand, and looked up to see Sonya, standing alone under the first palm grove. She smiled and blushed as he ran to meet her.

"I'm sorry I'm late," he said. "I got distracted back there."

"But you came from down the shore, not from town."

"Right, I did. I didn't mean I got distracted back at the house. I got distracted down the shore."

"What were you doing over there?"

"Uh, I was just looking around."

"We were planning a nice walk for our date. Did you decide to go without me?"

"What? No! I was—"

She burst out laughing.

"Relax, Brad. You're too easy to poke fun at."

"You're not mad at me?"

"Why would I be? Don't worry, I want to be here."

"I know," said Brad, "but believe me, I was here earlier. The truth is I ran off to chase a cat."

Sonya laughed again. "A cat? There are no cats here."

"There's at least one."

She walked up to him and touched his ear. "And you ran after a cat? When you could have been here with me? I lost you to a cat?"

"Hey now," said Brad. "I came back, didn't I?"

"I suppose you did." Sonya took his hand in hers. "Come on, let's go on this date."

Brad nodded and began to turn around, but Sonya yanked him in the other direction.

"We're going this way," she said.

"Why?"

"You chased a cat somewhere back there. I can't have you spot it again and run off after it. Right now, you belong to me."

The breeze had grown stronger, enough so to cool him down,

making the temperature almost pleasant.

"This is so nice," said Brad. "I was nervous you wouldn't like me."

"We've known each other for years. Of course I like you."

"You know what I mean."

"I know. I was nervous too."

"You were?"

"I thought you didn't feel the same way about me. I'm glad I was wrong."

Brad felt her hand tighten around his, and he tightened his as well.

"Wow," he said. "All these years I had no idea. I wish I had said something sooner."

"Don't feel bad," said Sonya. "We have the rest of our lives to spend time together."

"We do. I guess we'll just have to make up for lost time. We'll get plenty of chances to do so, if the Bear's plan against the Anteaters works."

"Or even if it doesn't."

Brad paused. "We'll see," he said. "We'll see."

Chapter 13

"They know," said Ray. "They may not know they know, but they know."

Jess squinted at him. "What?"

It was an hour before sunrise on their fourth day with Tusk Pack, and the siblings had once again ventured out of earshot of the camp before the wolves awoke. Although neither had planned such, these early morning meetings had become a ritual, their only chance to talk freely before another day of deception.

"They know we're not wolves," said Ray. "I can see it in their eyes. They don't fully realize it yet, but somewhere in those little brains of theirs, they can tell something's not right."

"Only Marissa."

"Yes, Marissa. And Sam. And Ralph. And—"

"Not Ben."

"All right, Ben seems to like us for some reason. It's a good thing he's the leader, or else they would have turned on us by now."

"You're being paranoid."

"I'm being sensible. Aren't you supposed to be the sensible one? I'm trying to look out for us."

"Then what would you have us do?" asked Jess. "Drive away while they sleep? Throw away all the progress we've made?"

"Maybe we should. They won't find us. We could still finish the mission. We could find a different pack and fall in with them. Maybe this time we could get our information out of them before they start to suspect us."

Jess shook her head. "There's no saying that we'd be any better off with a different pack. We've come this far with this one. We can hold out for just a little longer."

"For how long? Until they discover us?"

"We'll arrive in Grand Oasis tomorrow. We'll get the information we need and escape at the first chance we get."

Ray sighed. "I don't like this. I'll go along with everything for now, but if things get ugly, we leave tonight." He paused. "If we even have that chance."

Jess opened her mouth to tell him it would be fine, but no words found their way out. Ray looked out over the dull blue hills beneath the reddening horizon, and then turned back to his sister.

"We should head back to camp. Do you need to use the bathroom again?"

"No, I'm good," she said.

"Then let's go."

Last night's campsite lay on flatter ground than before, and as such, the siblings had ventured farther away than usual for their morning conversation. After a good half kilometer, they had come across some rocks large enough to block any wolves from their view. As they walked back, Jess squinted at the figures that wandered between the tents.

She had seen at least one of the wolves, but as they got closer, she saw that there was only one. Before she could breathe a sigh of relief, she realized the wolf was Marissa. Even before they could make out the eyes, Jess knew the she-wolf was watching them.

The Anteaters veered towards their side of the camp, but Marissa walked up to meet them anyway.

"What you doing? Why you leave camp so early?" Her voice boomed through the campsite, prompting grunts and snarls from within the tents. Wolves weren't known for their courtesy, but even so, Jess thought her voice was particularly loud.

"We no sleep," said Ray. "We go take look around."

"Why you go so far from camp?" asked Marissa. "You run off to scheme against Tusk Pack!"

More rustles came from the tents. A zipper sounded from the other side of the camp.

"We no scheme," said Jess. "We just bored. We go explore to pass time."

"You lie! You say you afraid of rival pack. You say that why you wear liquids. If that true, you no run away, you stay here where safe."

Other wolves began to step out of their tents. One by one, they walked over to the commotion and stood behind Marissa, but none said a word.

"Look around," said Ray. "There no other pack for kilometers. We know we safe."

"Oh really?" asked Marissa. "Then take off liquids."

"Marissa? What going on?"

Everyone turned to see Ben emerge from his tent. The other wolves cleared a path for him as he walked over to join them.

"These two leave camp while everyone asleep."

Ben gave her a confused look. "They still here."

"They come back."

"Then what's the problem?"

"They run off to talk about us! They hiding something."

Ben chuckled. "You think they wake up and go on walk just to share insult about you? You too sensitive, Marissa."

Marissa bared her teeth and growled. "You say that they have to face trial to join Tusk Pack. It been four days. They act like they part of pack already, but they do nothing to prove worth. You no plan to test them at all."

"That not true. Don't worry, we give them trial."

"When?"

"Today," said Ben. "They face trial today."

With that, the leader turned around and went back to his tent. As soon as he disappeared, the rest of the wolves dispersed, some to tune their buggies, and some back to their sleeping bags. Only Marissa kept her eye on the Anteaters, and even she eventually snarled and walked away.

Ray retreated back to the tent to catch another hour of sleep, but Jess didn't bother. The buggy wasn't in need of maintenance, but she looked over it anyhow. She tweaked the power levels, cleaned the corrosion on the battery, and checked the cables about a dozen more times than she had to. Even when it was clear there was no more she could do for the vehicle, she stared down the engine block, as though pondering the source of a tricky malfunction.

Her brother awoke after a while, but as they couldn't talk openly, his reappearance brought little relief. Only once the wolves had packed up and the group had mobilized did Jess finally feel more at ease. The desert road was kinder than the circle of stares she had endured back at the camp.

Larger trees became more common as they progressed, and even sapphire pools began to appear every so often. A cluster of palms would indicate each new oasis long before they saw the water itself. A few of them were large enough for her to think they had arrived in Grand Oasis a day early, but as they passed the meager villages at each one, she saw that none could possibly be the fabled mercenary hub.

Even though none of the landmarks were Grand Oasis, each lake boasted at least a dozen structures and two packs of wolves. Separate packs often gravitated to opposite sides of the pools, although a few clans waged battles beneath the palms. Few wolves took much notice of the convoy, and those that did stood back in respect of Tusk Pack. Jess couldn't help but notice a few intrigued glances at the two armored wolves riding in the rear of the procession, glances she did her best to ignore.

She found herself easing off the accelerator. The buggies ahead seemed to be slowing down, and Jess did likewise, keeping a distance from the next vehicle. Another oasis loomed not too far away and Jess squinted through the eyeholes. There were only a handful of structures; it was barely a town, let alone a city.

A line of wolves came into view by the water. By their number, Jess guessed they were two distinct packs, but the group moved as one, without a hint of conflict among them. These wolves didn't back off at the sight of Tusk Pack as some of the previous packs had done. They walked out to face the approaching challengers, leaving the oasis behind.

The procession came to a halt. The other wolves turned off their engines and stood poised to leap to the sand, but they did not do so until Ben dismounted.

"Jess! Ray!" He looked over at the final buggy.

They froze for a second, and then hopped down to the ground. As the rest of the pack watched, they walked to the front of the line.

"Hurry now," said Ben. "We have enemy ahead. You stand by my side."

"Who they?" asked Jess.

"You no recognize them? That Black Sun Pack. They destroy

your old pack."

She looked up at the wolf in the front of the formation, marching up to the challengers. He was tall, taller even than Ben, and perhaps heavier too. Through his unkempt tufts, she could make out an angry glower, two eyes that locked onto those who violated his pack's territory.

The other members of Tusk Pack flocked into a line behind Ben and the two armored wolves. As Black Sun Pack approached, the Tusk Pack warriors at either end of the line inched forward, forming their half of the gauntlet.

"I wonder who fool enough to approach Black Sun Pack," said the shaggy wolf. "Now I know. It been long time since I see you, Ben. I glad to have chance to destroy Tusk Pack."

The wolves of Black Sun Pack snarled in approval. Ben shot Jess a quick smirk, turned back to the shaggy wolf, and spat at the ground. The angry wolf clenched his teeth and stormed up to Ben, grabbing him under the chin.

"You regret that."

Ben turned to the side, shrugging the hand from his neck. "I don't regret anything, Maurice. Tusk Pack have nothing to fear from Black Sun Pack."

"Black Sun Pack is strongest pack in land," said Maurice. "Second only to Warlord Pack. You insult our name. You challenge me to duel."

"Tusk and Black Sun duel, yes, but not you and me. There are two new wolves in my pack. They hate you more than I do."

"You afraid to face me yourself."

Ben turned to the two armored wolves. "This Wolf Jess and Wolf Ray."

"Why they wear liquids?"

"They wear to keep safe at all times. They wear because you plan to track down and kill them."

Maurice laughed. "I have plan to kill lots of people. I never met Wolf Jess or Wolf Ray."

"You kill their pack leader. You destroy their pack, Razor Pack."

"I destroy many pack," said Maurice. "I remember each one. I destroy Stone Pack and Vulture Pack. I destroy Scar Pack, Palm Pack, and Torched Sand Pack. I never heard of Razor Pack."

"What you say?" asked Marissa. "You never kill Razor Pack

leader?"

Before Maurice could respond, Jess stepped forward. "You lie! You slash Wolf Omar's throat and you pledge to kill his warriors!"

"If I kill him, then why lie? All wolf should fear Black Sun Pack. Each pack I destroy add to my honor."

"There no honor in destroying other pack," said Ben. "All wolf know that."

"All wolf idiot. Your ideas weak, Ben. You sound like old grandpa. As for Razor Pack, I sure it never even exist."

She didn't even stop to glance at Marissa. Jess lunged forward and punched Maurice in the face, sending him to the ground.

"You insult Razor Pack legacy! You think so little of fight with us that you pretend we not real? You think my fist not real?"

Maurice pulled himself back to his feet. "All right, we fight. But I warn you, those liquids no protect you from me."

Jess stepped forward into what was now a fully formed circle. Wolves began to snarl and howl in a way one could almost describe as cheering. Even the Tusk Pack warriors cheered in this manner, but whether they rooted for her victory or simply demanded blood, Jess could not say.

As they encircled one another, a bead of sweat fell into her eye, blinding her at the worst possible moment. Maurice bolted forward and landed a brutal tackle on her chest. Despite his earlier threat, the liquids cushioned the blow to a gentle push. Jess tottered back a meter or two, but kept her footing. Black Sun Pack barked in delight.

She focused on her foe, trying to wipe the sweat from her eyes. She wouldn't be able to land another head-on strike, not in the cumbersome liquids. Maurice moved too quickly. Her best option was to counter his next attack, which would still require far more focus than usual.

Her trained eye caught the turning of his heel the instant before he lunged at her. As he came in for a second tackle, Jess turned to the side just enough to dodge the blow. As he charged by, she swung out her arm and hit him across the nose, sending his feet into the air and his head to the ground.

Before he could get up, Jess grabbed him by the wrist and swung her leg around his arm. She fell to the ground, leaning back until she felt a 'pop' at his elbow. Maurice howled in pain, kicking her off to the side and struggling back to his feet.

Jess stood up as well, and the two circled once again. Maurice clung to his injured arm, laboring just to keep his eye on Jess and his step steady. Doubting he could dodge in his weakened state, she watched for an opening.

To her surprise, Maurice ran at her again, but this time in a clumsy, uncontrolled manner. She ducked out of his path and swung her foot into the back of his leg, knocking him to his knees. Jess stepped behind him, grabbing him in a chokehold. As much as he flailed, he could not break free. With her conquered foe at her mercy, she now faced Tusk Pack, looking up for their approval.

"It over," she said.

Black Sun Pack had gone silent while Tusk Pack had become a chorus of proud howls. All but Marissa cheered her victory. Even Ray did his best to mimic the howls, taking care not to overdo it. The loudest of all was Ben.

"You true warrior," he said. "Strong enough for Tusk Pack. Now kill him."

She flinched, nearly letting go of Maurice. "What?"

"You hear me. Kill Maurice. End evil of Black Sun Pack."

Why would he suggest such a thing? Dr. Wilson had made it clear: duels between wolves of separate packs were not to end in death. Was her research outdated?

"There no honor in killing him," she said.

"Maurice have no honor," said Ben. "He kill your leader and many other. You stay in fear as long as he live. End him now."

They should have come up with a different cover story. She and her brother knew the rules of the Wolves; they should not have suggested a wolf from another pack killed their leader. They could have invented a thousand other ways for the imaginary leader to die. Now there was no way out.

Her grip tightened. With a twist at the right angle she could snap his neck. Jess looked up at Ray, who watched with wide eyes. She looked to Ben, and then back to Ray again, and then her hold loosened. She let Maurice fall to the ground, barely conscious, but alive.

"It over," she said again.

The Tusk Pack warriors made room for her to rejoin the circle. At first there was only silence and confused looks, but gradually the sounds of approval returned. The pack howled in triumph, but a few wolves—and not just Marissa—kept quiet. Jess had held back and now they had seen through her façade.

Ray shot her a look, a look that said 'we need to talk, NOW'. She lowered her head and nodded, doing her best to quietly duck out of the group. She and Ray walked back toward their buggy. It was hardly a safe distance to talk, but she doubted it would be issue. She half expected Ray to just jump into his seat and demand they leave at once.

He turned to her. "All right, look—"

"Jess!"

Before Ray could finish his sentence, Ben ran from the group, calling for her. Before they even made it to the car, he had stepped between them.

"Ben."

"Jess, why you do that? Why you no kill him?"

She sighed, trying to sound conflicted. "I already tell you. I want to be true warrior. I do right thing."

"Maurice never do right thing. He think of way to kill you now, just like before. If you kill him, you be safe. It all right to do dishonorable thing to dishonorable wolf."

"No, it not."

Ben paused. "What you mean?"

"It wrong to kill wolf when he defenseless. It no matter who. I always do right thing. It who I am. I rather die than not be who I am."

Ben just stared at her with a blank look. Jess felt herself inching away back toward the buggy. Why had she felt the need to try to explain such a thing as morality to him? The wolves were a savage people. If he couldn't already tell something was off about her, he would now.

"No one ever say things like that to me before," said Ben.

Jess shock her head. "I no mean it. I only joke."

"Don't say that," said Ben. "I wish more could think like you. Jess, you very special wolf."

"What you mean?"

"Listen," he said. "There place to eat not far from here. Owned by monkey merchant. Great place to bring pretty she-wolf. You go with me?"

She could almost hear Ray's jaw drop, but no further sound

came from his mouth.

Chapter 14

"A date?" asked Ray. "You want to go on a date with Wolf Ben?"

"It's not a date," said Jess.

"He's taking you to 'place to bring pretty she-wolf.' Yeah, it sounds like a date to me."

The Anteaters sat on the hood of their buggy about a kilometer from the oasis. After the departure of Black Sun Pack, Tusk Pack had set up camp and the wolves were taking a much needed rest. Ben had been more than happy to allow the two newest members a chance to drive off and have a talk before Jess gave the suitor her answer.

"Do wolves even go on dates?"

"Apparently they do," said Ray.

"Dr. Wilson never said anything about it."

"That's because she didn't think you'd wind up DATING one of them."

She sighed. "Fine, you're right. I'm going on a date with Ben."

"You're going to say yes?"

"I have to. Ben is the only reason the entire pack hasn't turned on us. He trusts us, and I'd like to keep it that way. A few minutes ago we thought the entire pack was going to realize we weren't wolves. Now Ben actually likes me even more. I say we go with it."

"So you plan to spend a few hours alone with him. You don't think he might pick up some clues that you're not a wolf?"

"If he really is infatuated with me, he won't be looking to find anything wrong with me."

Ray shook his head. "I don't like it."

"Oh," said Jess.

"What?"

"I see what's going on. You're being an overprotective sibling."

"I am not!"

"Come on. This is just like the time you beat up that guy Marcus who kept following me around."

"I thought you hated him."

"I did hate him, but I never told you to hurt him."

"But he stopped creeping on you, didn't he?"

"Ray, you're only proving my point."

"I don't know what you're talking about."

"So you're telling me that your only concern here is the mission. If we weren't in danger, you would have no problem with me going on this date with Ben. Is that right?"

Ray paused. "I—"

"Yeah, that's what I thought."

"Look, it wouldn't be so bad if he weren't a pre-op."

"That's what's bothering you?" asked Jess. "You're one to talk. I never gave you any crap about you and Jenny."

"Hey!" She could tell Ray was blushing. "I was just a kid. I didn't know any better."

"She was your girrrrrrlfriend."

"Stop that! We were six years old. We were in kindergarten! At that age, anteaters and pigs are pretty much on the same level. It's also the age when kissing is still gross."

"That didn't stop you."

"Be serious, Jess. He's not good enough for you."

"I know that, dummy. You think I want to go on this date? I'm just playing along. We need him to trust us, so I'll just pretend to be interested and make sure he's happy."

"And what would that entail?"

Jess smacked him in the face. "Nothing you wouldn't have me do. Now come on. Let's head back before Marissa starts bitching about us again."

She grabbed the frame and hopped backwards into the driver's seat, turning the ignition before her brother had a chance to protest. He too got in his seat, and Jess shifted the buggy into gear and sped forward.

Most of the wolves were napping in the shade of the palms when they neared the oasis again. Even Marissa was sound asleep. A few of the wolves knelt at the shore for a drink, but none of them swam or waded into the water. Only one neither slept nor drank, and he greeted the returning buggy with a big smile.

"You have good talk?" asked Ben.

"Yes, it very nice," said Jess.

"We have nice rest here. Tusk pack have you to thank for chasing Black Sun Pack from oasis."

"It no problem for me."

"So, you have answer for me? You join me at diner?"

She could hear a disgruntled sigh from Ray. "Yes. I go with you. It sound fun."

"Great! We leave now, yes?"

"Now? No time to rest?"

"We camp here tonight, plenty of time to rest. It already get late. Place only open for lunch."

She paused. "All right. We go now."

He gestured to his vehicle. "We take my buggy."

She gave a final nod to Ray before following the pack leader to his vehicle. Jess headed to the driver side door, paused as Ben sat behind the wheel, and then walked around to the passenger seat. The car sped off into the desert, leaving Ray and the wolves behind in a cloud of dust.

They didn't have far to go. Jess worried that Ben might try to make conversation on the ride down, but fortunately he didn't try to shout over the motor. She knew her relief was fleeting; there would be plenty of chances for awkward conversation at the restaurant.

It took her a moment to realize they drove on something that resembled a road. Thousands of tire tracks had packed the dirt into a flat, solid pathway. Every minute or so, another buggy, or an entire group of them, would drive by in the other direction, and each time the passengers would stare at the wolf and his armored companion.

The diner lay beneath twin hills, positioned such that at any given time, it would lie in the shadow of one of them. Jess wondered if it would catch a gleam of sunlight at noon, but it was already too late to know for sure. A dozen wolves sat at tables in the shade, gnawing at slabs of meat. The words 'Lisa's Diner' hung over the door in crooked letters nailed to the frame.

She followed Ben through the doorway and into the establishment, where a fat monkey behind a counter greeted them with a smile. Lisa, no doubt.

"Lovely to see you, Ben!" she said. "Will it be the usual?"

"The usual," said Ben. "Get for her too."

Lisa glanced over Ben's shoulder at his guest.

"So you're with Ben?"

Jess cleared her throat. "Yes, I come here with Ben."

"So you really are a lady." Lisa raised an eyebrow. "I couldn't tell you the last time I saw a wolf in liquids. Are you afraid of walking into an ambush in my little diner?"

"No, I just—"

"She have her reasons," said Ben.

"I'm sure she does. I'm just thinking it must get mighty hot under there. Not to mention impossible to eat anything." She gave Ben a playful jab. "So did you get tired of the last one already? Whatever happed to that *darling* Marissa girl?"

"Marissa still with pack."

"But you brought this one—"

"Jess."

"Yes, you brought Jess instead."

"Jess different."

"She certainly is." The monkey shook her head and laughed. "Don't let me interrupt your little date." She reached under the counter and retrieved two wooden slabs of steaming meat. "Cooked just the way you like it. Go ahead and help yourself to any available seat outside; I'll add everything to your tab. And as always, if you must fight the other patrons, please do so off my property."

"Always," said Ben.

Jess grabbed her slab, averting her eyes from Lisa. She rushed back out the door, leaving Ben stumbling to catch up.

"Where you want to sit?" he asked.

"Distance from other wolf."

"Good idea. Space to ourselves."

They chose at a table on the edge of the patio, well within the shade of the west hill. The other wolves gave them a few odd looks, but soon went back to their meals. Jess placed her slab on the metal surface and took her place.

As soon as they sat, Ben attacked his steak, grabbing it in both hands and yanking it from side to side with his jaw. Jess examined and poked at her own meal.

"This beef?"

"Yes. Best beef south of salt."

What a relief. At least it wasn't fox.

"You no eat?" Ben mumbled through bites.

Jess pointed at her head covering.

Ben nodded and swallowed a mouthful. "You have to take off if you want to eat."

"I need to stay safe."

"From Maurice? You could say that your fault. You have chance to kill him earlier. If you had, he no longer be able to hurt you. Then you able to take off liquids. But you no kill him. Now you wear them rest of life until he die?"

"Wolf like him no live long."

"Ha! You right. Still could be year or more. Long time to wear liquids, but you do right thing. That why I like you. Your grammar better than most wolf too."

Jess's eyes widened. "No it not!"

"Yes, it is. Why you so shy, Jess? You very smart wolf. I bet you outthink fox if you have chance. You ever go to Fox Nation?"

"No."

"I hear it pretty. Very green. Great to visit if Fox no kill you." He took another bite and then stared as Jess's slab. "You still need eat, Jess. I never see you have food. You no hungry?"

She was hungry. Sneaking a can of bugs every morning hadn't done much for Jess. While the presentation of her plate was rather sloppy, the meat really didn't look all that bad. She had tried beef back in her academy days, and it hadn't made her nearly as sick as it had made Ray. She remembered it tasting all right, perhaps even preferable to canned termites.

"Why not take off filter and eat some?" Ben raised his eyebrows. "I protect you if Maurice show up."

Jess leaned forward and peeled back the filter, leaving it hanging in place just enough to obstruct Ben's view. She couldn't have him catch a glimpse of her flat teeth. She tore a little piece from her slab and placed it in her mouth, taking a moment to chew. It was a bit rougher than she remembered, but still manageable. She took a second bite, and then reattached the filter.

Ben watched her for a moment, then pushed his own slab back. "We no have to eat," he said. "Why not climb to top of hill with me? Great view from top."

It sounded better than sitting around and not eating.

"Sure."

She stood from her seat and followed Ben. He led her around to the side of the near hill and up the slope. The side facing the diner was far too steep to scale, and even the side they chose to climb proved difficult in the heavy liquids.

Jess felt the gravel give way beneath her feet. She felt tempted to let herself tumble the desert floor blow. The liquids would cushion her fall, but she could still feign enough injury for Ben to call off the date. Before she lost her balance, however, Ben caught her by the wrist.

"No worry. I got you."

"Thanks."

He pulled himself up to the summit and reached down to help Jess up beside him. She sat near the edge, letting her legs dangle over the side. It hadn't looked so high from the bottom, but now she could see for kilometers around.

"Look," said Ben. "It clear day. You see everything. There oasis where Tusk Pack rest."

For the most part there was nothing but desert, but she could see the oasis. Several other hills and mesas dotted the horizon, with dirt roads stretching between them. Groups of buggies moved here and there, so far away they really did look like ants—live ants scurrying around their anthill. Jess began to salivate.

She turned around to the other side of the landscape, to what lay ahead. More and more buildings filled the empty space of the desert, and on the edge of the world, she caught a glimpse of a deep blue. Grand Oasis perhaps?

"Wolf Maurice no sneak up on you here."

She turned to him. "What?"

"Black Sun Pack have no flintlock. No one hurt you from ground below. Maybe you take off headpiece here."

"There nothing for me to eat here."

"That not why I suggest it," said Ben. "I want see your face. I sure you very pretty."

Jess laughed. "Yeah right."

"You no think so? If you no take mask off, then how I kiss you?"

"You don't." She said it with a smirk, hoping it would come off as jocular and not as frustrated. Then she realized he couldn't see her expression through the liquids. Ben didn't seem to mind though.

"Maybe someday," he said. "If you no want kiss, why not you tell me about yourself?"

"I did. Black Sun Pack destroy old pack, and Ray and I find Tusk Pack."

"Tell more. You have family?"

"I have Ray. Other family dead."

Ben paused, waiting for Jess to elaborate, but she remained quiet.

"I tell first then," he said. "I grow up in Grand Oasis before joining pack. Mother from Buzzard Pack. Father from Sandstone Pack. Both pack leader before they leave to start family. Many strong warrior in my family. My great-great-grandmother Wolf Lynn the Mighty."

The name sounded familiar. "Really?"

"She become Warlord of Wolves at young age. Monkey Empire come down to conquer Wolves, just like three thousand years ago. Lynn no surrender. She face and defeat priest and soldier. She cut off supply line and let monkey starve in desert. Empire retreat after year. Monkeys call it Second Folly of Desert."

Jess made herself chuckle. "Yeah. I know."

"Lynn remind us that we strong," said Ben. "Monkey say we too stupid to rule land. They call us pre-op, and all pre-op should follow monkey because they formal and they so smart. But wolf nothing like pig or sheep or cat. We proud and we strong. We defeat monkey on battlefield, and even after Monkey Empire fall, we remain forever."

He turned to her. "I see many wolf weak and violent and stupid, and I wonder if we deserve future. But then I meet wolf like you. You give me hope, like Lynn."

They sat in silence for a moment.

"I have strong descendant too," said Jess. "My grandfather. His name Wolf Anton."

"I no hear of him."

"He skilled warrior. He stronger than monkey priest, stronger than any fighter on Earth. He fight monkey in their own land."

"He member of Wandering Swords?"

"No, he fight in Autumn Revolution, help to end rule of Temple. He defeat monkey and set all nation free. He mighty hero, he inspire Ray and me every day." She paused. "But he make enemy. They hunt him down. Hunt whole family down."

"You still alive."

"And I wear liquids," she said. "There are worse out there than Wolf Maurice."

There was silence again. Strangely enough, Ben didn't seem to perceive it as an uncomfortable silence. As they sat and watched the view, Ben shifted closer to Jess until finally he put his arm around her waist.

"We safe now. We here together."

Jess let the arm remain for a moment, but then shrugged his hand from her side and stood up.

"I'm sorry, Ben."

"What wrong?" he stood up as well. "You no like me?"

"I like you. It just—"

"Just what?"

She sighed. "We not the same, Ben. Maybe you not see, but you and me different."

"I know."

"You do?"

Ben nodded. "Everyone different."

Chapter 15

The doll fit in the palm of her hand. She didn't remember them being so small, but then again, it had been many years since she had played with one. The maker had put an impressive amount of detail into the monkey's features, more detail than she would expect from a craftsperson of the Fox Nation.

"That's one of our best. Can I ring it up for you, Friar?"

Sky turned to the storeowner, a skinny, light-haired fox. He beamed and took another one of the dolls in his hand.

"I don't think so," she said. "I'm just browsing."

"Are you sure? None of these come from a factory. There's a guy right here in town who makes them." The clerk brushed his hand over the doll's thick hair and ran his fingers across its tail. "The monkey dolls always come out the best. He makes amazing pigs as well, but I've never had good sales with those. You seem to have taken a liking to that one anyway."

"It's beautiful, but I'm a little old to be playing with dolls."

"I know that, but maybe you have a little sister who would like it? In a few years, maybe even a daughter?"

"Not for a while," said Sky. "I do have a sister, but even she is too old for dolls. I haven't seen her in years."

"Well, you can't blame me for trying," said the clerk. "You priests always carry good copper. Thought maybe you'd feel like splurging."

"Not this time. I need to save what I have to get to my new home."

The door chime rang and a draft followed. The clerk turned to front of the store, but it was only one of the other customers leaving. He turned back to Sky.

"And where would that be, if you don't mind me asking?"

Sky didn't want to boast, but she couldn't suppress the big grin forming across her face. "I'm heading southeast. They've chosen me to serve at the Sand Monoliths."

"Have they? How exciting! Have you been there before?"

"No."

"Well, I'm sure you'll love it there. Beautiful site."

"Have you been?"

"Why, yes. I suppose I was only a child at the time, but I remember it all quite well. The Monoliths were bigger than anything I had ever seen, other than the Temple, of course."

"Only priests are allowed near the Monoliths."

"Nowadays, sure, but I'm talking about back before the First Vulpe-Simian War, back before the Second Order."

"Are you serious?" asked Sky. "I just, I mean I didn't—"

"Didn't what?"

"You don't look that old."

The clerk let out a hearty laugh. "Is that so? Well, I take it as a compliment. I do what I can to take care of myself. Just ran my seventh marathon last month. You'd never guess that I was over fifty."

"Do you remember the revolution?"

"No, I was just a baby. I grew up in the aftermath though. My family didn't migrate with the rest of the Foxes until years later, so I saw many things. The Bears opened all the sacred sites to the public. It was really sad how they turned a blind eye to all the vandalism, but hey, it's a good thing those monuments are indestructible."

"I guess so."

"I promise you, my family and I had no part in any of that desecration. We just wanted to see the holy places for ourselves, though we did keep our distance." He paused for a moment. "And then there was the pact and the genocide. I may not remember the revolution, but I remember the wars that followed. We got out of there fast, and it's a good thing we did. The native citizens didn't take kindly to foxes after the first Vulpe-Simian War broke out. Once Edward humiliated the Monkeys in battle, anyone with orange fur and a busy tail had to keep an eye out when walking home." He flinched. "I mean no offense of course—"

"It's fine." Sky put her hand on his shoulder. "Thank you for sharing your story."

"It's been my pleasure—"

"I think I will take the doll."

The clerk's face lit up. "Wonderful! Step right up to the register and I'll ring it up for you."

The setting sun turned the windows and checkout counter a bright yellow. A spotted dog sorted through the candy bars near the register, but made room for Sky to step up. The clerk swung behind the counter and took the doll.

Sky dropped a copper coin in front of him. "This should cover it. Keep whatever's left."

He took the coin and bowed. "Blessings be upon you, Friar."

She returned the bow. "To you as well."

Sky felt tempted to stay longer and ask more questions of the clerk, but the dog seemed to be edging toward the checkout. It was time to get moving anyway.

She opened the door to the ringing of the bell and made her way back onto the streets. It was a charming old cobblestone downtown neighborhood, glowing in the evening sun. Fox couples and families strolled across the avenue, all enjoying the cool weather. While everyone else found their way to shops and restaurants, Sky headed south towards the station.

Apart from a few passing glances, none of the foxes paid her any mind. It didn't seem to bother anyone to see a monkey walking among them. Sky almost felt embarrassed that she had been upset at the two scowling bears back at the dock. Surely most had forgotten the old hatred, and she could deal with those who hadn't. She had already done what most couldn't: she had passed the final trial and become a priest. Handling the uncivilized few in a calm and respectful manner would be no issue for her. Master Nyah was right; the Celestial Monkeys were all that mattered to Sky, and under their watch, she had nothing to fear.

Her evening in town had proved a welcome change to what had started as a rocky priesthood. The little boy who had died at her prayer still haunted her, but the Celestial Monkeys had their reasons, mysterious as they may be. Soon enough she'd be studying and leading prayer at the Sand Monoliths, with plenty of other things to think about. Years down the road, she'd be a wise master like Nyah, and the story of the sick lamb an anecdote about the trials of faith for her to tell to a new generation of trainees.

After few blocks in a less sightly neighborhood, the station loomed ahead. It was an ugly building, but it looked better than the abandoned and condemned structures around it. A bus pulled out of the garage as Sky crossed the road and made her way to the front door. It swung open before she could grab the handle.

Another monkey stepped out in front of her. She found herself smiling at him as she grabbed the door.

"Hi!" she said.

The other monkey responded with a snarl. It was only then that Sky noticed how hideous and unkempt he was. Patches of missing fur speckled his upper body and a deep red scar, too large and jarring to be ruggedly attractive, stretched across his shoulder. He wore black trousers beneath his belt, odd considering it was still far too warm for thermals.

The ugly stranger gestured back to someone behind the door.

"Move your fat ass, Cecile! Let's go!"

A large bear with a blank expression waddled after him. Despite her companion's insult, this bear didn't appear all that fat to Sky. She was big, yes, but her weight seemed gathered in her arms and chest.

Sky held the door for them, keeping her smile as she did. As soon as they had passed, she stepped through the doorway and let it close behind her. Other than a few sleepy travelers using their suitcases as pillows, the station was deserted. Sky walked up to the counter and rang the bell for the ticket agent, who looked almost as lively as the costumers.

"Yes?" she asked. "What are you here for?"

"I'm looking to purchase a bus ticket."

"Yes, I know. Where are you going?"

"The Sand Monoliths."

The agent gave her a blank stare. "Check the time tables, honey. Do you see anything heading to the Monkey Nation?"

"No."

"In case you weren't aware, things haven't been so friendly with the Monkey Nation recently. We cancelled all the outbound routes months ago. If you want to go there, you'll need to take a rental."

"Yes, my master and I got here on a rental."

"Then why'd you come into the bus station? The rental garage is next door. Big building. Can't miss it."

"All right, thank you."

Sky gave a quick bow that was closer to a nod, and headed back for the door. There was a big building next door, the one with boarded up windows. Sky checked the sign on the door, and sure enough it was still open and in business. She vaguely remembered coming through the bus station with Nyah on the way down. Perhaps there was a connecting passageway between the buildings that the agent had neglected to mention.

She stepped through into the spacious brick room to see a row of beat up old cars and buggies. The garage was vacant, other than a lone fox cranking a wench at one of the vehicles.

"Hello?"

No response from the fox. She walked up to him.

"Uh, hello?"

He turned to her. "Yeah? What do you want?"

"Is there anyone here I can talk to about renting one of these?"

"You can talk to me." He went to the other side of the buggy and slid beneath the engine, wrench in hand.

"So then, can I rent one?"

"Let me think about that," he said as the cranking continued. "Hmmm. How about no."

"What? Why not?"

"Because I said so."

"I didn't even say where I was planning to take it. I'm going to the Sand Monoliths, by the way."

"That makes no difference to me. These rentals can go wherever the company has a garage. They just won't be taking you."

"I came here on a rental."

"A different rental. These ones don't leave unless I say they do. These are mine."

"No, they belong to the company."

He rolled out from under the car and stood up to face her. "Maybe you didn't hear what I just said. You're not renting one of my cars."

Sky glared at him. "It's because I'm a monkey, isn't it?"

"It's not because you're a monkey. It's because you're a priest."

"I have copper."

"I have copper too. I think I can get by without yours."

"Fine. Then I don't need your help either."

She turned around and nearly bumped into someone else. She looked up to see the ugly monkey from before, along with his bear friend.

"Don't bother talking to that guy," said Sky. "He won't help you."

The ugly monkey ignored her and walked right up to the mechanic.

"Yeah? What do you want?" the surly fox said.

Sky shook her head and started towards the door. Before she could step outside, a thud echoed through the garage, and a painful groan followed. She turned around to see the mechanic collapsed on the floor and the other monkey standing over him.

"Listen closely, because you're going to do exactly what I tell you to. I want the keys to your two fastest buggies."

The massive bear stepped up within a half meter of Sky's face.

"You didn't see us—"

Sky landed a swift strike on the bear's forehead. The blow was enough to a knock smaller opponent unconscious, but the enormous bear managed to keep herself upright. Her beady eyes widened, more out of surprise than pain.

Before her foe could punch back, Sky spun around, swinging her foot into the bear's temple. The behemoth flailed as she fell to the side. It was not a clean knockout, but it would have to do for the moment. Something else demanded her attention—someone else's fist coming at her face.

Sky ducked just in time to avoid the ugly monkey's punch. A second fist came right after the first, and this one she only had time to block. She leaned in for a punch of her own, but her opponent landed one first. Sky managed to take the hit in the chest and stumble back without losing her footing.

She drifted back and assumed a defensive stance. The other monkey lacked neither speed nor fury, but his set of moves was familiar. Sky remembered the sequence from one of her old dojo masters—a sequence that always began with a right jab. Her foe charged again, and sure enough, he led from his right.

This time, Sky turned out of the way, grabbing the ugly monkey by the wrist and elbow. She pivoted her heel, poised to slam him to the ground, but heard something from behind—heavy footsteps that could only be the bear accomplice coming in for a tackle. Instead of planting her opponent into the floor, Sky yanked the other monkey around, bringing him headfirst into the charging bear.

"That's enough!"

Sky turned to see the fox, a massive blunderbuss in hand, standing five meters from the skirmish.

"Nobody move, unless you want to be my new wall decoration." Just as Sky breathed a sigh of relief, the fox's eyes darted to her. "I said nobody move! That goes for all of you!"

The ugly monkey and the bear clenched their fists as they ground their teeth at the fox, who glared back at them through the dark bruise across his face.

"What a bunch of morons," he said. "If you're going to rob me, you should wear your liquids. The cops will be here any moment."

Just as he said it, Sky heard sirens growing closer. The mechanic must have triggered a silent alarm as they had fought. The quick response still impressed her, but it made sense that a squad car would be on patrol in this neighborhood.

The door swung open, and half a dozen foxes with raised flintlocks burst through.

"Drop the weapon!"

The mechanic let the shotgun fall and raised his hands. "It's all right. I work here. I'm the one who made the call."

He slowly held out an ID card, which one of the cops checked before turning to Sky and the robbers.

"And those three?"

"They're the ones who assaulted me. They were here to steal my buggies."

"He's lying," said the ugly monkey.

"I have security footage."

The cop walked up to the monkey and stared him in the eye. "I recognize this one. Wandering Sword soldier, the one they call Pretty Gustav." He turned to the mechanic. "The detectives will be here soon. They'll want a word with you and they'll want to see that footage, but if you're telling the truth it will all check out."

"Lovely. Now the sooner you get these thugs off my property, the sooner I can get back to my job."

The cops took out their handcuffs and proceeded to restrain the robbers. One grabbed Sky by the wrist, with a set of cuffs ready. Before she could protest, the mechanic spoke again.

"Wait."

"What is it?"

"That one wasn't with the mercenaries. She tried to help."

"She's missing her tail."

"Check her tattoo. She's a real priest, not a reject."

The cop glanced over at her mark and sighed. "Let her go. She's not with these two."

Sky jerked her arm free and stepped out of the circle of radio chatter. As two of the officers led the criminals away, the mechanic gestured to her.

"Come over here."

"Why should I?"

"I have a gift for you. You can take it as soon as this circus wraps up."

She sighed and followed him down the row of vehicles.

"Crazy evening, right?" The fox didn't turn back to her as he spoke. "Wandering Swords. Explains why that monkey was so pissed off at you."

"What?"

"He lost his tail the same way you did, but he didn't get the tattoo he was hoping for. Probably didn't make the cut for the Disgraced either, so he found his way south of the salt instead. Things must be going pretty bad for the Wandering Swords if they have to steal just to get buggies. Must have been months since their last contract."

"Yeah, sure."

"Here." He slapped the hood of one of the buggies. "We're not renting out this beauty anymore. I was about to salvage it for spare parts, but the company supplies my needs either way. So take it. It's yours to keep."

"You want me to have this car? Does it even still run?"

"You'd be surprised how long these things last. No one will rent it because it makes some funny noises, but it still runs just fine. I'll even fill the trunk with some extra power cells, enough to make it from here to the monoliths—that is, if you take a very direct route."

"Look, I don't mind renting one of the other buggies. I'll pay you and everything."

"What? No, keep your copper. Here, I'll show you." He produced a key from his belt and turned the ignition. Sure enough, the buggy made a horrible whining noise, but steadily growled to life. He turned it back off. "See? Works just fine."

"All right, all right. I'll take it."

He tossed her key. "Great! Now if you'll excuse me, it looks like the detectives just walked in. Once we finish that business, I'll get the car set up for you right away!"

Chapter 16

"You have rest of day to meet with families," said Ben. "I wish we have more time, but Warlord have plans. Meet here tomorrow at sunrise."

The pack howled, and Jess and Ray howled along with them. They couldn't produce the most authentic of wolf calls, but the shouts of louder wolves drowned them out. Ben waited for the silence before speaking again.

"Tusk Pack make me proud," he said. "Enjoy the afternoon."

The wolves dispersed, most moving towards the vast array of sandstone buildings nearby. Only the two armored wolves remained with the vehicles. The Anteaters stood there in the makeshift parking lot, waiting for the pack to leave earshot. Ray glanced one way and then the other before he finally spoke.

"Wow. Check out this armada of buggies. I've never seen a bigger parking lot."

"Every pack in the city leaves their buggies here," said Jess. "Any one of them could return at any moment, so we'd better talk while we can."

"All right. Well, we did it. We made it to Grand Oasis. You can say 'I told you so'."

"How about we just figure out the plan."

"We should be fine as long as we don't sleep through sunrise," said Ray. "Tomorrow morning, the pack will meet with the Warlord and we'll find out what he has planned."

"Yes, but what should we do until then? We need to make use of this time. Maybe we can find some more clues as to what's going on."

"Yeah, great idea. How about we go hang out with the Warlord now and he'll tell us everything. We won't even have to go to that meeting tomorrow."

"What about Ben?" asked Jess. "He's warmed up to us. I bet if we talked to him some more, he'd be willing to fill us in."

"Really? Are you that eager for a second date with him?"

"Be serious, Ray."

"I am being serious. The less time we spend with Tusk pack, the better."

"All right, then. What would you suggest?"

"If we want to find out what's going on, we'll have to hear what the people of Grand Oasis have to say. I vote we go to the one place where everyone will be talking: a bar."

"Good idea. Let's do that."

"Really? You agree with me? Can I hear that again?"

"Don't push your luck." She started towards the city and yanked him by the arm. "Come on, follow me."

They made their way towards the sandstone houses and the growing noises of a bustling town. There was the slight stench of rotting meat, but after wallowing in her own grime for almost a week, Jess barely noticed the new smell.

As they walked through the town, Jess stared up to marvel at the sights. Some of the structures towered five stories above the dusty streets. None matched the buildings back in Beni, but engineering such a structure of sandstone was an impressive feat. The grainy, brown towers captured the late afternoon sun with a certain majesty.

"How they, I mean, how *we* build such tall building?" asked Ray. "We wolf not very smart. You know many engineer wolf?"

"I think we wolf not build them. There plenty of other people here we pay to build."

Sure enough, for every two wolves they saw, there was at least one member of another species. Bears appeared to the most common of the foreigners, some of them clean-cut merchants grinning over stacks of copper as they negotiated with pack leaders, and some of them as filthy and unrefined as the wolves themselves. The next most common were the monkeys, most missing their tails, but all way too hairy to be priests. There was even the occasional fox, but those she saw moved through the marketplace with more caution than the other species did. One of the smaller foxes openly displayed the flintlock on his belt, and wore a full set of liquids. Seeing his thin, flexible armor, Jess couldn't help a twinge of jealousy.

As welcoming at it was to see the other species, Jess found her eyes wandering back to the wolves. Many of them were obviously in packs, but a good number stayed near their homes, talking to their neighbors or playing in the streets. There were families with wolves too young or too old to be off hunting and raiding, wolves that didn't even growl when she and Ray veered closer than they should have. One of the tiny wolf pups ran up to sniff at her armor, but Jess did her best to ignore her and walk on.

An odd-looking wolf caught her eye, a wolf half a block away with a coat of brown instead of gray. She squinted and tilted her head. It wasn't a wolf, it was a dog.

"This place look good?"

She turned to Ray. "What?"

He pointed to the sign hanging from a nearby building. "Xiang's Tavern. Looks like bar to me, and it sound open. What to check it out?"

She looked back down the road, but the dog was gone. "Sure. Let's take look."

Ray pushed open the door and Jess followed him into the cool shade of the building. She could tell the bar serviced mostly the non-wolf species. Circles of tail-less monkeys drank beer and chatted, while a few bears played darts in the corner. The few wolves there were, more likely career mercenaries than pack wolves, fell in with the groups of monkeys.

A number of patrons kept themselves too concealed for Jess to discern their species. Some wore liquids, not nearly as bad as the ones she wore, but bulky enough to blur the line between a short bear and a fat monkey. A few wore dark cloaks, which looked great for protection from desert sun, but came off as unsettling in the shade of the tavern. One of the cloaked individuals in the corner turned towards the anteaters as they entered the room, watching them behind a pair of black sunglasses. Jess did her best to ignore the onlooker and stepped closer to Ray.

"There not many wolf here," said Jess. "We try other bar?"

"There enough. Smaller piece of pack easier to talk to. I try those over there." He pointed to three wolves by the window.

"All right. I try at the counter. Try not to get in fight."

"Get in fight at bar? How big of cliché you think I am?"

"Just be careful."

Ray headed over to the group at the booth while Jess walked up to the bar and took a seat. The bartender, an overweight fox even larger than Edward, grunted as if to ask for her order.

"Water," she said.

"Two small copper."

She sighed and tossed the coins his way. Water fetched itself quite a price in the desert. The bartender filled the cup and placed it in front of her.

"Thanks."

The stool next to hers screeched on the tile floor as someone sat down. She turned, expecting to see Ray already rejected from his group of wolves. Instead she saw the cloaked stranger in glasses staring at her.

"Why are you here?" It was a woman's voice.

"Me?"

"Yes, I'm asking you why you're here."

She sat only a meter away, but Jess still couldn't recognize the stranger's species. Jess could make out the eerie purplish tint of her hair, but somehow the stranger didn't strike her as a Tromian. She had long ears, but they pointed to the floor rather than the sky. She caught the glimmer of light on sharp teeth, teeth almost too big to fit in her mouth.

"Are you deaf? I asked you a question."

"I not deaf. Pack stopped in Grand Oasis for night. Leader give us time to visit city."

"Why are you really here?"

Jess raised the cup. "I here for drink."

"Please stop talking like that." The stranger pushed back her sunglasses. "I've had to endure the idiotic babble of wolves since I first arrived here. I don't need to hear it from you as well."

"I'm sorry you no like my voice."

"You can drop the act. Wearing wolf liquids doesn't make you a wolf. You're no pre-op."

Jess pushed back her water and stood up. "I no have to put with this trash. Enjoy your drink."

The stranger tapped on the chair. "Sit down. You have a secret, and I imagine the last thing you want is to make a scene. If you value your secret, you'll do as I say."

Jess looked back at the barstool. If she swung it fast enough, she imagined the stool would do some damage to those pretty shades. No doubt someone who wore such an outfit indoors had some secrets of her own. She clutched the rim of the barstool, checked to see if anyone was watching, glared back at the hooded figure, and then sat back down.

"What do you want from me?" Jess asked.

"That's much better. I knew you could talk like a civilized person."

"Do you work for the wolves?"

"No."

"Then stay out of my way. My business doesn't concern you."

"I wouldn't be so sure," said the stranger. "You see, there are those out there who want me dead, and many others who would do far worse. When I see two disguised individuals with an uncertain objective—well, I didn't stay alive as long as I have by assuming their objective never involves me."

"I don't even know you."

"And I don't know you either. So why should I trust you?"

Jess leaned in closer to the stranger, tightening her hand around the cup. "If I tell you why I'm here, will you leave me be?"

"I'll consider it."

Jess sighed. "As I said before, we're not here for you. We've come only to observe the Wolves."

"Go on."

"We're agents from the Fox Nation. The Wolves have grown more aggressive in recent years and we need to make sure they don't pose a threat. We're pretending to be wolves so we can fall in with a pack and learn their plans. The packs are gathering, and if they mean to march on the Fox Nation, we need to warn our superiors."

For a moment, the stranger stared at her and said nothing. Then she burst out laughing, as though Jess had just told her the funniest joke she had ever heard. "Shoot, I really scared you, didn't I? Agents from the Fox Nation? Oh my goodness."

"Excuse me?"

"That all was dreadfully rude of me. Sorry about that."

"Is this some kind of joke to you?"

Jess stood up and reached over to grab the stranger by the collar, but a clawed hand blocked her. The wiry purple hand squeezed around Jess's wrist, and the jagged, blue claws sank into the liquids. "Hey, easy now," said the stranger. "I meant what I said about people out there who want me dead. It was just a precaution, nothing personal."

"You're not going to blow my cover?"

"No, of course not. You're clearly not anyone I should be afraid of."

Jess scowled.

"Relax. As of now, I'm a friend. Sit down, finish your drink, enjoy my company."

She sat, but didn't lose the scowl. "How did you know I was a formal?"

"Honestly? You pay too much attention to your surroundings. Wolves are creatures of action; they don't stop and consult their companions before they make a move."

"That's not always true."

"And I've never seen a wolf order water at a bar."

"Uh huh. So who are you?"

The stranger pulled back her hood, not enough to reveal herself to the bar, but enough to give Jess a better look at her bristly purple fur, her rigid, pointy ears, and her shining fangs. Her glasses dropped enough for Jess to see that the stranger had no pupils. "Why don't you see for yourself?"

"Do you have a name?"

The hood came back on. "I do, though it's been a while since I've used it. It wouldn't mean anything to you."

"And why are you here?"

"In this city? Because there's someone who needs my help."

"And your friend asked you to come to Grand Oasis?"

"He's not a friend, he's family. Actually, he doesn't even know I'm here and he'd hate me if he knew I was, but that doesn't matter. You don't abandon your family, and he needs my help now more than ever."

"Whatever." Jess stood up.

"Wait."

"What now?"

"Look, I really didn't mean to cause you any trouble. I'll make it up to you."

"How?"

"I can tell you what you want to know, at least part of it. You were right, the Wolves are gathering for something."

"Go on?"

"The Warlord has been calling more and more packs back to Grand Oasis. They're massing for something, but it isn't a march on the Fox Nation."

"Then why are they gathering?"

"They have a client, a very rich client who seems to want some people taken care of and seems to think hiring an army is the best way to do it. More than that I cannot say."

Jess nodded. "Appreciate it."

"Good luck in all your endeavors."

The anteater walked away from the bar as fast as her armored legs would allow. Ray met her by the door.

"I got nothing from wolves at booth," he said. "They almost as friendly as Marissa."

Jess grabbed him by the wrist and pulled him along out the door. "Come on, we're getting out of here."

"Hey, quit that. What you find out?"

"The Wolves have client," said Jess, "and I have feeling we'll meet this client tomorrow."

Chapter 17

One of the wolves let out a loud yawn. Ben walked over and smacked him in the face.

"Quiet. We in presence of Warlord. You show respect."

"No we not. Warlord not here yet."

"He be here soon. Until then, you be ready. I hear no more from you."

The wolf kept quiet and Ben returned to the head of the group. Tusk Pack stood in a rough formation on the balcony of the Warlord's dwelling. It wasn't what she'd call a palace, but it outdid the smaller buildings around them.

Although she didn't say it, Jess couldn't help but feel bad for the yawning wolf. Wolves didn't stand at attention, but Ben had instructed everyone to keep still in their columns and it had been nearly an hour since their arrival. If she stood in just the right way, all her weight pressed down against the bulky liquids such that they did the standing for her. She made sure not to relax too much, lest she doze off.

Within the all-concealing sleeve of her armor, Jess held the tiny camera. Ray had agreed to take care of the microphone, so all she need to do was acquire a few pictures. With precise, silent movements of her fingers, she positioned the camera against the claw holes of the glove. She made sure she could hit the capture button, testing it on a picture of the Warlord's guards. All seemed in order; all she had to do now was wait.

Each of the guards was bigger than any wolf in Tusk Pack, even

Ben. It surprised her that neither of them wore liquids. While strolling about the city she had seen a wolf or two in liquids, but it seemed the Warlord's pack didn't bother with them. It couldn't be a question of expense, as their pack could certainly afford the hefty blunderbusses hanging from their belts.

The balcony door swung open and out walked a wolf. He looked no bigger or fiercer than any other, although he struck her as better groomed. He stood there, a mere dwarf next to the guards, looking back and forth as though examining the pack.

Ben stepped forward. "Warlord Lance, you give great honor to Tusk Pack."

He extended his hand, but not far enough for a handshake. The rigid manner suggested some sort of salute, but Dr. Wilson had mentioned no such custom. She angled the camera and pressed the button as the Warlord extended his own hand—or rather the stub where his hand ought to be.

"Hello, Wolf Ben."

"Tusk Pack report as ordered. What you command of us?"

"You know why I ask you here. We have job to do."

Ben nodded. "Yes we do."

"When I find out client expect me to present strongest pack, I call for Black Sun Pack right away. Only then I hear other pack already defeat them in standoff. When I hear of this defeat, I already know who responsible." The Warlord cracked a smile. "I always expect great things from you, Ben. You do not disappoint."

They shared a laugh. "I owe all to my pack," said Ben. "Especially newest warriors."

Jess cringed, but the Warlord kept his eyes on Ben and not his pack.

"Pack only as strong as leader," said the Warlord. "Much like entire nation. All of Wolf not be strong unless I let us."

"And you do let us. We have easy job from client now. We do it and then we rich."

"Yes, my friend. Enough to buy flintlock for all pack. More buggies too."

"And rebuild Grand Oasis. Use money for our families."

"We sort it out after job done. For now, we make sure all go according to plan."

"I not worried. We no have to fight army, only two targets."

Jess stopped taking pictures. Did she hear him right? The stranger at the bar had suggested the Wolves' contract only targeted a small group, but only two?

"It more difficult than you think," said the Warlord. "Targets live in Fox Nation. Wolf can never go there. We need bring them us."

"How we do that?"

"Client have idea. He say he know how to lure them here."

"I hope so," said Ben. "Hope wolf recognize them. Most of my warriors never met an anteater before."

Had her glove not concealed the camera, she would have dropped it to the ground. Anteaters? Two anteaters? She fought the urge to show any hint of surprise on her face, though she knew the headpiece covered her expression. There were only two anteaters the Wolves could possibly be after, only two that posed any threat, only two in whom the Wolves could possibly have an interest, but what could that interest be? Had they discovered the infiltration? Had the pack been playing them the entire time, luring them back for the kill? No, that couldn't be it. No group of pre-ops could carry out so elaborate a deception.

The Warlord turned back toward the doorway. "Ah, here come client now."

"Sorry I'm late. For all your late night howling, you wolves planned this meeting rather early for my taste."

She knew that voice.

"Hello," said Ben.

"Ben, meet newest client. His name Bear Theo."

"Please, don't be so formal. Just call me 'the Bear'."

There he was, standing before the pack, with the same maniacal grin he had worn the last time she saw him. The Bear looked different in the morning light, with his smooth fur shining and waving in the desert breeze, yet it only took one glance at his smile for Jess to know it was him. It was him all along. The entire mobilization of the Wolves had been the Bear's plan to get rid of them. At least for the moment, he seemed clueless about his targets' real whereabouts, despite his cocky grin.

"I honored to fight for you," said Ben. "But I may I ask question?"

"You just did," said the Bear.

Ben gave him a puzzled look, but then continued. "These anteaters you have us kill, what they do to you?"

"They didn't do anything to me."

"Then why you want them dead?"

"I have my reasons. Does it matter to you?"

"Yes, it matter."

"Old family business," said the Bear. "I'll leave it at that. I didn't think any of you would care, as long as I paid you."

"The money is help. All of us Wolf cost so much for such small job. I think there be cheaper way."

"Ben," said the Warlord. "You no say things like that."

"Oh, it's quite all right," said the Bear. "I assure you, you have nothing to worry about. I've already made up my mind about hiring the Wolves, and you'll have your money as soon as I have the Anteaters."

"Where you get so much money?" asked Ben.

"The spoils of an empire, my friend," said the Bear. "The spoils of an empire."

He turned toward the pack; something had caught his eye. Jess stood as motionless as she could, for what little good it would do. The Bear walked past Ben and the Warlord, past the front row of Tusk Pack warriors, and stopped face to face with Jess.

For a moment, she didn't even breathe. The Bear looked down her side, examining every corner of the unusual armor. Then he stared back into her eyes.

"Soldier, what are you wearing?"

"They liquids," said Ben. "Armor against musket or—"

"I didn't ask you, I asked her." The Bear's gaze never left her.

Jess silently cleared her throat, straining to sound gruffer than usual. "Ben right, they liquids. I wear for protection."

The Bear's eyes widened at her voice. "These are liquids?" he asked. "They look much bigger than the ones I'm used to."

"It hard to get same model that formal make. We build our own version of liquids."

"Can you even fight in those things? Can you even move? I have no place for useless warriors in my army."

"I can fight. I beat leader of Black Sun Pack in duel while wearing."

"Black Sun Pack," said the Bear. "Why does that sound

familiar?"

"Black Sun Pack fiercer than all my other pack," said the Warlord. "I plan to have you meet them, but then Tusk Pack beat them first. Then I have you meet Tusk Pack instead."

"Is that so?" asked the Bear. "So you're telling me you fought one of the toughest wolves in the land, and you won while wearing that?"

"Yes."

The Bear paused for a moment, doing another visual run-down of the armor. Then he turned and took a few steps back toward the door.

"So, do they work?"

"What you mean?"

The Bear's hand shot out, yanking the blunderbuss from the nearest guard. Before anyone could react, he swung the weapon around, took aim at Jess's chest, and fired.

The next thing she knew, Jess was lying on the ground, staring up at the sky. Her head spun and she could make out shouts over the ringing in her ears. A sticky liquid coated her skin, although she couldn't tell if it was sweat or blood. Something pushed against her side, shaking her arm.

She brought her head up just far enough to see what was going on. The one at her side was Ray, kneeling down and asking her something. The Bear also lay flat on ground. Ben, the ill-used blunderbuss in hand, stood between her and the Bear, shouting something at him and bearing his claws. The Warlord appeared to be yelling at Ben as well, but his commands went unnoticed.

Little by little, the feeling returned to her chest. She slowly twisted from side to side and felt no pain. The dampness was far too sparse to be blood. The blast had knocked the wind out of her, but that was all; the liquids had done their job, hardening in time to catch the shot. At least they were good for something.

"—no respect for Tusk Pack!" Her ears began to sort the sounds coming from Ben's mouth into words. "No one threaten any of my warriors!"

"That's enough, Ben!" The Warlord stepped between them.

"Everything all right." Jess sat upright. "I not hurt."

Her eyes darted to Ray, warning him to get back in rank before anyone commented on his lack of discipline. Ray gave a small nod and stepped back into his spot, while Jess stood up and did the same.

"You see, she's fine." The Bear lifted himself back to his feet and scowled at Ben. "Warlord, don't worry about this one. He's just looking out for his soldiers, and I'd have nothing else from a leader in my army."

"So you still let us have the job?"

"Yes, of course."

"Warlord," said Ben. "We done here. I ask that me and pack leave now."

He nodded. "Go."

As the pack formed a line and began to file back through the balcony door, Jess felt the camera jostle at her fingertips. She had almost forgotten about it! As she passed through the exit, she turned her hand and snapped a quick round of shots of the Bear and the Warlord side by side.

The morning was still young when the pack stepped back onto the city street. Perhaps Ben would give them another day off, which would give her and Ray the perfect chance to disappear. They didn't need any more evidence, and this mission was clearly more dangerous for them than anyone had thought.

It took Ben another minute to join them outside, and when he did, everyone turned to him for orders.

"Tusk Pack leave at once," he said. "We get into position now, and await more Warlord instructions. To the buggies!"

The pack howled in acknowledgement. The two newest members were silent.

Chapter 18

The plane touched ground with a bump, jostling the cabin. Edward grabbed the water glass on the table, and held onto it longer than he had to.

"Fear of flying?" asked Stewart.

Edward shook his head. "Please."

"Listen, I know it's your first Armistice Triumvirate, but you'll do fine."

"You think so? The last time I was face to face with a Monkey national, it was on the battlefield."

"Well, this isn't just any Monkey national. This is the High Priest."

"Thanks for reminding me."

"Sorry about that," said Stewart, "but really, don't worry about it. We're in the Bear Nation, neutral ground. The Monkeys can't pull anything funny."

"The thought never crossed my mind."

"It will be easy. Just you and them, no audience, no cameras, nothing."

"It won't be like that next year. The media's begging to get in on it."

"Then consider this session your practice round. It'll all be done soon."

Edward sighed. "Thanks. Honestly though, I'm just not all that good at this sort of thing."

"Sure you are," said Stewart. "I wouldn't be here with you now if you weren't."

The plane rolled to a stop and the side door opened, letting a stream of yellow light into the cabin. Stewart gave his shoulder a quick squeeze.

"They'll be waiting for you, Mr. President."

"You know you don't have to call me that."

"I know. Are you sure you don't want me to come with you to the State House?"

"I'll be fine."

Edward unbuckled his seatbelt and stepped up to the exit. His eyes adjusted to the light, and he spotted his limo at the connecting street. As he descended the steps, he noticed another fox awaiting him at the bottom.

"Tammy?"

"Good to see you, Edward," she said. "How was your flight?"

"What are you doing here?"

"Same as you. I'm here for the Triumvirate."

"Maybe you didn't see the news a few months ago. The Council appointed me as president, not you."

"No need to be snotty, Mr. President. I assume you've familiarized yourself with the Triumvirate rules and proceedings?"

"I have."

"Article five, section two states that each leader may bring a top government official of their choosing to assist with the meeting. In our case, that would be a fellow councillor."

"What's your point?"

She held out her hands. "Well, here I am."

"Tammy, it calls for a councillor of my choosing. I don't recall choosing you."

"Then whom did you choose?"

"No one."

"So you're turning down free help?" asked Tammy. "I didn't expect that from you. Shame, you had so much bipartisan support."

"What?"

"My fellow Developmentalists won't be too happy when they hear about this. I'm sure they'd understand if you simply wanted another Defender at your side, but to turn me down when I'm all you have?" she adjusted her glasses. "Listen Edward, I like to think of myself as a good reader of people. I can tell you have your preferred way of doing things and that you'd rather keep this meeting as small as possible. I get it. I'm afraid, however, my party isn't as understanding as I am."

Edward said nothing.

"If you really don't want me, we can call up one of the other councillors to fly over here and take my place. I'm sure the Chancellor and High Priest would understand if you had to delay the Triumvirate."

Edward sighed. "Come along. We don't want to be late."

She followed him as he started towards the limo. "Don't worry Edward, you made the right choice. I assisted at every Triumvirate for the last five years under President Mairéad. I'll get you through it."

It was a long drive to the State House. Edward had only visited the Bear Nation twice before, and he'd never had the time to see the sights. The day grew cloudy as they drove, but he still found his eyes drawn to the grassy downs, cut into squares by trees and waist-high stone walls.

As much as he wanted to enjoy the view, Tammy insisted his attention didn't wander too far. She spent the entirety of the trip drilling him on his agenda for the Triumvirate. Stewart had already gone over everything, but he went along with Tammy anyway. To his surprise, she made no attempt to suggest any changes in his platform, and whatever condescending remarks she had, she kept to herself.

"That's enough for now," said Edward. "We're nearing the city."

"If you insist."

To Edward's surprise, they were even closer than they had thought. The State House stood on a hill on the outskirts of the capital, overlooking the city and the river. As the limo pulled to a stop, an elderly bear broke from the crowd on the sidewalk and walked up to meet them.

"President Edward and Councillor Tammy, may I be the first to officially welcome you to the Bear Nation. I am Bear Piripi, attendant to Chancellor Pegasus."

"Pleasure to meet you."

"The High Priest has not yet arrived, but the Chancellor would be delighted to have a chance to meet you before we get started. If you would follow me."

"Of course. Lead the way."

As they followed the attendant into the building, Edward was surprised to find that he and Tammy weren't the only foxes there. As they walked up the staircases and through the corridors, he spotted at least two or three of them. The other foxes sat in offices, conversing with their bear co-workers.

The state house was a fine piece of architecture, but Edward found it not nearly as extravagant as his own domain back in the Fox Nation. He spotted only a few portraits, and no statues. The hallways were narrower and the ceilings were lower, but not to the point of inconvenience.

They found the door to the Chancellor's office open.

"Come in, Piripi," came a voice. "Have our honored guests arrived yet?"

Piripi stepped aside. "May I present to you President Edward and Councillor Tammy of the Fox Nation. Mr. President and Madam Councillor, you stand in the presence of Chancellor Pegasus."

The horse who stood in the middle of the room boasted a coat of pure white, and a mane so smooth and fine that Edward couldn't discern any individual hairs. Half a dozen times he had seen Councillor Helen in the hallway before a Council session, fretting while her stylist fought kinks in her hair, but Pegasus was different. Edward got the sense that this horse had never needed a comb in his life. He was handsome to say the least, and looked almost a little too young to be a head of state.

As the Chancellor walked over to greet him, Edward smiled and tapped his foot twice. Pegasus shook his head.

"I insist, there will be no need for that."

"Are you sure?"

Pegasus held out his hoof within arm's reach of Edward. "Don't worry, I assure you a handshake is no trouble for me."

After Edward and Tammy had shaken his hoof, Pegasus turned to the bear who had been waiting with him in the office. "I'd like you to meet Vice Chancellor Donalyn. She'll be accompanying me at the Triumvirate."

"Nice to meet you." She too shook their hands.

"It seems our guests from the Monkey Nation haven't yet arrived," said Pegasus. "It's nothing to worry about, though. I'd been hoping for a chance to become acquainted with the hero of the

Foxes. Edward, I was aware of your reputation as a fierce soldier, but goodness, you're even bigger than half my citizens."

"Really? How many citizens do you have?"

The horse laughed. "Tell me, how is everything in the Fox Nation?"

"We've never been better," said Edward. "Our borders are secure, pre-op unemployment is virtually nonexistent, and we've recently elected our first horse councillor."

It took a moment for Pegasus's face to light up. "Oh right, now I remember! Councillor Helen, was it? How is she faring on your council?"

"She's certainly an opinionated person," said Edward. "Helen always brings new ideas to our table, ideas we never would have discussed otherwise."

"Come to think of it, I recall her from a few of your broadcasts," said Pegasus. "I admire her spirit, if nothing else."

"What do you mean?"

"She gives off a certain disdain for the political system. She should know that she'll never pass any of her laws if she doesn't play nice. From what I saw, I had gathered that the two of you had grown rather impatient with her, and I wouldn't blame you."

Edward laughed. "Well, I would be quite the hypocrite if I criticized her for refusing to play the system."

"There is a line," said Tammy, "and not all of us can walk it so elegantly. It's hardly our place to judge those who can't."

"Tammy, it is good to see you again," said Pegasus. "Tell me, how is Mairéad doing?"

"She is well, although I don't get the chance to visit as much as I'd like. Last I checked, she'd taken up fishing."

"Well, that certainly sounds quieter than this sort of life. I had hoped to see her again, but if even the two of you can't find time for a reunion, my chances for one with her would appear truly abysmal."

"Maybe not. Send her a line. I'm sure she'd love to hear from you."

There was a knock on the door.

"Mr. Chancellor?" said Piripi. "The High Priest has arrived."

"Very good. Send her in."

Piripi stood aside and in walked two monkeys, all but their heads cleanly shaved. The one on the right, the older of the two, wore a tiny copper chain from her right ear. The other, younger priest spoke first.

"Chancellor, I must apologize for our tardiness. We have many important matters to discuss, but our plane had engine trouble—" she paused, staring at Edward. "What are you doing here?"

Edward flinched as all eyes turned to him. "Me?"

"What are you doing here, General Edward?"

"I don't understand what you're asking me. I'm here for the—"

The priest turned to Pegasus. "Chancellor, what is the meaning of this? Why would you insult Her Holiness by inviting someone who has slaughtered thousands of her people?"

"Please," said Pegasus, "I meant no disrespect. My only intention is to hold the Triumvirate."

"You should have reconsidered. Peace talks have no place for a fox such as him." The priest turned back to Edward, but Tammy stepped between them.

"Forgive the interruption," Tammy said, turning to the older priest. "Your Holiness, may I ask a question?"

The first monkey turned to the High Priest, who remained silent for another moment. Finally, she spoke with melodious, almost deep voice. "Ask your question."

Tammy tilted her head toward the younger priest. "Is that your Priest of War?"

"Grand Master Delia indeed holds the honor of that title."

"You should fire her."

"I beg your pardon?" The Priest of War stepped forward, but the High Priest held out her hand.

"Councillor, I imagine you would relish the chance to clarify," said the High Priest. "It is not in your nature to make insults."

"No insult intended," said Tammy. "It's merely a suggestion. It's your Priest of War's job to inform you on all matters pertinent to defense and foreign affairs. In my opinion, being unaware that the former general had been elected president would be an unforgivable oversight. You'd be better off with someone who could keep you informed."

"The entire Monkey Nation knows of Edward's current office," said the Priest of War. "Her Holiness doesn't need me to tell her that."

"So you were aware? And yet you acted so surprised upon seeing him here."

"I thought it most likely that Chancellor Pegasus would rescind the invitation of the Fox delegates for these special circumstances. At the very least, I assumed the president would send an alternate."

"Likely, maybe, but not enough to warrant such a shock. I don't appreciate what your priest is saying, Your Holiness. Her intention was to shame President Edward and put us on the defensive."

The Priest of War stepped forward. "Even if that were true, I would be justified in doing so."

Edward opened his mouth to say something, but Tammy beat him to it. "How so?" she asked. "His armies killed many monkeys, but that was only in defense against your invasion. The Monkey Nation was the aggressor in both Vulpe-Simian Wars, and unless I'm mistaken, at the First Armistice Triumvirate eight years ago, Your Holiness officially condemned your nation's actions in both conflicts and issued an apology. How can you accuse a man for fighting to defend his own country?"

The Priest of War said nothing.

"I won't have it. President Edward is a hero to my nation and a symbol of hope for my people. I will not stand by and let you slander him like this."

Edward closed his mouth.

The High Priest bowed her head. "Forgive the words of my advisor. Dire matters from home weigh heavily on her head."

"Her Holiness speaks the truth," said the other monkey. "We come today to discuss a most urgent matter, one that does not concern the Foxes."

"The Foxes have every right to be here, just as you do," said Pegasus.

"In that case, let us get on with it." The priest gestured to the circle of chairs by the window.

Edward followed Tammy to the circle, avoiding eye contact with either of the priests. He waited until everyone else had taken their seats before taking his own spot on the couch next to Tammy. Pegasus made do with the floor, and he looked left and right to make sure all were comfortable before turning to his assistant.

"Piripi, tea for my guests please?"

"I'll be right back with it, Sir."

"Thank you." He turned back to the circle. "Allow me to reiterate what I said before. This is to be a peaceful meeting. The wars of the past are behind us. Everyone will say what they came to say and the Triumvirate will come to a decision as one."

Edward's eye wandered over to the two monkeys, although he still kept his gaze low enough not to make eye contact. He stared at the Priest of War for a moment, but soon found himself drawn to the High Priest herself. She sat there, eyes closed, head slightly bowed, as if stealing a moment of quiet meditation. He found his eyes fixating on her neatly shaved skin. The tradition of hairless priests had made it easier for Edward to identify the enemy officers on the battlefield, but he hadn't much experience with anyone sitting up close. Most people her age would make an effort to hide their wrinkles, even going so far as to wear thermals in summer to hide any hair loss, but the High Priest bore it all without reserve. Her eyes opened, and Edward turned away.

As Tammy leaned forward, Edward leaned back. He adjusted from side to side, but she just wasn't nearly large enough to obscure the monkeys' view of him.

"Your Holiness," said the Priest of War. "Now is the time. They must hear of our great affliction."

"Proceed," she said.

"Pegasus," said the Priest of War, "we need to talk about the disaster."

"What's there for me to say?" asked the horse. "I know very little about it. My nation has kept true to our treaty and stayed clear of your holy site. We didn't even send in emergency crews—we waited for your own priests to respond."

"You can drop the pretense. I could hardly blame you for investigating that which is within your own borders."

"I'm sure you wouldn't, but there's nothing to blame us for. The smoke on the horizon is all anyone in the Bear Nation has seen. If you want to discuss anything, you'll have to disclose the details."

The priest eyed him for a moment, then glanced at the foxes, at her High Priest, and then back at Pegasus. "Very well. I'll tell you what happened. The Ancient Circle is gone."

There was silence for a moment. "What do you mean, 'gone'?" asked Pegasus.

"The entire structure has ceased to exist. Something destroyed it."

"Let us be clear. You are saying that the indestructible stone monument at which you initiate your priests has vanished."

"Yes."

Edward turned to Tammy and leaned in close to her ear. "Did you know about this?"

She shook her head. "No."

"How is that possible?" Pegasus asked the priest. "Nothing can destroy the Ancient Circle. It has withstood explosions without a scratch."

"I'm well aware of your nation's early tests. As irreverent as these experiments were, they did prove what the faithful already know: the Celestial Monkeys made each of the Five Monuments, and only the Celestial Monkeys can unmake them."

"Are you telling me the gods destroyed it?"

"I don't know. Our team found only a smoking crater and a few leftover stone shards. Two priests have been missing since the incident: one was an initiator, and the other was an old master who had recently settled in the area."

"Perhaps they saw what happened."

"If so, I doubt either is still alive."

Pegasus nodded. "All the same, I'd like to do what I can to help. We'll continue to stay off your sacred grounds, but I can assign a task force to look for those two priests."

"The Temple would appreciate such a gesture."

"The Fox Nation would be happy to help too," said Edward. "We could send a few operatives of our own to join the search."

"That won't be necessary," said the priest.

"With your permission," said Pegasus, "I'd like to address my people concerning this event. Any followers of the faith will want to offer their prayers and support."

"Her Holiness would ask that you refrain for the time being, as she has not yet informed her own citizens. Other than the priests and initiates at the scene, only the Chief Attendant, the Quadrad, and the other grand masters know."

"When will you let the rest of your people know?"

"When the time is right. The Quadrad must first come to a conclusion as to the meaning of this calamity; no doubt there will be panic once we reveal the truth, and our people will look to us for guidance." She paused, running her hand across her brow.

"She speaks the truth," said High Priest, "and as with all things, this consensus will take time. I speak for all of us when I say this turn of events has been trying on my soul."

"Yes," said the Priest of War. "The Ancient Circle fell at the hands of either petty vandals, or the gods, and I'm not sure which of the two has the worse implications."

"May I remind everyone where we are," said Tammy. "The Armistice Triumvirate has a secular charter, so I shouldn't have to tell you that in this room, we do not recognize the existence of the Celestial Monkeys."

"Show some decency, Councillor," said the Priest of War. "Someone has dealt a major blow against the foundation of our religion and way of life."

"Forgive me for not being a shoulder for you to cry on," said Tammy. "We're in a place of business and I thought you wanted to get to the bottom of this mess. Now as I was saying, I won't entertain the notion that your gods reached from the heavens to smite the Ancient Circle. We called the structure indestructible, but that was only because our scientific principles couldn't explain it. Clearly, someone has made a few advancements."

"Then who?" asked Pegasus. "It would take the resources of an entire nation to come up with the necessary technology. Are you suggesting the culprit sits here in this room?"

"Not at all," said Tammy. "There are other nations and factions out there."

Edward's ears perked at a growing whirring noise from outside. He glanced out the window, but saw nothing.

"Whom does that leave?" asked Pegasus. "The Wolves? They don't even know how to make flintlocks. The Horse Nation? They take no interest in such matters; they keep to themselves in the East. Perhaps Tromia though—"

"If this be the work of mortals, then the answer is clear," said the Priest of War. "It was the Disgraced. No one hates the Temple as they do."

Pegasus leaned back. "The Disgraced. Forgive me, but I

doubt they have the means for such an attack."

"The Disgraced are no longer a mere mercenary group. They control Golem's Pass and all the surrounding regions. There are non-combatants among their numbers, not just farmers and miners but scientists and engineers."

"If you're so sure, why come to us?" asked Tammy. "Go ahead and march on the Disgraced. Put an end to their blasphemy."

"You'd like that, wouldn't you?" said the priest. "Monkeys killing other monkeys. No, my armies would never oppose them alone. Ever since the Shroud, my soldiers wouldn't dare step foot in their lands."

"I doubt you'd see a snowstorm in the middle of summer, not to mention you outnumber them many times over. Send them in—don't good soldiers follow their leader's orders?"

"And good leaders do not needlessly send their soldiers to their deaths." The whirring sound had become much louder, loud enough that the priest had to shout for all to hear. "That is why I bring this matter to your attention. A joint army, from all three of our nations, could finally eliminate the Disgraced!"

"You're asking us to send our soldiers where yours fear to tread?"

"As you said, numbers make a difference. If we thoroughly overwhelm their forces, no one will have to fear another disaster."

"And why should we help you?"

"For peace." said the High Priest. She didn't shout, yet everyone could hear her voice above the noise. "For the beginning of a lasting friendship between our nations."

At first, no one spoke. Then Tammy shouted something back, but now the noise had become too much for anyone to make out her words. She tried again to voice her comment, and gave up mid-sentence, turning to the window to catch a glimpse of what was making the horrible sound. One by one, everyone else did the same, and this time Edward was the last to do so.

At first, he saw nothing. Then a shadow descended from above, hovering behind the window and staring down the Triumvirate. It looked vaguely like sort of aircraft, but none Edward had ever seen before. As he stepped back, there was a flash of light, and his world went blank.

He came to on the floor, moments later. It took a second to

remind himself where he was and what had just happened. His ears rang, but he pushed himself up, conjuring enough feeling and control in himself to move.

The window had shattered, and three figures stood before them. Edward made out sharp teeth and dull purple fur—Tromians. An all too familiar feeling came over him; they were under attack. The tromian closest him reached for something on his belt—a weapon perhaps.

As disoriented as he was, Edward ran up to the intruder and punched him hard across the jaw. The tromian tried to shove the fox away, but his attempt did little against Edward's massive arms. Giving that up, the tromian jumped back and tried to reach for his weapon again, but he stepped a little too close to the open window. Another punch from Edward was more than enough to send the tromian plummeting to the ground below.

Edward looked up to see that the High Priest also had sprung into action. She had engaged the tromian on the other side of the window in combat, barraging him with well-placed punches and kicks remarkably fast for a monkey her age. With a final foot to the chest, she sent the tromian out the window to join his comrade below. Only the tromian in the center remained.

The final Tromian already had his weapon drawn, and Edward found himself wishing for his old liquids. Too far away to make a safe strike at him, Edward ducked around the stone pillar beside the window. Most fools with a gun tended to waste their shot and leave themselves defenseless.

He heard a gunshot—and then another. And then another, and another, and another. The shots came so quickly that they almost blended together to make the sound of an untied balloon, only a thousand times more terrible.

Edward peered out from around the pillar. The tromian's finger stayed pressed against the trigger, and a stream of fire burst from the barrel. The intruder hadn't taken much care to aim—no one from the meeting appeared to be in his path, but the gun showed no signs of stopping. There was another flash, but this one wasn't an explosion—it was Pegasus.

The white horse charged the tromian head on. The intruder fired at him, but somehow the shots didn't seem to hit their mark. Pegasus slammed into the tromian, knocking him out the window just like the rest.

It took a moment for Edward to convince himself that the tromians were gone. As the ringing in his ears subsided, he realized that he was breathing rather heavily. The strange aircraft had vanished. Pegasus ran to his desk and slammed his hoof against the intercom.

"Guards! Where are the guards? Find those tromians and track that plane!"

A buzz of radio chatter answered him. Edward took a moment to look around and make sure they were all still there. The High Priest peered out from behind her own pillar and Tammy was already up and walking over to where he stood. The other priest and the Vice Chancellor were on their feet as well, and as far as Edward could tell, both looked unharmed. Then Edward saw him.

Piripi sat against the doorframe, in a pile of shattered china and a puddle of tea and blood. More blood trickled from several holes in his chest, and his eyes watched the side wall with an unblinking stare.

"Oh no." Pegasus galloped over. "Piripi? Can you hear me?"

There was no response.

"Dammit!" Pegasus turned down the hall. "I need a medic! Guards! Anyone!"

Chapter 19

The terrain grew rockier as they progressed. Steep hills intruded further and further into their path, gradually forcing the convoy of buggies to weave around them. Grand Oasis had long since disappeared behind them.

"Now?" asked Ray.

"Not yet," said Jess.

The second to last buggy in the procession was already fifty meters ahead of them. Little by little, Jess eased off the accelerator, allowing the distance between them to grow. Even as the minutes passed, none of the wolves ahead looked back to check on the pack's newest members.

The road ahead snaked its way around the peak of the next hill, twisting sharply enough that, for a moment, the rest of the procession disappeared around the corner. Jess let the buggy slow even more.

"How about now?"

"Not quite."

The buggy cleared the corner and the rest of the pack reappeared on the next stretch of road, although they were even farther away than before. The Anteaters could barely see the wolves sitting in the next vehicle.

Another sharp turn loomed ahead at the base of the next hill. As the buggies disappeared around the corner one by one, Jess took her foot off the pedal altogether.

"All right," she said as the last one vanished behind the hill.

"Now."

She turned just before the cliff, swinging the buggy almost completely around and slammed on the accelerator again. The vehicle zoomed off in the evening shadow of the peak, breaking away from the line. Ray watched behind them as the trail grew smaller, and soon enough it was out of sight.

"Nice work," said Ray. "We did it. We're home free."

"I wouldn't be too sure just yet," said Jess. "I'd like to put some more distance between us and them before we start celebrating."

"Fair enough. Even so, I guess I owe you an apology. The intel from Grand Oasis was worth the visit, and we made it out without an incident."

"Only if you don't consider the Bear shooting me an incident."

"Oh, right. Well, that turned out all right too. He's still clueless, and you were wearing armor."

"Crappy armor," said Jess. "I can feel a bruise on my chest. These liquids aren't much better than those old pre-dilatant vests they used to wear."

"Speaking of which," said Ray, "why don't we take the liquids off?"

"Are you serious?"

"Yeah, think about it. If Tusk Pack comes looking for us, they're looking for two people wearing wolf liquids. They won't suspect two anteaters."

"Ray, the Bear hired the Wolves to hunt us anteaters down. If we take off the liquids, we'll be a target not only to Tusk Pack, but to every pack out there."

"Huh. I guess you have a point. Some fresh air would have been nice though."

They rode in silence for a few minutes, negotiating the last of the hills as they made their way to flatter ground. The route was not the same path they had taken on their way to Grand Oasis, but it didn't matter at the moment. Jess wasn't taking them anywhere specific just yet.

"It's kind of funny, isn't it?" said Ray. "We spent all that getting to know our good friends in Tusk Pack. Now we're disappearing without so much as a goodbye."

"We don't have much of a choice."

"You never got to bid farewell to Ben or thank him for all his help."

"I suppose I didn't," said Jess. "I hope he doesn't take it too hard. The poor guy seemed to like me."

"He's a tough wolf. He'll manage."

From out of nowhere, another buggy sped across their path, screeching to a stop on the dirt. Jess slammed the brakes, lurching their own buggy to a halt. Shaken, Jess looked up and glared at the other driver.

"Hey, watch it!"

"Jess?" Wolf Ben stared back at her.

A chorus of whirring motors emerged as a stream of other buggies followed, circling the two in the middle. Jess looked back, double checking that the terrain offered no cover for a hundred meters in every direction. She couldn't believe she had been so complacent. The circle of buggies slowed to a stop as Ben jumped out to meet her.

"Where you going, Jess?" he asked. "You get lost?"

She nodded. "Yes. We lose you around corner."

"It easy to get lost back in rocky trail. You need keep up with group. Your buggy need repair?"

"It slower than usual."

The rest of Tusk Pack had parked and begun to venture into the circle. The first among them was Marissa.

"I try to tell you something wrong with new recruits," she said. "Now you see? They run away."

"Calm down, Marissa," said Ben. "Jess and Ray have motor trouble. That all."

"They no have engine trouble," said Marissa. "They head in completely wrong direction. They try to escape from Tusk Pack."

"Jess and Ray go through so much trouble just to join Tusk Pack. Why they try to leave?"

"They hiding something! They disappear in mornings, they no take off liquids, they spare Black Sun Pack leader, now this! You no see something wrong?"

Several of the wolves began to growl at her words, but Ben walked over to Jess and put his hand on her shoulder.

"Leave Jess alone. That's an order, Marissa."

Marissa's eyes widened and then she snarled. "You regret this." With that, she stormed off.

Ben turned to the rest of the pack. "It late. We camp here tonight. Ralph, Gabrielle, start campfire."

Still under the gaze of half the pack, Jess got out from the driver's seat and walked around to the back crate. She unbuckled a spare power cell from the bin and took it to the motor block. The old cell wasn't even half depleted, but she got to work replacing it anyway.

Ray stayed in the passenger seat until the rest of the pack left and went about their business, setting up tents and unwrapping packages of meat. When the last set of eyes turned away, he got up and sidestepped over to Jess as she undid the last bolt and yanked the old battery from its mount.

"That too close." He was barely loud enough for her to hear. "We need leave as soon as possible."

"When pack go to sleep," said Jess. "We keep quiet. Sneak away. We have hours to get head start then."

Ray's eyes darted between the wolves of the pack. For almost a minute he remained silent, then he turned back to Jess.

"That longer than I like, but we no have much choice."

"No."

He stood there for another minute and then turned back to the buggy. He stepped into the passenger seat again and adjusted himself several times before finally sitting still. Even then, he kept a hand on the frame, squeezing it between his fingers.

Jess pretended not to notice anything her brother was doing. She placed the old battery onto the sand and reached behind her for the new one. The new battery was gone; in its place she felt a foot.

"You fool Ben," said Marissa. "But you no fool me."

Jess looked up at her. "Yes, Marissa. I know."

"You no fool anyone else either. If I was leader, you and your brother both be dead."

Jess stood up. "Well, that prove Ben better leader than you."

Marissa paused for a moment. Jess almost thought she was about to walk away and leave them alone, but the rage never left the wolf's face.

"Ben sometimes idiot, but he great leader," Marissa finally said. "He strong, and not just in fight. He inspire me, inspire everyone to be better wolf. He done so much for me. That why I must tear you to pieces. Ben my mate. Ben mine."

"So?"

"No act stupid. I see him with you. I know he take you to Lisa's diner and spend time with you."

"You know what? I don't care. You take Ben. He all yours."

"That some kind of insult? You take Ben from me then make fun of me by saying you no care? You think you better than me?"

"Yes, Marissa, I am better than you. I'm a functioning person who makes an actual contribution to the world, not some whiny savage like you. And you know what else? I stay out of matters that don't concern me."

Marissa's eyes widened. "Why you talk so fancy all of sudden? You think you some formal or something? You think me stupid?"

Heads began to turn towards the commotion. Jess took a quick look around. Where was Ben?

"Enough of this. You die tonight. I rip liquids off your ugly face and stab you with my knife. Maybe if your brother behave, I let him live."

"You be sorry if you try."

"Jess, no."

She turned around to see Ray, standing up in the passenger seat and shaking his head. Just as she took a deep breath, something clamped down on her hand.

It was Marissa, snarling and digging into the thick gloves with her jagged teeth. Although Jess could tell it was a forceful bite, she could barely feel anything through the hardened liquids.

She clenched the wolf's jaw between her fingers as hard as she could. As Jess held her in place, she thrust a powerful kick into her chin, sending the wolf flying into the air. Jess managed to keep a firm hold on a single tooth, ripping it from its socket as Marissa soared away.

As soon as she had hit the ground, Marissa was back on her feet, growling as the blood tickled from her lips. She reached her hand into her mouth and felt around for her tooth, only to find the empty socket.

"You pay for that! We duel now!"

A circle of wolves had formed around them, snarling and cheering the same way they had when she had fought Black Sun

Pack. Ben still didn't appear among them, but Jess had no time to search him out. Marissa was charging at her.

She lunged at Jess without half the control that Maurice had displayed in the previous fight. Even with the liquids, it took no effort for Jess to step out of the way, grab Marissa by the nape of her neck, and slam her face-first into the engine block. She hit the motor with a clang that made even Ray shudder from the passenger seat.

Jess freed her hand from Marissa's neck, but oddly enough the wolf did not go limp at the brutal blow. She stood up tall, bruised and cringing, eyes still locked with Jess's. Clearly she didn't know when to quit.

The wolf charged again, and this time Jess met her with a fist to the face. The punch was so forceful that she could feel her liquids harden across her elbow and shoulder to absorb the blow. Marissa landed flat on her back, but still fumbled around, struggling to get up. Jess didn't give her the chance.

She pinned Marissa down, her knees against the wolf's elbows. With the weight of both anteater and armor, the wolf wasn't going anywhere. Jess reeled back and landed punch after punch into her face. Marissa struggled at first, trying to yank her arms free, but that only made Jess punch harder. Finally, the struggling ended. Marissa continued to breathe through her mess of a nose, but the fight was over.

Jess stayed were she was, taking a moment to catch her own breath. As the outside world came back into focus, she looked up to the see the pack still growling and cheering. They were cheering for Jess.

She began to ease off Marissa's arms, but almost immediately the cheering subsided. There was only one way a duel within a pack could end. They wanted blood.

She looked back down at the barely conscious wolf, still laboring for air. Jess tightened her fist, but then felt it loosen again. She looked up at Ray, who stood wide eyed, doorframe in hand. She looked back down to Marissa, who was whispering something to herself. She couldn't make out the words, but she sensed repetition, the same chorus of hushed sounds over and over again. Jess's hand wouldn't clench into a fist again. She grabbed the buggy frame and stood back up.

The snarls of disbelief from the wolves quickly turned to

snarls of anger. Ray jumped out of the buggy to meet her and pulled her to the side. She ignored the growls from the pack as she and her brother made off a few meters from the group to talk.

"Jess, you remember pack rule—"

"I know."

"We need leave now. We have no option."

She glanced up to see Ben, who looked to be returning from a walk off in the distance. Why couldn't he have returned when she needed him? "There Ben. We go ask him to leave."

"We tell him we cause discord in pack," said Ray. "We tell him we need go away before things get worse. It the truth."

Jess nodded. "All right."

"You!"

They turned around to see Marissa, her face still a bloody pulp, standing firm before them. The pack stood behind her, baring their teeth at the siblings.

"How dare you insult me like this!" she said. "You hate me so much you rather see me live in shame than kill me? That give you sick pleasure? What kind of wolf do that?"

"I won't see you at all anymore Marissa," said Jess. "We leaving."

"No. Now you both die by my knife."

"Get lost."

Jess and Ray turned back and walked to meet Ben, whose pace had quickened as he saw the commotion.

"Jess? What happen?"

"Ben, we sorry, but we need leave Tusk pack. The other wolves and us—"

Before she could finish, someone grabbed her by the shoulder and yanked her to the side. Marissa glared at her through her swollen black eyes, knife drawn.

Jess reached to shove her away, but someone from behind caught her arm. She slammed her elbow back into the wolf behind her, but then she felt another pair of hands on her, then another, then another. As she tried to fight against the swarm of wolves and her own cumbersome liquids, Marissa charged, and this time, she tackled Jess to the ground.

"Get off her—" Ray's shout cut short, as she heard a series of thuds from his direction. She couldn't see anything as the pack closed in around her, piled on her, held her down. If only the armor hadn't held back her arms, she might have been able to punch herself free of the mess.

"What you doing?" Ben's voice rang among the snarls. "Marissa, everyone, stop!"

No one responded to Ben's order. Jess could feel claws beneath her mask and chest piece, digging at the buckles. She jerked her head and body from side to side as much she could, trying every way to slow them down. Little by little she heard a tear building—and then her face felt fresh air.

"What's this?" Marissa stood above her, the liquid mask in one hand and the knife in the other. "You not wolf at all. What are you? Anteater?" The snarls began to subside, but Marissa didn't back away. "You and your brother, are you both anteater that Bear talked about? It no matter. You die either way."

There was a flash of sunlight as the knife fell. It took all the strength she had, but Jess managed to jerk her shoulder forward, protecting her neck. She didn't even sense the pain at first, but she could feel the tip of the knife sink beneath her shoulder blade.

"Marissa!"

Ben shoved Marissa to the side, and stood over Jess. His eyes widened as he stared at her face, and for the first time that she could remember, Tusk Pack fell completely silent. It felt like hours before he finally spoke.

"Remove liquids and tie them up. And someone contact Warlord. We found them."

Chapter 20

The buggy cast a shadow in the glow of the campfire, but the flames flickered too far away for any of the heat to make it to the Anteaters. As the night air wafted between the ropes around her body, Jess felt something she hadn't felt in a while: cold.

The thick layers of ropes held them tight against one of the buggies. Whether it was their own buggy or it belonged to a wolf from the pack, Jess couldn't tell. She faced the other way, with nothing to see but pitch black desert. The breeze carried the laughs and chants of Tusk Pack, but every now and then, she could hear an exhale from Ray as well.

She tried to move, but the ropes held tight, and to her every twitch her shoulder responded with a jolt of pain. The sticky sensation of dried blood told her that the bleeding had stopped. She was no longer in danger of passing out from blood loss, but the risk of infection still loomed, and it had already been several hours.

"You were right."

"What?" She tried to turn her head towards Ray, but her shoulder screamed for her to stop.

"You were right," Ray said again. "Under those liquids, we smelled terrible."

Jess sighed. "Ray, I'm sorry."

"There's nothing for you to be sorry about."

"If we had left back when you said we should have, none of this would have happened."

"No, we did have to go to Grand Oasis to find what we needed.

Don't blame yourself for wanting to finish the mission. I'm the one to blame."

"You? Why?"

"I couldn't fight off the pack when they turned on us," said Ray. "I let them beat me."

"Really, Ray? There's nothing you could have done. They swarmed us before we could make a move."

"I could have taken them all. Easily. It was those damn liquids—I couldn't move when I was wearing them. I hated that armor the moment I put it on! I never would have lost otherwise!"

They sat in silence for a minute. Another burst of laughter broke out from the campfire.

"Do you think I should have killed Marissa?" asked Jess.

It took Ray a moment to respond. "Do you?"

"I don't know. It would have gotten the wolves off our back."

"Then maybe you should have killed her. It wouldn't have been the first time."

"I know," said Jess. "But it was different this time. She was already down on the ground, just like Maurice was. Anton never would have done it."

"No. No, he wouldn't have," said Ray. "Maybe you could have made the problem easier and ended her in the heat of battle. When she charged you, you should have hit her head just a little harder."

"You think I wasn't trying?"

Ray said nothing.

"Not that any of that matters now," said Jess.

"Of course it still matters. We'll get through this. They're not going to hurt you, Jess."

"And why do you say that?"

"Because I'm your big brother. I won't let them."

"And how will you stop them?"

"I'll figure something out. I always do. Just trust me, Jess."

"All right, Ray. I believe you. Everything will be all right. But whatever happens, don't forget that I love you."

Ray said nothing.

Jess looked up into the night sky, this time ignoring the pain in her wound. It was a moonless night, just like the night she and her brother had picked to see the Mr. Explorer movie. When she squinted, she could see one of the galaxies in the distance, just like she had seen that night. She recalled their conversation from that evening, every line of that cheesy spiel her brother had made about the millions of unexplored worlds. Strangely enough, just as she did then, Jess felt the urge to laugh, and this time she made no effort to hold it back.

"Jess?" asked Ray.

Before she could respond, her ears perked at approaching footsteps. She didn't have to turn her head. A few moments later, the bruised face of Marissa stared down at her, along with the faces of several of her friends.

"Tough little anteater not so tough anymore," she said. "What you do now? Huh?"

Jess feigned a look of surprise. "Is that you, Marissa? You're much prettier than I remember."

It took a moment for a response from any of the wolves. One of them started chuckling, but Marissa punched him in the face. "I look better than ugly anteater. Besides, these wounds all badge of honor. They show I was the one who stop spies from Fox Nation. I was the one who stop biggest targets in history of Wolf."

"Badge of honor? Whatever happened to you living in shame? I seem to recall you lost that fight against me. You shouldn't even be alive."

"If I lose to wolf from Tusk Pack, it right that I die. But you never part of Tusk Pack. You from biggest, stupidest, ugliest pack of all: Fox Pack."

Jess burst out laughing. Marissa scowled. "What so funny?"

"You are. That was a good one."

"You laugh now, but you no laugh when Bear come for you."

"Yeah, the funny thing is I've met the Bear once before. We didn't have long to talk, but he came across as a complete idiot. It makes sense that he would find a home among the Wolves."

"He better wolf than you. You no act like wolf at all. I should have attacked you from beginning. You never smell right either, but I not sure at start. I never smell anteater before."

"About that, I've been sweating non-stop the entire time I've been here," said Jess. "You're standing a little close to me. How's that keen wolf sense of smell treating you now?"

"It no bother me."

"And by the way, thanks for finally taking those crappy liquids off me. Those things were torture. I don't know how any of you fight in them."

"We don't."

"But do you know what's an even bigger relief? Now I can finally speak like a civilized person again. You have idea how agonizing it was making myself talk like a pre-op and pretending to be some brainless wolf."

"Marissa, Akiko, Pablo, Ralph, Tina, leave now." It was Ben's voice.

Marissa looked as though she might throw in one last comment, but this time she obeyed her orders and the others followed her. Ben stepped into her view, and only once the rest of wolves were long gone did he speak.

"I make sure they leave you alone. Our instructions are bring you to Bear alive."

"Ben, can you stay here and talk to me for a minute?"

"I can talk."

"Then please listen to me. You don't need to do this."

"Yes, I do. I need follow Warlord orders, and we need money from contract."

"No you don't, Ben. I know you're better than that."

"How are you one to say thing like that?" asked Ben. "You lie to me. You lie to me from moment I met you. I believe you real wolf, I turn against own pack when they tell me they no like you, and I let you spy on us all along! I have many good talk with you, but that was all lie too. I still no understand. You trick me, you not even wolf, and yet I still—" he paused for a moment. "I still have feeling for you."

"Oh my goodness." The voice came from the other corner of the buggy.

"Ray, please." She stared up at Ben. "Yes, you're right. I lied to you. We had to do it to protect ourselves and blend in, but I promise you, we mean no harm to you or your pack. You are all innocent—I see that know. The Bear is the one we are after. We have no quarrel with the Wolves."

"Well, it now seem Wolf have quarrel with you."

"You don't have to. I don't hate you, Ben. I know you're good. All this time, you protected us because you're a good person."

"I protected you because I was idiot. That what you mean, right?"

Jess shook her head, again ignoring the pain from the wound. "No."

"You understand what I feel? Everything I tell you on that hill was true. I so badly want bright future for Wolf, but it seem like all I see are violence and savage. I wonder if we really as bad as formal species say we are. Then I meet a wolf who different from others. She smart and cunning, she care about doing right thing, and she best fighter I ever seen. She seem too good to be true. I guess she actually was too good to be true. The best wolf I ever met turn out to not be wolf at all. How I be so stupid?"

"Ben, you're not stupid. The Wolves may very well have this bright future you speak of, but it won't be because of me. It will be because of you, Ben. It will be Wolves like you who bring about this change. I know you believe in your kind, and I know you can't be the only one. As long as you're here, there will be hope for your people."

"You mean that?"

"You know I do."

He shook his head. "No, I don't."

For a moment, she wondered if he was about to leave.

"If you can't set us free, there is another way you can help me."

"How?"

"Bring me my belt."

"I no untie your arms."

"You don't have to, just bring it over here so I can see it."

In a minute, he was back with her belt. The compartments still bulged with their contents.

"What now?"

"There's something I need you to get from one of the pockets."

He reached for the central compartment, the one with the camera and recorder.

"No, not that one. Open the first one down to your left."

"This one?"

"Your other left."

"What?"

"The one on the other side of the one in the middle."

When Ben finally opened the right pocket, he pulled out a small box. "Is this it?"

"Yes, that's a first aid kit. Marissa stabbed me and the wound still needs treatment. Are you willing to fix it up for me?"

"I will."

"Thank you. Now I need you to follow my instructions very carefully. First, take out the bottle of antibiotic—"

"You no need tell me what to do. Wolf get wound just like formal."

He spent the next few minutes dressing the stab wound. Jess cringed as he worked the needle through her skin, but she never once had to stop and correct him. When he had finished, he left the kit and the belt where they were on the dirt.

"The Bear is a bad person, you know," she said.

"Is he?"

"He is. He plants bombs in public areas, bribes politicians, and as you know, he's trying to have Ray and me killed."

"I see."

"You don't have to work for someone like him. No wolf does. If you believe in the goodness of the Wolves, in the goodness of yourself, you will let us go. You know it's the right thing to do."

Ben said nothing.

"You don't have to do what they tell you to," said Jess. "You have a choice, Ben."

He turned to her one last time. "I know I have choice," he said. "The Bear bad, yes. He also very rich. The money he pay us good for Wolf, and not just for weapons and buggies for pack. We use it for homes, for schools, for our children. I wish I able to let you go free, but don't tell me what's better for my people."

And with that, he walked off into the night.

Chapter 21

The clouds outside darkened. The wind picked up and lightening flashed off in the distance. Sky shuddered at the sight, although she wasn't quite sure why it bothered her. She had to turn away from the window.

Other things were on her mind now. She was hungry. She could really go for a ripe banana, and she figured they had a few left.

There was no fruit on the counter, so she opened the refrigerator. It was empty, other than a heavy looking knife sitting on the middle rack, made from some weird metal she didn't recognize. It didn't look at all like a kitchen knife; it looked more like a weapon, or maybe even a ceremonial piece.

She closed the door, still finding herself as hungry as before. Then she looked in her hand to see that she had been holding a banana the whole time. Sky was too overjoyed to feel stupid.

As she ate her snack, Sky pulled up a chair and sat down. As she did, she felt a sharp pain where her tail used to be.

"Good morning, Sky."

She looked up to see her master in the doorway.

"Good morning, Master Nyah."

"Would you care for some company?"

"Please, take a seat."

She sat down opposite Sky and looked at her with the relaxed, kindly face that Sky had missed in the stressful months leading up to the initiation.

"Have you managed to get some rest? You seemed like you

needed it after the ceremony."

"Oh, yes. I'm doing fine now."

"Nothing more is bothering you?"

"Only my tail stump. It really hurts."

"Have you been applying your ointment?"

"Yes."

"How many times since you woke this morning?"

"Just once."

"Then perhaps it's time you applied more. You must take care to be thorough in this task. An infection in that area is a shameful burden for a young priest."

"I could understand why."

"Also, when you're feeling better, be sure to practice your fighting forms. With your tail gone, you have lost an instrument of balance. It will take time to reorient yourself, but I'm sure it will prove no challenge for you."

"Yes, Master."

"Sky, you don't have to call me that anymore."

"You are a Master though."

"Yes, but I'm no longer your master. I'll always be your mentor, but you are a priest now, just like me. You passed your initiation."

"I know."

"But you have a hard time believing it has finally come to pass?"

Sky nodded. "How did you know?"

"Such is the way of many a young priest," said Nyah. "So fervent in faith in the Celestial Monkeys, yet struggling to grasp the plainer truths in life."

"It's a little bit of a shock, yes," said Sky, "but I still know it happened. I know I'm a priest now. It's just that, other than my missing tail, I don't feel any different."

"Are you suggesting that such a change within you could occur in an instant? No, the path to the priesthood is a long and trying voyage, far more than the flick of a knife. Young ones like you see every year as an eternity; only when one becomes old like me does one see the entire journey. Remember when you stood vigil at the shrine on Whinson's Night last year? When you organized the schedule for volunteers at the refugee shelter and spent four months repairing the building? When you won the junior division sparring tournament within your first year of training? All of those things made you into a priest just as much as did getting your mark."

"But it all could have ended right there by that bonfire. If the initiator had deemed me unworthy, I wouldn't have become a priest at all."

"You're looking at it the wrong way, Sky. You passed the final test because of your years of training. Those years made you into the person you are now, someone who would triumph before the initiator's blade. That morning, you woke up guaranteed to succeed."

"Actually," said Sky, "I don't think I woke up at all that morning, because I don't think I even fell asleep the night before."

"Oh?"

"I'm not sure I should tell you this."

"I sense you will regardless."

Sky thought for a moment and then looked back up at Nyah. "I was scared that morning. It may have been for only a moment or two, but despite all my training, I was terrified of losing everything I had worked for. I know the initiator saw my fear, but he gave me the mark of honor anyway."

Nyah laughed. "Of course you were scared, Sky."

Sky paused. "What do you mean?"

"You were scared, as you damn well should have been. I know I was scared at my own initiation."

"Then why didn't I get a mark of disgrace? Didn't he see my fear?"

"I imagine he did. As I said, the initiator will see any fear within you and then deem you worthy or unworthy, but I never said that he made said decision based on said fear."

Sky sank into her chair. "Please tell me you're joking."

"Your entire future revealed to you in a moment. What sane person wouldn't be nervous?"

"So you and the rest of the priests tricked me this whole time?"

"Trick you? Never. Sky, clearly you should have asked some more specific questions when I gave you the chance." She put her hand on Sky's shoulder. "Cheer up. I'm not going to call up the initiator and have him come cross out your tattoo. You're a priest now. You earned it and no one can take it away from you."

"You are kind, Master. Twisted, but kind."

"I'm not your master anymore."

"I know."

Darkness engulfed the room, and the sides of the building began to creak in the wind. Sky turned her head to the window to get a look at more clouds rolling in. That was when she saw another flash of lightning.

"Lightning," came Nyah's voice. "A bad omen."

Sky turned back to Nyah, now enveloped in shadow and not looking half so cheerful as she had a moment ago. "What did you say?"

"I said the lightning is a bad omen," said Nyah.

"That's what the initiator said."

"And he was right."

The windows tried to rattle free of their frames as the booming thunder roared by.

"But everything turned out all right, didn't it? I still became a priest."

"You did."

"So then there's nothing to worry about. All that's left for me to do is devote my life to serving the Temple."

"No."

Another wave of thunder shook the dishes on the counter.

"What?"

"No Sky, your actions will bring no service to the Temple. The bad omen truly was of your priesthood. You becoming a priest will bring about a terrible future for our people. You will bring about the downfall of our Temple, the downfall of our faith, and the downfall of our very way of life. Curses of the Celestial Monkeys upon you, Friar Sky."

"What are you saying?"

A final blast of thunder yanked the house from its foundation. The windows shattered. The drywall cracked and then shattered as well. The wooden beams within the walls screamed as they bent and twisted and finally snapped in a shower of sawdust. The furniture, the rugs, the remnants of the walls, all were gone in an instant.

Master Nyah was the last to disappear. The thunder blew her away, like paper in the wind. And then Sky was alone.

She stood atop a tower, looking out over a burning city. A scorching wind rustled her tuft of hair as she gazed up into the blood red sky. She was back home in the Monkey Nation, back in Quadrus. And there, in the middle of the city, stood the Temple.

Its foundation took up several blocks of the inner district, and its spires towered well above every other skyscraper. It towered beyond the clouds and into the glowing sky, so high that she couldn't even see the summit. Truly it stood as a work of art both ancient and modern, with marble pillars bolstering the bottom and a skeleton of cobalt alloy interspacing an endless vertical field of glass paving the way to the heavens. The majesty of coppers and greens and blues still glistened off its tinted windows even in the harsh red of the sky.

The Temple remained untouched by the fires of the city, yet somehow Sky could feel its vulnerability. At the same time, she felt something else: a notion of complete control. All the power in the world rested in her hands, and she could with it as she pleased. The Temple was in grave peril, but she, Sky, had the power to save it.

And yet, she stared straight at the Temple before her, and said three words.

"Let it fall."

There was a flash of light in a narrow vein running up the tower, and then it was no more. The pieces remained, but any semblance of structure was gone. Glass, cobalt, marble and copper all fell to the earth as if from a waterfall in the sky. Before all the shards could even reach the ground, a white light enveloped the city.

Sky sat up from her sleeping bag, gasping. She yanked her legs out of the bag and jumped to her feet. Her eyes shot around but saw nothing but dark desert. The city was gone.

It took some time for reality to fade back to her. It had all been a dream. She wasn't in the Bear Nation or the Monkey Nation. She was in the Wolf lands, south of the Great Salt Pan, on her way east to her first assignment at the Sand Monoliths. It had gotten late so she had stopped to rest for the night.

She ran her hand down her back, and sure enough, her tail was gone. She felt beside the stump to her mark, which also still hurt. From the most painful regions, she make out the shape of three lines forming a simple arrow. She was a priest.

Everything back in the Bear Nation had gone all right. She had passed the final trial, spent some time in recovery, and parted ways with Master Nyah without incident. There had been no destruction of the Temple, no burning of the city, and no tearing away of kitchens. All was well.

As her breathing calmed, she began to shiver in the chilly night air. She lay back down and pulled the sleeping bag over her. She turned belly down and closed her eyes, trying to fall back asleep.

Try as she might, Sky couldn't shake the horrifying image of the Temple collapsing. Every morning of her training, she had looked up to the mighty structure on her way to and from the barracks. As far as she was concerned, it had been there forever and always would be, just like the Five Monuments. The Celestial Monkeys may not have built the Temple themselves, but they had inspired their faithful servants to do so in their name, and didn't that mean just as much? She shuddered at the thought of seeing it fall to pieces.

She rolled onto her back, a position in which she seldom found sleep, even before she had lost her tail. Her eyes scanned the sky until she spotted a speck halfway to the horizon. Staring into the heavens often brought her comfort, but tonight the tiny blip did little to draw her thoughts; the drug-like influence of the dream still clenched her by the heart.

Just as disturbing as the temple's destruction were Master's Nyah's words. Why couldn't her mind have picked a less endearing figure for the horrifying message?

She thought back to the start of their exchange. The beginning portion was from a real conversation she and Nyah had had, almost verbatim. The morning after the initiation, Nyah had indeed lectured her about cleaning her wound and practicing her martial arts skills without a tail. True to her word, Sky had done both.

The next part, in which she had dreamt that Nyah had explained how it was normal to feel fear during the initiation and how the initiators judge the initiates solely on other matters, had never happened. It sounded sort of like something Nyah might say, but she could think of nothing in the real world that suggested the idea held any truth. In the dream, Sky had had to slowly wrap her head around this crazy new idea; now, she had to slowly unwrap it. If one showed fear, one wouldn't become a priest. End of story.

She didn't even want to think of the final piece of their conversation, but she couldn't keep it out of her head. Why would Master Nyah say such horrible things to her? All she wanted was to lead a generous and spiritually fulfilling life as a priest—how and why would she possibly destroy everything she held dear? She refused to accept it. There was one thing Sky believed in even more so than the Celestial Monkeys, and that was her own free will. If she resolved not to destroy the Temple, no power on heaven or Earth could compel her to do otherwise.

Destroy the Temple? Somewhere in her mind she knew the whole idea was absurd. It was the dream delirium, still clawing away at her. She would get no more sleep that night. The only thing to do was to walk it off.

She stood up again and looked over at the buggy, little more than a ghostly outline in the moonless night. If she were going to take her mind off these thoughts, she might as well put in a few more hours on the road. Eventually her head would start to nod behind the wheel, and she could pull over for some much easier rest.

She rolled up the sleeping bag and tossed it in the crate. The cold breeze made her shudder again. Being a priest and having very little hair proved no help keeping warm on desert nights. She yanked a thick thermal cloak from the crate and wrapped it around her body, dropping the hood over her head. Much better.

When she turned the key, the motor responded with a pathetic cry and then went silent.

"Oh no."

She turned the key again, harder. The motor whined even louder than before, but it finally hummed to life after a few seconds.

She had gotten lucky this time, but she wasn't sure how long her luck would last. That was what she got for trusting that sleazy mechanic back in the Fox Nation. She made a mental note to avoid shortcuts and stick to the trail between the string of towns leading to the Monoliths.

Though there was little to crash into, she knew she wouldn't get anywhere without the headlights. It was so dark she could barely see her own hands. With the lights on, there would be enough warning to avoid any wolf packs, and they would probably leave her alone anyway.

After about half an hour behind the wheel, Sky didn't feel nearly as disturbed about the dream as she had before. By midday, the words and images would have faded into the fog; such was the manner of dreams. She probably could have pulled over right then, but she was making good progress and at that point she felt curious to see when the morning sun would rise.

For a while she saw nothing but dirt in the two narrow beams from her headlights. Once every so often there was a rock or shrub to avoid, but nothing gave her any trouble.

Then the vehicle hit a bump, and something new came into view: two figures sitting by a buggy about two hundred meters away. There were more buggies behind that one, maybe a dozen or so. A pack.

She slammed on the brakes, switched off the headlights, and turned the key. She heard nothing. No one from the pack could have seen her. Only then did she realize she hadn't made things much better by stopping. To get away from the wolves, she would have to start the motor again. The horizon now revealed a deep blue—perhaps it would be just light enough for her to see the path if she were to sneak around them with no headlights.

As she reached for the key, another thought crossed her mind. Why were two of the wolves sitting against their buggy? It seemed a very uncomfortable position for sleep. Hadn't she heard somewhere that most wolves sleep in tents?

Before she knew it, Sky found herself hopping down from the driver's seat and wandering toward the pack. The Master Nyah in her head gave her a dozen reasons not to do so, but her curiosity drowned out the voice. It was her duty to pursue knowledge, was it not? Sky wanted to know what those two figures she saw were doing, and besides, she had never seen a wolf pack before.

She paid mind to her footsteps as she neared the camp. There was still no sound from anyone ahead, so the slightest noise she made could very well be the loudest. The blue glow above had advanced on the black, so she dropped to the ground to crawl the rest of the way. Thirty meters would be enough for her to get a good look.

The two figures sitting against the buggy didn't look much like any wolves she had imagined. She couldn't make out any sharp teeth, and their noses were much longer than expected. It took her longer than she cared to admit to realize that they were both tied to the buggy, each secured with a thick cord of rope.

They weren't wolves. They were anteaters.

That brought more questions than it answered. Who were they? Pilgrims? Salespeople? Mercenaries? Were they unwitting victims, or had they done something to make the pack turn on them? Given the nature of wolves, it probably wouldn't take much.

Perhaps the two did deserve to be captives. Maybe they were violent criminals that the wolves had finally apprehended. Or maybe they weren't. Maybe they needed her help. From where she lay, Sky had no way of knowing.

But she intended to find out.

Chapter 22

Jess thought she had seen a flash of light for a moment, but now it was gone. Had her mind been playing tricks on her? The embers of the campfire behind her had long since flickered away, leaving the camp in total darkness. Any light would be impossible to miss. She fixed her eyes on where she thought she had seen something, but there was nothing there.

Jess let out a sigh, and then had to force her eyes open again. She couldn't fall asleep. Fall asleep, and it would be over. Fall asleep and she would wake up face to face with the Bear and his maniacal grin.

She could hear nothing from Ray. Though she never knew him to be a silent sleeper, he still seemed too quiet to be awake. She could hear something though: a slight rustle in the sand. Had she made the sound herself? No, it seemed a few meters from the buggy.

A palm slapped over her mouth, muffling any sound that might escape her lips. Jess felt someone lean in near her ear.

"If you want to get out of here, do exactly as I say." The whisper was barely audible. "When I take my hand away, you will make no sound. You will step as quietly as you can and follow me back the way I came. Nod if you understand."

Jess did so.

"Good. Now I'm going to cut you free of these ropes, and then I'll do the same for your friend. Remember, not a sound."

After a slight tug on the ropes, she felt them release and collapse to the ground at her feet. She stepped forward, still clutching her arms to her sides, careful not to let her deep exhale betray her.

As the mysterious figure moved over to Ray, Jess stole a glance back at the pack. There was some light now, just enough to see that everyone was still snug in their tents. She turned away and shuffled forward to feel something at her feet. It was her belt, still sitting where Ben had left it. She picked it up, but didn't risk snapping the buckle within earshot of the camp.

She felt a hand on her shoulder and turned to see Ray, or the dim outline of him, standing beside her, and the stranger beside him. As the shadow made off into the night, the Anteaters followed, laboring over every footstep. Only once they had cleared a hundred meters did they resume their normal gait.

Jess spotted something not too far away: another buggy. She flinched at first, but the stranger hurried towards it, so she followed suit. No one else was in the vehicle, so clearly it belonged to their new friend.

The figure jumped into the driver's seat and motioned towards the two seats in the back. Ray was the first to comply, and after a moment, Jess stepped up into the seat next to his.

A horrible whining shriek filled the air and then whimpered away. The Anteaters cringed in the moment of silence that followed. There was a second shriek, and then the happy purr of an electric motor. The frame shook to life and lurched into gear.

Still in the shadow of the very early morning, the driver made a ninety degree turn and took them in a circle, giving the pack a generous berth. Jess kept her eyes on the blurry encampment for any signs of a reveille, but all remained as still as before. Gradually the pack became smaller and smaller, until at last it disappeared over the horizon. Only a few minutes after that did the driver finally turn on the headlights.

It wasn't long before the driver turned them off yet again. A pale light had made its way to the eastern horizon, rendering the land deep blue, but visible. Jess tried to get a better look at their rescuer, but whoever it was wore a thick thermal cloak, rippling in the wind. Jess shivered. She leaned in next to Ray, and this time he let her.

She still clutched the belt in her hands. Jess reached into the various compartments to find that everything was where she had left it. The camera, the recorder, the flare, and all the other supplies were neatly packed in their places. She could sense from Ray's glances a twinge of envy that she had gotten to retrieve her belongings and he hadn't.

They continued on for what she guessed was an hour or two before the sun finally appeared in the sky. After another ten minutes, the air began to warm.

"That cave there," said the driver. "That should do."

It took Jess a moment to spot the cave. It sat beneath a rock formation, a circle of vegetation obscuring its entrance.

The buggy slowed as they approached the mouth, and as they got closer, Jess could see that the cavern could easily accommodate the vehicle. The grass parted as they drove through, and with a great bump, they disappeared into the cave and screeched to a stop.

The interior only went back about ten meters, but it was tall enough to stand in. Most of the floor was flat and rocky, with a patch of sand here and there. The driver dismounted and walked over to the tire tracks in the grass.

"They'll be looking for you," she said, leaning down to push the leafy blades as far upright as they would go. "We'd best lay low while we can."

Jess was the first of the siblings to jump down to join her. "You saved our lives," she said. "I don't know how we can ever repay you."

"There's no need to repay me." The cloaked figure stood up again, still facing out into the desert. "It sure got warm all of a sudden. Much too warm for these thermals."

She let the cloak fall to the ground, and then the Anteaters saw. She was a monkey, an almost hairless monkey. Jess's eyes shifted down to the stump below her spine and the arrow tattoo on her hip. A priest.

"Now that's much better."

"Who are you?" asked Ray.

The priest turned around and smiled at the siblings. She was young, perhaps about their age. "My name is Sky."

Jess bowed her head. "I'm Jess, and this is my brother, Ray."

Sky bowed as well. "Jess, Ray, You two are lucky I came along when I did. You're safe from the wolves for now, but before anything else, you'll understand if I have to ask you a few questions."

"Why?" asked Ray.

"Isn't it clear? That pack was holding you prisoner. For all I know, they may have had good reason to do so. I have to trust the two of you not to stab me in the back, so I need to know now: why did the wolves tie you up?"

"Someone hired them," said Jess. "Someone is paying them a lot of money to capture us."

"Why?"

"We don't know."

"Then what were you two doing in the Wolf lands in the first place?"

"Well, what were you doing here?" asked Ray.

Jess turned to him. "Ray!"

"No, it's all right," said Sky. "It's a fair question. The Temple has assigned me to the Sand Monoliths for the next few years. I'm on my way there now—this desert is the quickest route other than a straight shot through the Salt Pan. That just about sums it up. Now I'd like you to tell me why you're here."

"That may not be possible," said Jess. "I'm promise I'm not just saying this, but a lot of that information is classified."

"Then tell me as much as you can."

"All right. We're from the Fox Nation and we work for the government. Our concern is the safety of our borders." She reached for her belt. "We have identification badges, or at least I do—"

"That won't be necessary. I believe you."

"Glad to hear it."

Sky walked back from the shrubs and joined them in the shade of the cave. "So then, we need to a plan. By now, your pack has probably discovered your absence. They'll be out searching the desert for you, so we'd do best to rest here today and travel by night. Beggar's Station is the nearest town, and the residents aren't very friendly with wolves, so you should be safe there. It's about a day's trip from here, and from there, you should be able to secure passage to wherever you need to go. Does that work for you?"

"I suppose so. Ray?"

"I'm not so sure. I didn't see many other caves on our way here. If I were looking for someone, this is the first place I would look."

"That's why one of us is going to stand watch," said Sky. "I slept most of the night, so I'll volunteer for the first shift."

"Well, so did I," said Ray. "So don't trouble yourself. I'll stand guard."

"I didn't sleep at all," said Jess. "So I'm going to bed."

Jess stepped aside and scanned the cave for a spot smooth enough to serve as a suitable sleeping area. Ray and Sky didn't budge.

"I mean it," said Sky. "I got plenty of sleep, so I'll keep watch."

"I meant it too," said Ray, "and since there's no point in both of us standing guard, you might as well go to sleep now."

The priest sighed and went over to the buggy. She yanked a bundle from the crate and handed it to Jess.

"I only have one sleeping bag, but seeing as no one else will be needing one, you might as well have it."

"Thanks." Jess rolled it out on a patch of sand that looked almost large enough for her to stretch out her legs. "Wake me up when it's my turn."

As she lay down, Jess stole a final glance across the cavern. The glaring sun had grown brighter already, but she could still make out the two silhouettes at the mouth of the cave: her brother on one side and the priest on the other. Jess wasn't one to argue if neither one of them wanted to sleep; she was exhausted.

She pulled the sleeping bag over her, turned toward the back of the cave, and closed her eyes. Despite all that had happened, she felt too tired to be worked up, and sleep couldn't come soon enough.

"What was that?" Ray's voice bounced off the walls of the cave.

"What was what?"

"I saw something move. Look, way over there."

"I think that's just a bush moving in the wind."

"Are you sure?"

Jess rolled over and squinted in the light. "What's going on?"

"It's nothing," said Sky. "Your brother thought he saw something, but it's nothing to worry about."

"I'm just being cautious, all right?" said Ray. "I hope I didn't bother you, Jess."

"No, don't worry about it," said Jess. "It's not like I'm trying to sleep or anything."

"Sorry."

She turned her back to them again and closed her eyes, and this time, they stayed shut.

Chapter 23

He pressed his thumb against the wheel and spun it once, twice, three times. No spark. He pressed it harder than before, only to have the lighter slip free of his hand. He lunged to grab it, but the lighter eluded him, falling past the railing, bouncing off the balcony, and disappearing into the deserted street below.

"Dammit."

He had only brought one lighter with him; he had figured he would only need one. The Bear pulled the cigar from his mouth and rolled it between his fingers. It was useless now; it might as well have been one of those candy imitation cigars they made to hook kids, and even in that case he might have at least had himself a snack. Now he would have to run down the stairs and comb the street just to retrieve the lighter. Or maybe not. Perhaps the Wolves had stocked the guest suite with all the usual provisions and he'd find what he needed by his bedside—no, that would be ridiculous. Sure the Wolves doted upon their esteemed guests, but they knew nothing of the finer points of stocking hotels. He could check the nightstand, but he was as likely to find a book of matches as he was the Book of Whinson. The only option was walking all the way down to the street.

And yet, he stayed where he was. The sun had just climbed over the horizon and he couldn't help but watch it glimmer off the lake in the breeze. In the heat of the day, the sandstone buildings always looked so bland and sterile, but now the rising sun painted everything vibrant shades of orange.

The silence too had such a pull on him. Every night, he had had to cover his ears with his pillows to escape the howling of packs camped outside the city borders. Wolves were creatures of the night, but in the early morning, all was silent.

"Hey Bear!"

He turned to see two dogs standing on the balcony of the adjacent room. Brad had one arm around Sonya's waist, and with the other, he waved.

"Good morning," said the Bear. "You're up early."

"So are you," said Brad. "We got up to see sunset. It was pretty cold until a few minutes ago, so we just watched it from the window. Is that why you're up too?"

"No, I'm just out here for a smoke." He walked over the edge nearest Brad and Sonya's balcony. The space between them looked just close enough to jump, but the Bear had no intention of attempting it. "Do you have a light?"

"No."

"Huh. Figures."

"Don't you have one?" asked Sonya.

"I did, but I lost it."

"Well, that's too bad," said Brad. "Still, you could just enjoy the sunrise with us."

"Yeah," said the Bear. "The sunrise and the silence."

Brad opened his mouth to say something, but then stopped midway. Sonya gave him a squeeze around the waist and he turned back to her, looking into her eyes. Then they turned back to the rising sun, and for a minute, all three said nothing as they watched the view.

Even though he didn't admit it, the Bear found he really was enjoying the sunrise. He almost didn't mind that he couldn't enjoy the moment with a lit cigar. Almost. As Brad and Sonya held each other closer, the Bear averted his eyes. Brad planted a kiss on her forehead and the Bear shuffled a few paces away from them. Perhaps it was time to make a discrete exit.

He had gone halfway back to his door when Sonya turned to him.

"Do you think the Wolves caught the Anteaters yet?"

He chuckled. "I doubt it. The Wolves can't catch the Anteaters while they're still up north in the Fox Nation."

"So how do you plan to get them to come down here?"

The Bear stepped back over to the edge of the balcony. "Haven't I gone over this already? The Anteaters have an eye for me now, so I'll lure them here myself."

"You want to provoke them and then have them chase you back to the Wolf lands?"

"Or just the salt pan. Somewhere there won't be any Foxes to save them."

"What if it doesn't work?"

"It will."

"I know," said Sonya, "but it's still a lot of money, and that's on top of everything you're paying Tammy. We could do a lot of other things with that kind of money."

"It's pocket change," said the Bear. "If I have to alter the plan again, I'll just shell out some more."

"What if we all spent it on a luxury vacation instead?" asked Sonya. "I've always wanted to stay in one of those spa resorts in Port Sable."

"If we see this through, I'll buy you all your own vacation homes on the beach. We've come this far already. Don't you want to see the job done?"

"Yeah, Sonya," said Brad. "Is something wrong? You sound like you even don't care about giving the Anteaters what they deserve."

"Of course I care, Brad. I know how important this is to you."

"This isn't about me. This is about Phil."

"And you think this is what Phil would want?"

"If he ever wakes up, I'm sure he'll be happy to hear about what we did here. If the Anteaters hadn't ditched that game, Phil wouldn't have had to sub in for them, and those jackasses from Kraphton Beach wouldn't have busted his spine."

"I know, Brad. I was there."

Brad just shook his head. "He wouldn't have lost the last seven years of his life."

The Bear let out a sigh. "Are the two of you going to need to sit this job out? Pack up and go home if this is all too much for you."

"No, Bear," said Brad, "we're in."

"And what about you?" asked Sonya.

"What do you mean, 'what about me'?" asked the Bear.

"You must have a reason for hating the Anteaters too. Why do you want them dead so much?"

The Bear laughed. "Don't you know who I am?"

"Uh…"

"So Brad never told you?"

She turned to Brad. "Who is he?"

"Um," said Brad. "You're the Bear?"

"No—"

"Bear Theo?" asked Sonya.

"No! Just shut your mouths and listen!" He waited a moment to make sure the two dogs were silent. "My full name is Bear Carson Theodore. I'm the grandson of Julia and Lazarus."

Brad stared at him. "You mean Bear Julia and Bear Lazarus?"

"I don't think his grandparents were foxes," said Sonya.

"That's right," said the Bear. "My grandmother was Bear Carson Julia, the last angel of the First Order, leader of the Autumn Revolution, and the greatest warrior the world has ever known. My grandfather is Bear Carson Lazarus, the most brilliant mind of our time, scourge the treacherous Anteaters, and known to all as the Great Bear."

"The mass murderer," said Sonya.

"My grandfather was not to blame for the genocide. In the Pact, he asked only for Anton and his family, but the Monkeys got carried away."

"So Bear," said Brad, "if Julia and Lazarus really are your grandparents, then how come you're so bad at fighting?"

The Bear put his fist down on the railing. "Why don't you hop over to my balcony? Then we'll see just how bad at fighting I am."

Brad flinched. "Hey, chill out, Bear. I'm just messing around."

"So they're your grandparents," said Sonya. "What does that have to do with anything?"

"I've been doing some digging. It turns out that those two anteaters are the last living descendants of Anton. The Great Anteater himself might be out my reach for now, but I will fulfill my destiny, and that begins with eliminating the last of his progeny. Then Lazarus will finally realize my potential."

"Have you ever actually met him?"

"Only once. It was many years ago, and I didn't even know who he was at the time. I thought he was just some mysterious old bear who had some strange interest in my family. Now I know that he was evaluating me, trying to decide if I was worthy of his legacy. I know I disappointed him. He was much more interested in my older sister, Amanda. She was so smart and strong and good at everything she did. She had everything, yet still she turned him down. She had no interest in becoming his apprentice."

"Makes sense to me," said Sonya. "Why should she want to get herself involved in some feud?"

"Because she was a Bear, and because she was a warrior. She turned down an opportunity that most people could only dream of having. Lazarus couldn't see past her before, but he'll see me now. Especially since she's out of the picture."

"What do you mean 'out of the picture'?"

"I took care of her," said the Bear. "She won't be an issue anymore."

Sonya looked down at her feet, her arm around Brad's waist clenching him harder than before. Brad gazed out into the sunrise, smiling as though no one had said anything, and for another minute, no one did.

"Enough of that for now," said the Bear. "I have anteaters to catch, and you two have my money to blow."

Just as he opened the balcony door, he heard a knock from across the room. Someone was pounding on his front door, nearly shaking it from its frame.

"All right, all right, I'm coming!"

He scurried across the suite, nearly tripping over the nightstand as he made his way to the door. He fumbled with the bolt and then swung the door open to reveal a tall, scruffy wolf.

"Yes, what do you want? It's early."

"Bear, sir, sorry to bother at this time, but something urgent come up."

"Well, what is it? I'm listening."

"Warlord receive messenger from Tusk Pack. They found the Anteaters."

He couldn't have heard that right.

"The two anteaters I was looking for?"

"Their names Anteater Jess and Anteater Ray. They agents for Fox Nation, just as you say. They hide in pack for last few weeks by pretending to be wolf."

"And where are they now?"

"Tusk pack capture them. They tied up right now, just awaiting your arrival."

So it was true. His luck had finally turned, making up for his entire life of misfortune. Nothing good had ever come to him, and even when he had taken matters into his own hands, his plans still screwed up. But no longer. Now his grand scheme, the scheme Tammy had called idiotic, had worked better than he had ever dreamed it would.

"Have my buggy prepared at once," said the Bear. "And make sure the Warlord has ten packs ready to escort me."

"Right away."

"You'd better make it quick. The sooner I get my prize, the sooner you all get your payment."

When the Bear left the building a few minutes later, the silent street had become a muddled crowd of wolves, shoving and clawing at each other as they fought to stay with their packs. The Warlord's herald bellowed instructions to the pack leaders, the pack leaders barked orders at their soldiers, and the soldiers snarled at anyone who got in their way.

"Sir, follow this way." A she-wolf waved from the crowd.

The Bear followed, doing his best to dodge the scrambling packs. His escort led him down a quieter street, a narrower branch of the central marketplace. A few of the bear and monkey merchants already stood by their shops, craning their heads to get a better look at all the excitement.

At the end of the road where the sandstone faded to sand, his private buggy awaited him. The driver nodded at them and the escort jumped into the passenger seat, leaving the more comfortable back seat for the honored guest.

"Ten packs standing by," said the attendant. "We leave now and they join us on road after we clear outskirts."

"Bear!"

He turned around to see a brown dog rushing to meet him.

"What is it, Brad?"

"Is it true? Did they really capture the Anteaters?"

"It appears so. I'm about to go see for myself."

"Are you going to let me come with you?"

"I suppose so," said Bear. "I suppose you also have a stake in witnessing their demise. If you want to see it happen, you'd better get in this buggy with me."

"What about the other dogs?"

"What about them?"

"They might want to join us too."

"Well then where are they?"

"Sonya's back in her room," said Brad. "She didn't say anything when I asked her to come along. I know Fuzz and Larry want to be there, but I haven't seen them. They're probably still asleep."

"Too bad for them. This buggy is leaving now, so you can hop on board or stay behind."

Brad hesitated, so the Bear turned to the driver. "Go ahead."

"Wait!" He jumped into the buggy and took the seat next to the Bear. "Sorry. We can go now."

"Well, what are you waiting for?" the Bear asked the driver. "Go!"

The buggy lurched into gear and sped off into the desert. They made their way around the oasis and past the clusters of swaying palms.

"How far will it be?"

"Tusk Pack have almost full day of travel from Grand Oasis before they catch Anteaters," said the attendant. "With smooth ride, we make it there by late afternoon."

Several hours of desert left no shortage of time for his mind to wander. How had the Anteaters pretended to be wolves? The messenger had mentioned the pack that caught them was Tusk Pack—wasn't that the pack the Warlord had displayed to him? None of those wolves looked anything like anteaters. But of course. The two in liquids. There had been something off about those two and only now did he realize what it was.

The Bear reached into his belt and pulled out a heavy dagger. The intricate patterns on its hilt glimmered in the early morning sun.

"I've never seen a metal like that," said Brad. "What is it?"

"This?" asked the Bear, holding it by the blade to display the grip. "This is element 79."

Brad raised an eyebrow. "I did flunk chemistry, but I thought there was no element 79."

"That's not entirely true. It is a stable element, but it doesn't occur in nature. The Monkeys call it gold."

"How did the Monkeys get it?"

"That I don't know, but this knife was one of the sacred treasures they kept at the top of the Temple. My grandmother plundered it in the Autumn Revolution. I thought it only fitting I use her blade to avenge her."

Brad leaned closer to get a better look, but the Bear placed it back into his scabbard. The dog had seen enough.

A few minutes later, they shared the road with well over a hundred buggies from the escort packs, but the rendezvous was the last interesting part of their journey. The boring desert went on and on, and it always looked the same.

He hadn't had a chance to eat breakfast and the journey would last well past lunchtime, but he'd be damned if he asked them to stop for a bite. He had a granola bar in his belt, hardly a meal, but it would last him if he rationed it.

He spend the ride alternating between bites and fitful naps. The trip seemed to take forever, but little by little they chipped away at the hours.

"Hey Bear, wake up." Brad shook his shoulder. "We're here."

The Bear yawned, stretched his arms, and squinted at the camp. The escort packs had parked their buggies in a wide perimeter around the grounds, leaving a noticeable gap between them and Tusk Pack. Strangely, the camp didn't look that crowded.

He jumped out of his seat and started toward the pack. He didn't see the Anteaters among them, but perhaps the wolves held them in one of the tents. As he approached the pack, the few wolves he saw began to scurry around. He heard shouting.

"Hey Bear," said Brad, running up to join him. "What—"

"Shhh!" He put a finger to his mouth and tilted his ear toward the camp.

"Here he come! What you do now? What you have for him?" It was a she-wolf's voice.

"Just wait one more minute! I send Yuval north, I send Ralph east, I send—"

"We no have one more minute! He here now!"

"Just, just quiet! I try to think."

The camp went silent as the Bear, Brad, and the attendant walked up to meet them. That was him all right, the wolf he had met back in Grand Oasis, tall and strong, but not looking quite so confident anymore.

"I received the good news," said the Bear. "You've just made your nation a whole lot wealthier. Show me the Anteaters."

The Wolf dropped to a bow, as though he thought he were a monkey or something. "I so sorry, Bear. It all my fault."

"What is?"

"The Anteaters are gone."

"What do you mean gone?"

"They escape their ropes and run away. We can't find them."

"When did this happen?"

"No one know. They gone when we wake up this morning."

"How could you let this happen? How hard is it to watch two prisoners? You pre-op idiot!"

The Bear hit him across the face, almost as hard as he would have in a real fight. He didn't think the blow would hurt a wolf that size very much, but the wolf still winced in pain.

The Bear turned back to the attendant. "Send out all the packs. Someone contact the Warlord and get him to send out every pack he has left. Track them down before they get too far. Someone bring me those Anteaters!"

He shoved a cigar in his mouth and reached for his lighter. The lighter wasn't there.

"Dammit!"

Chapter 24

"Hey Jess, wake up."

She opened her eyes and turned her head. The cavern was much darker than before, but she could see Ray standing over her.

"Is it my turn to keep watch?"

"Uh, no. It's nighttime now."

She sat up. "Really? You know I would have taken a shift if you had woken me earlier."

"I know."

"So why didn't you?"

"Well, the priest didn't want to take a break, so I didn't take one either."

"You were both up all day?"

"Yeah."

"Did you see any wolves?"

"No."

"Did you say anything to each other?"

"No."

Jess stood up and stretched her legs. "So both of you just sat there when only one of you had to. Well suit yourself, and don't blame me when you collapse from exhaustion. Where is she now?"

"Over there, praying."

He pointed toward the mouth of the cave, where Sky sat with her head bowed and her legs crossed. Jess walked over to meet her, but paused when she got close enough to see that the monkey's eyes were still closed.

The sun had gone down, but the horizon still cast a silhouette against the eerie pale green glow. The faintest sliver of a moon followed the receding remnants of sunlight.

"Glad to see you're up. Did you sleep well?"

She turned back to Sky. "Yes, thanks. I had hoped you would get some rest too."

"I'll be fine."

"Even so, you should probably catch up on sleep now. I'll drive us."

"That won't be necessary."

"I insist."

Sky nodded. "In that case, thank you." She stood up, donned her thermal cloak, and walked over to the buggy. "Have you driven one of these before?"

"Of course."

"Good. I verified our location on the map last night. Beggar's Station is almost directly east of here, so keep an eye on the compass and you'll be fine. We'll check our bearing at the halfway point, and we should reach the town before daybreak."

"I won't have a problem driving the whole way."

Sky turned back into the cave. "Ray! Come over here. It's time to go."

"All right, all right, I'm coming."

Jess jumped into the driver's seat and Ray slid into the passenger seat beside her. This time Sky sat in the back.

Jess turned the ignition and the motor let out a terrible squeal. She had to cover her ears. "What the hell?"

"It does that sometimes," said Sky. "Remember from this morning?"

"This car clearly needs new battery cables."

"Unfortunately I don't have any on hand. Just try again and it will work."

A second piercing squeal.

"One more time."

Finally the motor responded with a much happier sound. Jess eased onto the accelerator and held on as the buggy pulled itself back up the slope and out of the cave. The pedal was more responsive than the one on her last buggy.

The moon had already hidden behind the horizon. After holding her finger over the knob for a moment and taking a final look around, she turned on the headlights, checked the compass, and sped away.

A minute passed, and then another, then another, and still there were no wolves. The endless desert was far too vast for a finite number of packs to cover. Jess leaned back a little more in her seat, still keeping an eye out on either side.

Ray was already snoring in his chair. Jess couldn't help but smirk a little; he hadn't been fooling anyone trying to pretend he wasn't tired.

"I forgot to mention," said Sky, "the compass is a little off. You want it to read about five degrees clockwise from your actual target bearing."

"Got it." She gave the wheel a slight nudge.

The drive went on for some time, and Jess found it not nearly as monotonous as before. She squinted in the dim headlights to dodge rocks and pits, and scanned the horizon for any sign of wolves.

With no sun to indicate the time, Jess wasn't sure how long it had been, but it felt like several hours. Her stomach growled, and only then did she realize she hadn't eaten in over a day.

"You must be hungry."

"Sky? Are you still awake?"

"Stop the buggy here and I'll get you something from my supplies. It's about time to verify our location anyway."

"What time is it?"

"A little after midnight."

Jess looked around for a tree or larger rock or some other suggestion of shelter, but seeing none, she stopped the vehicle right in its path. Sky jumped out and began to rummage through the crates in the back.

"You can turn off the headlights. I have my flashlight."

"Got it." The path in front of them disappeared, leaving only a wavering beam of light from the back.

"Here we go," said Sky.

Jess got out and walked over to Sky, who held out three bars in wrappers.

"Thanks."

"What's going on?" asked Ray.

"Get over here, lazy," said Jess. "Do you want something to

eat?"

"Sure." He walked over and snatched one of the bars from Sky, unwrapping it and taking a bite before Jess even had a chance to take a bite of hers. "Ugh. What is this?" he asked. "It tastes awful."

"These are just the standard nutrient rations they give out in the Temple," said Sky. "They're safe to eat for all species, but I'm afraid they don't taste all that great. What can I say? That's the life of a priest for you."

"Oh please, don't give me that."

"I beg your pardon?"

"Eating gross rations once in a while doesn't mean you have a hard job."

Sky smiled. "It's not just the nutrient bars. We priests live lives of service and sacrifice."

"Sacrifice? How so? I know what things are like for you priests. You all live in big houses and fancy apartments and make ten times the money of any other monkey. You're free to marry and have children. You're the only voice in your government. What are you sacrificing?"

"Ray!"

"Our lives," said Sky. "Everything we do is in service of the Temple. If Temple orders us to go somewhere or do something, we have no choice but to obey."

"The same goes for any other citizen. The only difference is that you're the one giving the orders, and you do it in the lap of luxury. I ask again, have you really sacrificed anything?"

"Yes, I have!"

She turned around and dropped her cloak to show them the stump of her tail. For once, Ray had no response.

"Ray, that's enough!" said Jess. "Sky saved your life! Why don't you show her a little respect?"

"No, Jess. It's all right." From what Jess could see from the back, it looked like Sky had her head down and her eyes closed, but when she turned back to face them she was smiling again. "Your brother has some really important questions and he deserves some good answers."

"Really Sky, you don't have to do this."

"I'm fine," she said. "I didn't study the Celestial Monkeys' teachings my entire life just to shy away from an argument."

"See, Jess? She's fine."

Jess sighed and leaned back against the buggy, munching on her disgusting snack. Sky took a slight step forward.

"Ray, you don't like me very much, do you?"

"No, I suppose I don't."

"Is it because I'm a monkey?"

"It's not because you're a monkey. It's because you're a priest."

She laughed.

"What's so funny?"

"Nothing much," she said. "It's just that I've been a priest for less than a month and that's already not the first time someone has said that to me."

"It's not hard to see why."

"Listen, it's clear to me that you have some issues with the Temple and the Priesthood. Why don't you take some time to tell me how they have wronged you, and then I will explain our actions and our way of life the best I can."

"Oh no, I see what you're doing. You want to make sure you get the last word in. You want to give yourself time to break down my argument and tell me why I'm obviously wrong. If you're so sure of yourself, then how about you go first?"

"All right then," said Sky. "I'd be happy to. Without knowing your specific grievance I can only say so much, so I'll keep it short and tell you what you probably already know. Every aspect of society across all nations owes everything to the Temple. Our language, philosophy, science, and technology is all based on the teachings and relics the Celestial Monkeys left behind. Before the Quaternity, the Earth had fallen into a savage dark age. The turmoil of the last half century notwithstanding, the Temple reigned over a peace that lasted over three thousand years."

"The last fifty years is quite an omission," said Ray. "What about the atrocities during the Autumn Revolution and the Vulpe-Simian Wars? Do you deny them?"

"Not at all. All I can say is that the Second Order has acknowledged and repented the sins of the past. We are now content to focus only on ourselves and let the other nations be as they are."

"So you don't want us all to follow your religion?"

"We always want more people to see the truth, but faith seldom blossoms by force."

"And why does it matter what we believe?"

"Because it is the truth."

"I can see why you'd want to think that. It is a religion that claims monkeys are superior to all other species."

"That's not what we believe."

"Yes it is. You claim to be made in the image of the gods—you even named your gods after yourselves."

"The only reason we call them the Celestial Monkeys is because they happen to look more like monkeys than any other species. Monkeys do tend to be particularly spiritual and open to inspiration, but each of the four species has their place in the divine plan. We each symbolize part of the self and therefore must respect and care for one another. As the quaternity goes, the Fox represents the mind, the Bear the body, the Anteater the heart, and the Monkey the soul. In the early days of the First Order, there were always four High Priests, one of each of the formal species."

"And within a few hundred years, only monkeys could hold that distinction. A few hundred years after that, the other species couldn't even become regular priests. I know my history."

"Then how come you got a 'C' in that class?" asked Jess.

"Jess, you're not helping. I'm trying to make an argument."

"I don't see why you're doing this now. Need I remind you we're on the run?"

"Don't worry," said Sky. "There are no wolves in sight and we have plenty of time to make it to town before dawn."

"Don't change the subject," said Ray. "Isn't it true that you believe pre-ops don't have souls?"

"That's a common misconception," said Sky. "No matter what you've heard before, the official stance of the Temple is that pre-operationals do have souls."

"What do you mean by 'official stance of the Temple'? Isn't the answer written clearly in the Book of Whinson?"

"If you want the bluntest answer, the texts indicate that only the Celestial Monkeys themselves have souls. The Temple's interpretation is that the Celestial Monkeys have the greatest souls, while we formals have souls that are not quite so vast."

"And concretes and pre-ops have lesser souls than we do?"

"That's one way of looking at it."

"And what about tromians? Do they have souls?"

Sky paused. "The official stance is that they do not."

"Don't hide behind any more of this 'official stance' crap," said Ray. "I want to know what you believe, what Sky believes."

"What I believe," said Sky, "is that the Celestial Monkeys have imparted to us all the wisdom of their world. Their ancient scripts tell us many wonderful things about the different species, and not just the intelligent species, but about all animals. They tell of the species of today, of species long extinct, and even of mythical species that never existed. But never once do they mention tromians. Tromians are not part of the world the Celestial Monkeys created, so no, I don't believe they have souls."

"You're hesitating, and you're trying way too hard to justify yourself. Maybe they aren't in your books, but they exist and they're intelligent enough that you can talk with them like anyone else. Have you spoken to any immigrants from Tromia? Most of them are a bit on the rough side, but they're people like you and me. You're trying so hard to believe something that the rational part of you already knows isn't true."

"You're wrong," said Sky. "Faith isn't something where you can pick and choose whatever parts suit you best and ignore the rest. You have to accept it all. Sometimes things can be hard to believe, but that's why they call it faith. Even so, plenty of concrete evidence overwhelmingly indicates that the Celestial Monkeys are real."

"What evidence?"

"You pick. How about the liquid body armor we wear? Scientists still don't fully understand how it works, but we can make it by following designs the Celestial Monkeys left behind. What about the Five Monuments? They're made of stone, but somehow they're completely indestructible. How do you explain that?"

"I can't, but maybe someone will, someday. Just because we can't figure out the scientific explanation for something doesn't mean there isn't one."

"You call my beliefs ridiculous, but yet you believe that natural processes formed those invincible stone sculptures? Atheism takes faith too."

"I'm not an atheist."

"What are you then? A deist?"

"Maybe. I don't know."

"What do mean you don't know?"

"I haven't decided what I believe in yet," said Ray. "I still have time to figure that out. All I know is that I sure as hell don't believe in the Celestial Monkeys."

"You don't know that there's time to figure it out. For all you know, you might die tomorrow."

"Not if I have anything to say about it."

Jess managed the final bite of her nutrient bar. If nothing else, she certainly didn't feel like eating anymore. Ray still hadn't eaten anything beyond his first bite.

"I can tell this argument isn't just a rational debate for you," said Sky. "You're emotional about this subject. You feel that the Temple has wronged you personally. Am I correct?"

"You are."

"So tell me, what has the Temple done to you?"

"Not to me, but to my family."

Sky nodded. "Do you have ancestors who died in the genocide?"

"All anteaters do."

"It was nothing but a senseless tragedy," said Sky. "However, the ones who committed this atrocity were not the Temple. They were mostly bears."

"There were bears and monkeys involved."

"But the Second Order did not come into being until after the genocide. As soon as it did, the new High Priest rounded up all the monkeys involved and had them tried and executed for their crimes."

"But back before the genocide, during the revolution, that still was the Temple."

"Do you have family who fought in the revolution?"

"Not just any family. Our grandfather's name is Anteater Lee Anton."

Sky paused. "Anteater Anton?"

"As in, the Great Anteater. Have you heard of him?"

"He was a legendary warrior, one of the last angels of the Temple. He turned on his masters and led the empire into rebellion."

"That's right," said Ray. "The Temple only appointed the best of the best to serve as angels, and only rarely did they appoint non-monkeys, but Anton was in a league of his own. He practiced not only the Temple's martial arts, but also the brawling styles of anteaters and bears. He and his partner Bear Julia spent years wandering the Ghost Belt and fighting the Tromians who preyed on the remaining locals. When Anton and Julia reported back about the Tromian hordes, do you know what the Temple said to them?"

"Yes, I know."

"They said that tromians were only a myth. Their sacred texts never spoke of tromians, so therefore they must not exist. Once Anton and Julia saw the ignorance of the Temple, it was not long before they also saw the greed and corruption, the hypocrisy and injustice. The empire was no place for anyone but the monkeys, so they organized a revolution."

"And they had to forge an alliance with the Disgraced mercenaries," said Sky.

"That's not true. The only soldiers they needed were the Temple's own abused subjects. They defeated the Monkey army, stormed the Temple, and overthrew the priesthood. Finally the other species were free to form nations of their own and live in peace."

"The peace didn't last."

"That was because Julia began to take things too far. She saw it as her duty to punish the Monkeys for their crimes and had more priests killed. Anton didn't approve of what he saw, and when he confronted her, the only way to settle the argument was with a duel. In the end, Anton had to kill his oldest friend.

"Julia's husband Lazarus never forgave Anton. Lazarus and his supporters signed a secret pact with the Monkeys: if he returned the Temple lands to Monkey control, they would deliver Anton into his hands. It didn't go as smoothly as he planned. Anton escaped the ambush, striking down everyone in his path. Furious and desperate, Lazarus had the Monkeys round up every anteater they could find. He ordered them to kill any anteater who matched Anton's description, but the vengeful bears and hateful monkeys got carried away. First they killed every anteater who looked like him, then it was every anteater of his age, then all male anteaters, and finally, all of them.

"Anton never appeared among the bodies, and soon after, Lazarus went into hiding as well. He vowed to kill not just Anton, but all his descendants. Even as the years passed, Lazarus never forgot his promise. Jess and I were only children when he killed our father."

No one said anything.

"The former priests who signed Lazarus's Pact may have no longer belonged to a holy order, but they still out sold my family for their part in a righteous revolution. In the end, it was the corruption of the First Order that ultimately led to the genocide of my people. Enough of us survived to live on as a species, but there's a reason there's no Anteater Nation."

It was a minute before anyone spoke.

"We should probably get going," said Sky.

Ray nodded. "Yes. Yes we should."

Chapter 25

Jess stuck her arm out past the patio roof and held it there for a minute. When she pulled it back, her hair was soaked. Rain. She never thought she'd see such a thing in the desert, and if it kept coming down at this rate, the region would fulfill its precipitation quota for the next decade.

They had arrived in Beggar's Station the previous morning while it was still dark, just hours before the rain. Jess had spent the majority of the following day and night catching up on sleep, taking short breaks to eat and change the dressing on her wound. The gash beneath her shoulder hadn't bothered her much during the drive, but it had started hurting more once the rain began.

Understandably, the builder of the establishment hadn't bothered to install gutters on the roof, so the rainwater gushed right down from the shingles and plopped into brown puddles where the concrete met the sand. It came down so hard that Jess had to squint just to get a look at the watchtower across the street. A fuzzy shape moved beneath the canopy.

Jess waited for something close to a lapse in the stream from the roof and then bolted out into the downpour. She leapt over the murky trickles in the middle of the road and jumped onto the wooden ladder leading up to the hut. One fat drop after another made its way from the canopy to Jess's forehead as she climbed. A sharp pain ran through the wound on her shoulder, but she ignored it until she finally pulled her way onto the shelter of the platform.

"You're lucky I'm not feeling all that trigger happy today, the way you burst in here like that. I might have shot you if I thought you were a wolf."

"I'm sure you saw me coming," said Jess.

The sentry was a short but well-built fox. She wore a red headband and kept her hair a bit longer than the foxes back north, probably as a means to protect herself from sun and sand. Clearly neither was a concern on this day; now long hair meant soaked skin. However, the guard's hair was as dry as any hair Jess had seen.

The fox looked out over the railing, always keeping at least one finger on a flintlock. She carried three on her belt, one by her right hand and two by her left. The watchtower didn't look like much from below, but now Jess could see that it offered a full view and a clean shot of anywhere in the tiny town. The wooden tower was only a story or two off the ground, but even in the rain she could see for kilometers.

"I'll save you the trouble of asking," said the guard. "There are no convoys leaving for or arriving from the Fox Nation today."

"Dipika, was it?"

She nodded. "I'm surprised you remembered. You looked like you were ready to pass out when your crew rolled in yesterday."

"In my line of work, it pays to stay aware."

"As it does with mine."

"Listen, Dipika, it's very important that we make it back to the Fox Nation as soon as possible."

"I'm sure it is," said Dipika, "but that still doesn't change anything. Our next shipment of supplies won't get here until next week, and now isn't the time of year to expect unannounced visitors. No one here plans to leave anytime soon either."

"Is there any way we could send a message?"

"There are no lines across the salt pan."

"I didn't think so. I meant could we use a radio transmitter?"

"There's one in town that gives off a decent signal. There's a chance they could hear it in Marshton or maybe Friendship, if anyone's listening. Sorry to say though, we can't let you use it to call for help."

"Why not? The wolves don't have radio receivers."

"A few of them do, and all it takes is one to alert every pack. They would normally leave Beggar's Station alone, but if the word got out that their high-value targets were here, nothing would stop them from overrunning our little town." She shook her head. "I could never let that happen. Wolves are so brutal."

Jess stepped up to the railing alongside Dipika and looked out into the storm. The anteater lowered her head and closed her eyes. "They can be determined, that's for sure."

"When you've lived out here as long as I have, you see what they're capable of. I've lost neighbors to the wolves. I've happened upon dead bodies of merchants not a kilometer from town."

"If you hate wolves so much, why do you live here?"

"The town needed a guard and I needed a job. I could ask the same of you, why you made your way out here where all the wolves want to kill you."

"I couldn't tell you," said Jess. "All I can say is that the sooner we make it back to the Fox Nation, the better."

Dipika chuckled. "Sorry, I already told you it's not going to happen. I'd drive you there myself if I owned a buggy, but I'm afraid there's nothing I can do about it."

"I see."

"Cheer up. Not all travelers hate the summer heat. Might be there's a rogue pilgrim out there who will drive into town tomorrow, bound for the Fox Nation with two free seats."

"Summer heat…"

Jess shivered and clutched the damp skin of her forearms. It was hard to believe that only three days ago she had lived in a constant state of muggy grime. She had been too hot for too long, but at the moment she couldn't even remember ever craving the relief of cool air.

"Does it rain like this often?"

"I've seen a spell or two since I got here. It's rare, but I wouldn't say it heralds the end of the world."

A breeze swept beneath the canopy and made Jess's hair stand on end. The light from her window at the inn started to look more and more inviting. She sidestepped her way back to the exit and extended a foot onto the ladder.

"You'll be safe here," said Dipika. "If you're willing to lay low and wait it out, transportation will come. Stay quiet, and we won't let the wolves hurt you. You're a guest of Beggar's Station now."

"You have my gratitude."

Jess slid down the ladder and sprinted back towards the inn, hands shielding her face from the lash of rain. A particularly large gush of water nailed her on her way back under the patio roof, presumably to make up for the one she had dodged on her way out.

She burst in through the door and shut it behind her as she dashed right for the heater vent on the wall. As she soaked up the hot air, she reached over and grabbed the towel hanging over the top of the nearby chair and dried herself off as best she could. She heard a muffling knocking noise, but it didn't sound like it was coming from the door. She waited a moment, and then heard it again; it seemed to be coming from above.

Their room at the inn was small, perhaps even smaller than either of their rooms in their house back home. It was only just big enough to fit the queen size bed, chair, dresser, and mini-fridge, and still leave some space to walk around. She and Ray had had to share the bed, but it was worlds better than sleeping on the ground again.

A pile of messy covers lay strewn across the bed and a sliver of light escaped from beneath the bathroom door.

"Ray? Are you in there?"

"You can come in. I'm just taking a bath."

She opened the door to have a pleasant rush of steam meet her. Ray lay back in the tub with his hands folded behind his head.

"Good morning," he said.

"Didn't you already take a bath when we arrived yesterday?"

"I did. It was kind of chilly when I got up, so I thought I'd take another. It's not like they charge extra for the water."

A cold drop fell from the tip of Jess's nose. She heard the knocking sound again. "What is that noise?"

"Beats me," said Ray. "So what were you doing out there?"

"Just surveying our surroundings. I got a look from the watchtower."

"You probably met Dipika then."

"I met her yesterday."

"So did I. When I woke up to eat dinner, I ran into her and we had a nice chat. We're in good hands here."

"She says we're stuck here," said Jess. "She still insists that there's no way we'll get passage back to the Fox Nation until next week."

"That sounds fine to me."

"How could you say that?"

"Hot food and hot baths? I could go for a week of that."

"And what about the army of wolves out looking for us? A week ago, you were going crazy telling me we had to escape."

"That was when we were stuck in an actual wolf pack with actual wolves who were actually catching on to us. Now we're safe in a town the wolves never visit, a town we share with a particularly vigilant, gun-toting guard who hates wolves. Even if the Wolves are stupid enough to come here, they won't be a problem for us. We're not wearing those liquids anymore, so there will be nothing holding us back."

"Why do I get the feeling you want them to show up?"

"Don't be ridiculous," said Ray. "Besides, what other option do we have but to wait?"

"I don't know, but I'll think of something. I don't like waiting around at a time like this."

"Yeah, I can tell."

"By the way, have you seen Sky?"

"No, am I her keeper? Maybe she left already."

"Her buggy is still here."

"All right, then she hasn't left yet. I still haven't seen her."

"So then I take it you haven't apologized to her yet."

"Apologized? For what?"

Jess filled her hands with water from the sink and splashed Ray in the face. "You know what! For being rude to her after she went out of her way to help us."

"Hey, quit it! I wasn't rude to her. She and I just had a lively debate."

"Debate? Please, that was an attack. You were hostile."

"Sky didn't think so. She said she was happy to argue with me. She probably saw it as an opportunity to convert me to her religion."

"Are you at least going to thank her?"

"For what?"

"For saving your life!"

"Oh, that." Ray grabbed the sponge hanging from the faucet and started scrubbing his back. "Yeah, I already thanked her for that."

"When?"

"In the cave, when you were asleep and she and I were on guard duty."

"Bullshit."

"Fine, don't believe me. I don't need to answer to you."

"Ray, please don't be like this. We're professionals, on a mission."

"I know," said Ray, "and our mission does not include playing nice with one of our grandfather's oppressors. Our mission is to get our intelligence back to the Fox Nation. If you want to talk about that, I'll be as serious and professional as you like."

"I did talk to you about that. You said that you'd be fine sitting around for a week."

"And I meant it. Staying quiet and waiting it out gives us our best possible odds for survival."

"Whatever. I'm heading back outside."

"What for?"

"To find Sky."

"Cool, be sure to close the door behind you."

Jess slammed the bathroom door and walked over to the window. The rain didn't seem to be coming down as hard as before. She knew she had to change her dressing, but that could wait until after she found Sky.

She opened the door and walked out onto the patio. Sky had taken the room around the corner closest to theirs, so Jess wouldn't have to leave the shelter of the patio roof to find her. Jess went over to the next door and knocked twice.

"Up here!"

The voice had come from above. It was a single-story building. "Sky?"

"On the roof!"

Jess stepped back, venturing out into the rain once again as she peered up onto the roof. Sky held a hammer in one hand and waved to Jess with the other.

"What are you doing up there?"

"I'm fixing the roof."

"In this weather?"

"Hold on, I'm almost done."

Sky crouched down and held a nail to one of the shingles. She hammered it in with a thud echoing across the street each time the tool hit its mark. "There we go."

She slid down the shingles and dropped to the ground below, landing on her feet not a meter away from Jess.

"Won't the innkeeper fix the place herself?" asked Jess.

"Come on," said Sky, "let's not stand out here as we talk. You look soaked."

Jess followed Sky back under the roof.

"That's better," said Sky. "My roof was leaking and the innkeeper did offer to fix it, but I volunteered to do it myself."

"Why?"

"One of the advantages of having no hair is that I don't get soaked like most people do. Better I do it than that poor woman come out and freeze to death. That being said, I wouldn't mind a warm shower now."

"You'd better hurry before my brother uses all the hot water."

Sky laughed. "I'll keep that in mind."

"Listen," said Jess. "I spoke with the guard earlier. Ray and I might not be able to leave for at least a week."

"I see."

"I'd understand if you had to leave. I know you have to get to your job."

"Do you want me to leave?"

"No, of course not. I just don't want to be a burden, and we can handle ourselves from here."

"The Temple would understand if I were late because I had to help someone in need," said Sky. "If you don't mind having me around, I'd prefer to stay in town until I can properly see you off."

Jess nodded. "All right then. That works for me." A jolt of pain ran through her shoulder. "Ow. Sorry, I have to go change this dressing. I'll be in our room if you need me."

"And I'll be in mine."

Jess started back towards her door, but before she rounded the corner, she turned to Sky one last time.

"Oh," she said, "and thank you."

Chapter 26

"Sir? Wake up, sir."

The Bear squeezed his eyes even harder shut and dug his face into his pillow.

"Bear?"

"Ugh. What is it?"

"It time to go, sir."

He opened his eyes, only to have to squint at the sunlight bursting through the tent flap. A wolf's nose poked through the top of the opening.

"What time is it?"

"It seven o'clock."

"So early? You wolves never get up at this hour."

"Sir, you instruct us to spend little time sleeping and more time searching. Last night when I ask when you want to begin next day's hunt—"

"Yeah, yeah, I know, just give me a few minutes."

The wolf disappeared from the door and the Bear began to roll around in his sleeping bag. It felt so nice just lying there, but he did have things to do. The Anteaters were still out there and with every second he wasted they would make it further and further from his grasp.

The air inside the tent had grown stuffy, almost uncomfortably so. He kicked his sleeping bag off his feet to give himself some air, but it didn't do much good. He sighed, grabbed his belt, and stepped out of the tent.

A wave of heat met him on the other side of the flap. Most of the wolves in the pack had gathered to eat breakfast around the campfire, a bright orange flame that crackled as it fed on dry wood. One wolf was not among the group—she stood only three meters from the opening to the Bear's tent, waiting for him.

"Good to see you up, sir," she said. "I prepare morning status report for you. Will you join me by map?"

"Yeah sure, let's get on with it."

"Right over here."

An oversized map of the area lay spread across the boulder that sat in the middle of the camp. Several pebbles formed a circle across the top of the map, and the boulder was just flat enough that the rocks didn't roll off.

"Let me guess," said the Bear. "Each of these stones represents a pack?"

"Correct, sir."

"You didn't have anything nicer to work with? Like figurines or something?"

"We use what we have," said the aide. "Now see. Pack go out all direction from where we lose Anteaters. We sweep three hundred kilometers from start, even up to Great Salt Pan."

"That's not enough," said the Bear. "Assuming they have a vehicle, they could be halfway back to the Fox Nation by now."

"Tusk Pack report that the Anteaters leave their buggy behind when they escape. If they still on foot, they no make it far."

"Then why haven't you found them?"

"It take time to search big desert. We do what we can with number of available packs."

The Bear pointed to a cluster of pebbles some distance from the search perimeter. "What about those packs? What are they doing?"

"Those packs in Grand Oasis. Warlord order them to stay behind."

"What? I thought you had every pack sent out!"

"Every available pack, sir."

"The Anteaters are fleeing from us as we speak. Don't you see that we're going to miss our chance? Have the remaining packs sent to join the search effort."

"I can't do that, sir."

"Why not?"

"Warlord's orders."

"Can I speak with him?"

"Of course." The attendant turned towards the campfire. "Lora! Bring radio!"

One of the wolves eating breakfast nodded and then ran over to one of the tents. She emerged with a heavy black box with an antenna and cord.

"So you do carry a radio," said the Bear.

"Our pack does," said the attendant. "You lucky you ask at this time of day. Warlord always listen for pack updates in morning hours."

As soon as the radio landed at his feet, the attendant got to work adjusting the dials and tweaking the antenna.

"Warlord? Come in, Warlord."

There was no response for at least a minute, but the biting static finally faded and a wolf's voice on the other end came through.

"Are you there, Warlord? The Bear wish to speak with you."

"Of course," said the Warlord. "Good morning, Bear."

"Yeah, morning."

"The packs all make good progress on search. We find Anteaters soon."

"I'd feel better about our odds of finding them if you sent all the packs after them."

"I no understand. We do send all packs—"

"All of the packs," said the Bear, "including the dozen still sitting around Grand Oasis."

For a moment, all he heard was background static.

"I see," said the Warlord. "We all very sorry, but those packs stay put. Someone must keep Grand Oasis safe in case of attack from rogue pack or mercenary. You understand."

"That's not going to cut it. Have those packs join the search effort, or you can forget about receiving your payment."

"What good money do us if we no protect our own families? The answer still no. Will you cancel contract?"

The Bear paused. He looked to the attendant, still adjusting the antenna to maintain the signal without even a tilt of her ear to better hear what her Warlord or the Bear had to say.

"No, never mind," said the Bear. "Forget I said anything."

"I most glad to hear it. There anything else?"

"No, that's all. Goodbye."

The Bear reached for the dial and switched off the transmitter before the attendant had a chance to.

"Mobilize the pack," said Bear. "Come and find me when it's ready to move out. It had better only take a few minutes."

"Yes sir."

The attendant ran off and started barking orders to the pack. Within seconds the fire was out and tents across the camp began to collapse.

As the Bear leaned against his buggy, his stomach growled. He reached into the largest compartment and rummaged around, but he couldn't find any granola bars under the wad of old wrappers. Maybe he still had some leftover provisions in the supply crate.

"Hey Bear. How'd you sleep?"

He turned to see a dog with a bone in his hand, a bone still covered with lingering scraps of meat and dripping with grease.

"Brad, what is that you're holding?"

"It's a bone with some freshly cooked meat."

"Yes, I can see that. Why do you have it?"

"Come on Bear," said Brad. "When we left the city, I didn't think we'd be gone so long. I didn't get a chance to pack any food for myself. The wolves offered me some of their most recent kill. Do you want a bite?"

"Get that thing away from me."

Brad paused, then took one last bite from the largest chunk of meat remaining and tossed the bone aside. "I hate to see it go to waste," he said between chews.

"I'm sure a wolf will pick it off the ground."

The dog looked around. "The pack looks all fired up. Doris sure has them moving."

"Who's Doris?"

"You know who Doris is!"

"No, I don't."

"You talk to her all the time! She's the one the Warlord sent to relay messages and stuff to you."

"Oh, you mean my attendant? That's Doris?"

"Yeah, her," said Brad. "Her, right over there."

He saw her now. Doris, if that was her name, was indeed moving, but she was not nearly fast enough. He crossed his arms and waited for what must have been five minutes before she finally walked up to him to report.

"Pack ready to leave now," she said. "We begin move out and begin sweep formation. Please step into buggy."

"About time."

"Bear, wait," said Brad.

"What?"

"Listen, when I followed you out here, I thought we'd be done with this matter within the day. I haven't had a chance to talk to Sonya or the others—"

"Stop wasting my time. Just get to the point."

Brad nodded. "I'd like to go back to Grand Oasis. If it's all right with you, I'll have someone from the pack drive me back."

The Bear took a step closer to the dog. "You think we won't catch them?"

"What? No, I didn't say that. I was going to explain, but then you said I was wasting your time."

"You are wasting my time. You know we can't spare one of our buggies at a moment like this."

"Then how am I supposed to get back?"

"You can walk."

When the Bear jumped into the back seat he didn't have to wait for Brad to join him.

"We'd better find them soon."

"I will. Count on it."

With the remnants of the campsite nothing but a smoking pile of logs and a collection of tent-shaped imprints in the sand, the convoy departed. The procession of buggies began as a straight line, but one by one the cars broke off from the main formation. Gradually they veered away from their neighbors until the nearest buggy on either side was several hundred meters away.

Now each buggy had a perfect-sized strip of land to watch as they made they made their way across the desert, not that the desert had anything to hide. It had been a full day since the Bear had seen so much as a hill.

If the Anteaters had gone this way on foot, they'd have died of thirst by now. Such would rob him of the pleasure of killing them himself, but then again, dead was dead. He kept an eye out for shriveled bodies.

The buggy swung a sharp turn, so sharp the Bear nearly flew out of his seat. He grabbed the frame above and glared at the attendant.

"Hey! Why are we turning?"

"No worry, we be back on course soon. We just need to avoid obstacle."

The Bear squinted ahead. "What obstacle? There's nothing over there but more damn desert."

"Two kilometer east is Beggar's Station."

"What's Beggar's Station? A town?"

"Yes, and wolf not welcome in that town. They shoot on sight. Very dangerous, wolf stay away."

The Bear shook his head. "You morons. You worthless, pre-op morons."

"Sir?"

"Stop the car now!"

The buggy jerked to a stop, sending the Bear's head into the driver's seat in front of him. He scowled and fought the urge to rub the bump on his forehead.

"Now listen," he said. "Pretend for a moment that you were an anteater fugitive hiding from an army of wolves. Tell me, where would you hide?"

"Uh—"

"You'd hide in the one place wolves refuse to go! You'd hide in a town that would protect you!"

"Beggar's Station?"

"Yes! That's where they're hiding! Turn this buggy back toward the town. We're going there."

"Sir, the people in town outnumber us. We try and they kill us all."

"We have an army," said the Bear. "Send word to the rest of the packs and we'll overwhelm them."

"The packs out searching the desert as you ordered. If you bring them here, we lose more than entire day of search. You really think that worth it? What if they not there?"

"She's right," said Brad. "I don't think—"

"Shut up." The Bear thought for a moment. "What if we knew for certain they were there? What if I could confirm it for you? Would the Warlord risk his army on one little town if he knew the targets were there?"

"If it guarantee our pay, then yes. We warrior, and this is what we fight for."

The Bear stepped out of the buggy. "I'm going in. Send word to the rest of the pack to stay put until I return."

"Bear!" said Brad. "What are you doing?"

"What does it look like? I'm going to check out this town myself. After I find the Anteaters, the wolves will have their proof."

"Isn't that place dangerous? They'll shoot you."

"I'm not a wolf, am I?

"Won't you at least wear your liquids?"

"I'd rather not look suspicious. As far as the townspeople are concerned, I'm just another traveler."

"But—"

"Shut your mouth already," said the Bear. "I'll be right back."

He starting walking off in the direction of the town before Brad had the chance to say anything else. The Bear felt a grin creep across his face. This was it. He rubbed the hilt of the golden dagger on his belt. Yes, this was it.

Chapter 27

The baked earth crunched beneath his feet. The Bear squinted through the morning heat, trying to spot the town. He could make out houses and some sort of wooden tower somewhere beyond the shimmering sand. Hopefully it wasn't a mirage.

He stopped for a breather, reaching for the canteen on his belt and pulling it to his lips. Although he had made the perfect exit, now he wished he had asked the driver to drop him off a little closer to the town. Perhaps the wolves didn't want to go anywhere near it, but he might have talked them into another kilometer. He strapped his canteen back into place and resumed the march.

A few minutes later, the buildings had begun to take form. The end in sight, the Bear quickened his pace, ignoring the sweat under his belt. He didn't see anyone awaiting him on the street, so no one would notice if he slipped in. He took another drink, then another. His canteen felt half empty by the time he reached the border.

A warm breeze blew over his hair as he stepped onto the main road. The town consisted of a single strip with aged wooden houses on either side of the street. A few of the buildings had broken planks in their porches and windows boarded up. He noticed solar panels on several buildings, but they looked dusty and outdated. There were buggies parked in the alleyways, but all buggies were so rusty he couldn't tell a derelict from one that was still functional. Had the wolves been avoiding a ghost town? He wouldn't doubt it, considering their brains and his luck.

"That's close enough!"

He looked to the tower on his left to see a fox glaring down at him. She held a flintlock in her hand, aiming up at the sky.

"Hey, easy with the gun!" he said. "I'm not wearing armor or anything!"

"I wouldn't bother with the gun if you were. What's your business in Beggar's Station?"

"I'm just traveling through the area. I seek food and lodging for the night."

"And I suppose you walked all the way here?"

"My convoy is going on ahead to the next station. I opted to stay behind a get some rest, so they dropped me off."

She nodded and lowered the gun. "Shame. We were hoping for an unannounced convoy. Looks like we just missed out." She made a nudging motion with her head. "You'll find what you need at the inn over there. Enjoy your stay in Beggar's Station."

He thought about asking her of the town's other recent visitors, but decided against it. She had already retreated into the shade of the canopy anyway. He could go for some shade himself.

The third building on the right bore the word "INN" in big letters above the front door. If the Anteaters were in town, that was where they would be. But he couldn't just go knocking on all the doors. He needed a plan.

He spotted someone else on the other end of town, which was only a little ways down the street. She was a monkey, a mercenary by the look of her tattoo. Wait—no, an actual priest. She was carrying a bundle of wooden planks under one arm and a hammer in the other hand.

The monkey stopped where she stood and looked over at the Bear. It was too far away for him to discern her expression, but the Bear still pretended he hadn't seen her and made haste to the door of the inn.

A bell rang as he stepped into the air-conditioned room. There was no rug, no couch, no magazines, nothing but wood surfaces and a fat bear in glasses sitting behind the reception desk.

"Welcome to the Beggar's Station Inn," she said. "We offer the most comfortable lodging of anywhere south of the salt, the perfect place to rest for any traveler. How may I help you?"

He walked up to the desk. "Hi. I was wondering if I could ask a few questions about the people staying here."

"I just told you, sweetheart. The Beggar's Station Inn offers comfort and relaxation to travelers of all persuasions, from merchants to mercenaries, from—"

"Yes, I know. That's not what I trying to ask. I wanted to know if you could tell me about the people staying here now, as in at this moment. I have some friends also traveling through these parts and I thought there was a chance we might meet up here."

She took off her glasses. "Sir, while we may not have to deal with all the laws and regulations they have up in the Fox Nation, as a common courtesy we still do not disclose information about our guests."

"Come on, it's not a big deal. Do it for a fellow bear?"

"As long as you're not a wolf, I couldn't care less what you are. Now if you really do have friends somewhere nearby, you can leave a message with me and I will pass it on to all our current customers. Would you like to do that?"

"No, don't bother."

"That's what I thought. Now would you like a room?"

"Yes. I'll take all of them."

She paused. "All of them?"

He reached into a pouch on his belt and pulled out a pile of coppers. He dumped the fistful in front of the owner and didn't bother to pick up the ones that rolled off the edge. "You heard me. I'll take every available room for the night."

She stared at the glimmering pile of copper for a moment and then looked back up at him. "Are you stupid?"

"No, I'm just homesick. As you may have guessed, I'm exceedingly wealthy, so I'm used to sleeping in a mansion. Having all these rooms at my disposal is the closest thing I have to feeling at home."

"In that case, what about our luxury suite? It comes with a large master bedroom connected to a private patio, a whirlpool bathtub—"

"Yeah, I'll take that one too. Along with all the others. All right?"

"No."

"What do you mean 'no'?"

"Same thing 'no' usually means. You can't do that. I'm not going to rent out all my vacant rooms to you."

"Do you not see the pile of copper? I'm paying for this. Don't you want my money?"

"Sir, it's the first duty of the Beggar's Station Inn to provide accommodations to all weary travelers. If I let you have all our rooms, then we can no longer provide our service to those who need it most."

The Bear sighed. "All right then, Miss Goody Two-Shoes. I'll tell you what. If you give me what I want and then you happen to get another customer or two, you have my permission to free up as many of my rooms as you like. And you know what? I'll even let you keep my payment. How about it?"

She stared at him. "Fine."

"Now that's better. I'll be staying for just one night."

"In that case, I don't need nearly this many coins."

"Whatever. Take what you need, just give me my keys."

"Here, please fill out this form."

As the owner reached for the key rack on the wall, the Bear grabbed a pen off the desk and stared at the form. It asked for all the usual information: name, point of origin, and such. He put down a bogus alias for the first block, but remained truthful for the majority the questions.

"Here you go." The owner dropped a handful of keys in front of him. "The keys for rooms 1 through 12 and rooms 15 through 30."

"Yeah, thanks." He scooped the pile into a pouch on his belt and returned to the form.

The bell by the front door rang again and the Bear froze. He turned his head just enough to see the priest walk in. The planks she had been holding were gone, but the hammer in her hand was still there. He turned his gaze toward the corner and hunched over the form.

"Good morning, Sky," said the owner. "How are you today?"

"Good morning, Lucy," said the priest. "I just came in to let you know that the sink in room 14 isn't working."

"I'll get on it right away."

"No, don't trouble yourself. I'll fix it myself, but I just wanted to let you know in case you keep maintenance records."

There was a pause as the Bear scribbled in the last few items. He waited for the bell at the door to ring again, but the chime never came.

"What are you doing?" asked Sky. "Going through your

finances?"

"No," said the owner, "just dealing with another customer."

Keeping his head turned to the side, the Bear shoved the form back in front of her. "Here." He mumbled it as quietly as he could.

"And don't forget to take your change—"

"Keep it."

He turned, making sure not to make eye contact with the priest, and got back out the door as quickly as possible.

"Sir? This is too much. Sir! Come back—"

The door slammed behind him. He wasn't sure what had bothered him so much about the priest, but he didn't feel like sticking around to find out.

The fox in the watchtower glared down at him—yet another reason to get on with his task. He had all the keys except for rooms 13 and 14, and the monkey had just mentioned she was lodging in room 14. That left one option. The Bear hurried around the corner to find room 13, ran past it to room 12, and fumbled for the right key. As he shut the door behind him, he breathed a sigh a relief.

He shut the blinds, tossed the pile of keys onto the bed, and took a look around. It took a moment for his eyes to adjust to the dark room after the blinding desert. Despite the rustic exterior of the building, the room looked just like any other hotel room, though perhaps a bit smaller than he was used to. There was a bed, night stand, TV, all the usual comforts. His interest lay in amenities of a different nature; an adjoining door or even a heater vent shared with room 13.

As he scanned the wall, muffled voices leaked through from the other side. He saw nothing connecting them but a bare wall, so he pressed one ear against the wooden surface and closed his eyes.

"Has Sky left yet?" It was a male voice.

"Didn't I already tell you? She's not going to leave until we do." A female voice.

"She doesn't trust us to do as we say?"

"What are you talking about? No, she just wants to make sure we're headed back home safely."

"So she's just going to hang around for a week?"

"Looks like it."

"Doing what?"

"Haven't you seen her? She's been fixing up the whole town."

"Why? It's none of her business."

"Seriously? You're giving her crap for that? Sky could give money to the homeless and you'd still find fault in it."

"Actually, you're not supposed to give money to homeless people. You have no way of knowing that they won't spend it on beer or—"

The wall shook with a sudden crash.

"Ow! What was that for?"

"You, for being a jerk."

"Fine, I'll change the subject. Do you want to play cards?"

"No, I'm sick of cards."

There was a pause. The Bear adjusted the position of his ear.

"Whatever. I think I'll go for a walk."

"Have fun."

There was another loud sound, farther away this time, which the Bear guessed to be the slamming door. He waited another moment, and after hearing nothing more, sat back down on the bed.

That could have been them. Man and woman could have been brother and sister. Concern for their safety could have been in regards to the wolf army hunting them. The pieces fit into place, but he knew it proved nothing. Travelers came in all forms, and the land south of the salt withheld its perils from no one.

A shadow fell over the curtains, a shadow that paced back and forth before coming to a stop in the center of the window. The silhouette turned from side to side for a brief moment, ever so subtly hinting at a long nose.

The Bear knelt down beside the window and pulled back the corner of the curtain just enough for a peak. His eyes had barely just adjusted to the dark, and now they struggled again in the sunlight. Gray hair. Two white stripes, one black. A face that brought back memories of his miserable academy days. Anteater Ray.

The Anteaters were here. Trapped in a small town with nowhere to run. All that remained to do now was alert his army to their presence.

Ray leaned against the patio railing, staring out into the empty street. The Bear couldn't suppress a wide grin. One of his most hated enemies stood barely a meter away and had no idea he was there. The patio wasn't even wide enough for a pair to walk two abreast. If the Bear wanted, he could grab the anteater from the window and slit his throat.

Now there was a thought.

His cautious side told him no, told him not even to consider it, told him to run back to his wolves and order the attack from the safety of his buggy, but the opportunity seemed so perfect that he couldn't help but entertain the idea. He could take Ray out right here, and still leave Jess for the wolves. He had negotiated a separate payment for each anteater, so here was a chance to save half his money.

Then again, the money made little difference to him. Neither the full nor half payment would even scratch his bank account. It was money well spent. He knew that he should play it safe. Unless.

A vision flashed through his head, a scene he had imagined before, but one he had refused to acknowledge until now. The Bear saw himself reunited with his grandfather. He saw himself proud to divulge to the old man the deaths of the last descendants of Anton. Lazarus asked how such a thing came to pass, and when his grandson mentioned the mercenary army, the Great Bear shook his head. 'This young bear before me is no true grandchild of mine, just a boy playing with his family's money.'

The Bear removed the knife from his belt. He would start by opening the window in a leisurely fashion, as if to merely suggest a guest's desire for fresh air. He would pull the anteater in close with his left hand and cut his throat with his right. Finally, before anyone would notice, he would pull the body back into the room. Flawless.

The window put up more a struggle than he had expected, and when he pushed harder, it slid to the top of the frame with a clunk.

The anteater's ears twitched. "Hm?"

The Bear lunged forward, grabbed him by the shoulder, and yanked him back against the sill. He swung out the knife, searching for the flesh of his neck.

A sharp pain enveloped his right wrist and he felt a hand beneath his shoulder. The next thing he knew, the Bear's feet left the ground and the window jumped forward to meet him. He heard the glass shatter before he felt the gash on his face, and an instant later he felt the hard floor of the patio against his cheek.

Everything was darker, only a blur of dim light. He tried to sit up, but something held him back. The curtain had wrapped around his head. The Bear tore it off and leapt to his feet. He drove the knife towards the first shape that moved.

There was a thunk, not quite the sound of metal through flesh. He had missed his target and sunk the blade into the building. He yanked the handle as hard as he could, but the knife wouldn't budge.

He saw a foot swinging at his face, and his world went dark again.

When he opened his eyes, he saw not one, but two anteaters, along with a fox. It was Ray and Jess, and the fox he recognized from the watchtower.

"No kidding," said Jess. "It's really him."

"I didn't think he would find us here," said Ray.

"Where's Sky?"

"I don't know. Didn't you say she was out fixing stuff?"

"Anteaters," said the fox. "He's awake."

He could see now that Ray held the knife—his grandmother's knife—in his hands. The Bear was seated against the railing, facing the street. His hands wouldn't budge when he moved them. From the feel of the fabric against his wrists, he could tell someone had improvised bindings from the torn curtains.

"You're sure this is him?" asked the fox. "This is the bear who hired the wolves to kill you?"

"It's him all right," said Jess. "Hey! Can you hear me?"

The Bear nodded. "Yes."

"You should have thought before trying to stab me," said Ray. "Look where it got you."

"Ray, come on, focus." Jess turned back to the Bear. "Do any of the Wolves know you're here?"

He said nothing.

"They know," said Ray. "If he doesn't go back, they'll come looking for him."

"How many wolves know?" asked Jess.

He said nothing.

"We need to kill him." Both anteaters looked at the fox. "Like Ray said, the wolves will realize he ran into trouble. We kill him now and we dump his body outside of town where the wolves will find it. They'll realize there's no one left to pay them and ditch the job."

"No," said Jess. "He's tied up and defenseless. I won't murder him."

"That's fine. You won't have to." The fox drew the first of her three flintlocks.

"Dipika, stop!" Jess stepped between them.

"You realize it's him or you. It should be an easy decision."

The Bear smirked. "Mind if I make that decision easier?" All three turned to him again. "I've given one of my associates full access to my account, along with very clear instructions. Should anything happen to me, said associate is to take my place at the Warlord's side and pay the Wolves as promised when the job is done. And the job will be done, one way or the other. It doesn't matter what you do to me here."

His captors had nothing to say to that. The Bear wiggled his wrists. As tight as the curtains had felt at first, the fabric was a poor substitute for ropes. The knot weakened by the moment, until he could feel his hands all but slip free.

All he needed now was a chance to make a break for it. He may not have been a match for either anteater in a fight, but he had been a varsity member of the track team back in his academy days. Back at the movie lot in the Fox Nation the Anteaters had managed to chase him down by splitting up and cutting him off, but the open desert left no chance for that. He knew he could hold a near sprint until he reached his buggy, and then it would all be over.

"I do have another question," said Jess. "Why do you want us dead?"

The Bear laughed. "Don't you know who I am?"

"I have no idea."

"My name is Bear Carson Theodore. I'm the Grandson of Bear Carson Julia and Bear Carson Lazarus."

"Shit," said Ray. "I agree with Dipika. Let's kill him now."

"Ray!"

She turned to argue with him, and a moment later the fox joined in too. They didn't want their captive to hear more than he had to. Little by little, their backs turned to him. This was it.

He burst free of the restraints, pushed off against the railing, and took off down the road. He took pains to ensure his first movements were as silent as possible. Every step he took without them noticing made his escape that much more probable.

"Hey! He's getting away!" It was Ray's voice. A little too late for them, though. The Bear had already passed the last building in town.

For a moment, he thought he heard the patter of feet behind him, but the sound soon died away. There would be no catching him now. Even if they decided to head back for a buggy to run him down, his own buggy was only a kilometer or two away. The wolves would see him and come to pick him up before anyone else would have a chance to catch up.

There was the echo of a gunshot and a sharp sting at his left side. The Bear howled in pain, but never broke his stride.

As he ran, he felt around his ribs with and stole a quick glance at his blood soaked paw. The wound had felt more like a scrape than a puncture; the projectile had only grazed him.

He didn't have the luxury of time to look back, but he knew it had been the fox guard. How many guns did she carry? He only had to make it a little farther; flintlocks had terrible range.

There was a second gunshot and a second jolt of pain. This time he had no choice in the matter—his legs gave way beneath him.

He collapsed to the ground, screaming in agony as his blood painted the desert sand. It took another moment to realize the iron ball had lodged in his left calf. He cringed and fought just to push himself onto his knees.

"Jess, he's down! We can still catch him!" It was Ray's voice again, and it was growing louder. He could again make out the footsteps behind him.

The ball had stopped just short off the bone. He could still run if he had but the strength to fight through the pain. He forced himself to his feet and took off once more.

Despite everything he had, his sprint still bore a hint of a limp on his wounded leg. The weaker his calf grew, the wetter with blood his ankle became, the harder he pushed himself. He pushed and pushed until finally, the footsteps behind him faded once more. As he looked up toward the horizon, he thought he could see the tiniest speck of a wolf buggy off in the distance.

He never heard the third gunshot.

Chapter 28

A brown mass protruded from the yellow sand not far ahead.

"He's down!" said Ray. "Quick, let's get him before he takes off again."

Jess let herself slow to a jog. "Ray, I don't think he's going anywhere."

"I wouldn't be sure. He's faster than he looks." Ray came to a stop at the body. "Oh."

It was the Bear all right, or what was left of him. His limp body lay spread across the ground, his face flat against the sand. A mess of red caked the lower half of his left leg, but no more blood gushed out of the bullet hole on his calf. Almost hidden in fur, another bullet hole stared out of the back of his skull.

Still catching his breath, Ray kneeled down beside the body. He ran his hand over the Bear's head and turned his palm to see the smudge of blood. He then reached down and felt the side of his neck.

"No pulse."

"What did you expect?"

They stood there, and for a moment all was still but the scorching desert breeze. Jess felt something trickle down her shoulder.

"Crap."

"What is it?"

"I think I just tore one of my stitches."

"Dammit, Jess. You shouldn't have been running after him with your injury."

"It's not a big deal. We'll fix it up when we get back."

A long pause followed.

"We should probably take him back to the town," said Ray. "I don't know if the things he said were true, but if they are—"

"Sure," said Jess. "You carry him."

Realizing he still held the assassin's knife, Ray tucked it into his belt before stepping forward. He nudged the body and pulled it up by the wrist, looking for a good grip to hoist it up onto his shoulders. He hesitated for a moment, and then took the right knee in his other hand, doing his best to avoid the dripping blood. He grunted at he lifted the sagging mass up over his back.

As he did, Jess took a moment to scan the desert scene. A whole lot of nothing stared back at her in all directions, with the exception of Beggar's Station, and a distant speck on the other side.

They started back toward the town at a fast walk, neither feeling the urge to run. The buildings had grown surprisingly far away, enough so that they shimmered in the heat of the desert air. After a minute, she noticed her brother fall behind a step or two.

"He too heavy for you?"

"I'm fine," he said. "It's just the bastard ran farther than I thought."

Dipika awaited them on the outskirts of town when they returned.

"How is he?"

Ray lifted the body over his head and dropped it face down in front of her. "Dead."

Dipika knelt down to examine the wound, giving the slightest hint of a grin as she eyed the hole in the back of his head. "That was a one-in-a-million shot," she said, fondling one of her pistols. "I got these off a Tromian merchant. They can hit twice a far as your average flintlock, and I've been honing my aim for at least an hour a day. Even so, your friend made it quite a distance, and my guns still have rather terrible accuracy at that range. So as I said, it was a one-in-a-million shot."

"Congratulations," said Jess.

The fox stood back up, a more somber look on her face. "The wolves will come looking for him soon. He said earlier that he had worked out a deal with them, that if he were to die, someone else would pay them to finish the job. If he was telling the truth, then dumping his body where they would find it wouldn't help us. I think he was being a dirty liar, but I'm not taking chances."

"So what would you have us do?" asked Ray. "Put on a ventriloquist act? Dangle him from above like a marionette and have him convince the wolves to leave?"

"I don't know."

"Ray and I will keep them away from Beggar's Station," said Jess.

"We will?" asked Ray. "How?"

"We'll do what we have to," said Jess. "You took us in and kept us safe when we needed it. We won't let the wolves close in on your town."

Dipika looked down at the Bear's body and then back up at the Anteaters. "I wish it didn't have be like that. Should you need them, our resources are at your disposal."

"We need to get moving soon. But first, where is Sky?"

The Fox craned her head and look back at the town. The residents had begun to trickle out onto the street, peering towards the three standing by the body.

"Never mind. We'll find her."

The siblings left the fox and headed back through the center of the strip. They pushed past the growing crowd of townspeople as they scanned the faces for the priest.

"Are you planning on doing what I think you are?" asked Ray. "Do you want us to turn ourselves over to the Wolves?

Jess looked him in the eye. "Are you suggesting we run for the border and leave the town to their fate?"

"No, of course not. But there has to be another option."

"Like what?"

"I don't know. We could drive his body somewhere far away from the town and look for a derelict buggy to dump him beside. Then we could rig some explosives and destroy the buggy. The noise would draw the Wolves to the scene, where they would find the Bear and presume he died in a vehicle accident."

"That's too complicated," said Jess. "Too many things could go wrong and there's no guarantee the Wolves will come to the conclusion you want them to."

"But we have to try something. Anything is better than just

forfeiting our lives."

"We're not forfeiting our lives."

Jess thought she spotted Sky for a moment, but it turned out to be another fox, just one that was slightly more built than the others.

"It's not what the Bear said that worries me," said Ray. "There's no way he has someone else to pay the Wolves in the event of his death. I'm sure he just said that to buy time." The anteater paused. "What worries me is the Wolves. They'll finish the job and kill us even if there's no reward to be had. They have their pride and a twisted sense of honor, just as Dr. Wilson said."

"Has Dr. Wilson lived among the Wolves as we have? We know they're better than that. We'll present them with the Bear's body and they'll see it's pointless."

Ray ran his hands down his face. "I know it's what we have to do. But don't tell me it's going to end well for us."

At first Jess could only return a somber stare, and the silence between them drowned out the buzz of the curious crowd.

"There is one hope we have," she said. "We could find Ben."

"Ben Wolf?"

"You heard the things he said. He has enough pull with the Wolves and he wouldn't let us die over petty honor. If we let him know the Bear is dead, he'll see to it that we return safely to the Fox Nation."

"And how are we going to find him? He's one wolf out of millions."

"We'll start by heading to the last known position of Tusk Pack."

"They'll have moved."

"It's a start. We have to try. As you said, anything is better than giving up."

Ray barely returned a nod. His head drooped toward the ground before he finally looked up, a glimmer of recognition in his eyes.

"There's Sky," he said.

The monkey pushed her way through the crowd, moving a large fox out of her way with a gentle but firm shove. The tension in her face eased up when she saw the Anteaters making their way over to her.

"I heard all the commotion." Sky looked at Jess. "What happened? You're bleeding."

"I know," said Jess, though she had already forgotten about the torn stitches.

"The Bear is dead," said Ray.

They told Sky about the Bear's appearance in town, his attempts at murder and escape, and Dipika's lucky shot. She remained calm and quiet as she listened, but her eyes grew larger as they told her of the plan to bring his body to the Wolves and turn themselves in.

"It's the only option," said Jess.

Sky was silent at first, but finally she spoke.

"How will you make your way to find Ben? Do you plan to walk?"

"We don't know. We'll figure it out."

"I'll take you. In my buggy."

"No," said Jess. "This isn't your problem."

"Was it my problem when I found you two tied up in the desert?"

"You've done so much for us already," said Jess. "And we appreciate it more than you could know. But there's a possibility that we won't be coming back, and you being there will not change our odds of survival."

"All right," said Sky. "I'll stay behind. But I want you to take my buggy."

"You'd let us have your buggy?"

"What about your new job?" asked Ray. "Don't you have to get to that?"

"I will find another way to the Sand Monoliths, and if I am late, the Celestial Monkeys will forgive me. You need the car more than I do."

Jess took Sky's hand in both of hers. "We won't forget what you've done for us. If we all get through what lies ahead, I swear to you we will find a way to thank you. For everything."

"Give your thanks to the Celestial Monkeys. I am but their servant."

Ray too extended his hand for a handshake. "Well, all right. We appreciate it."

Sky's eyes wandered down to the glimmering weapon in Ray's belt.

"What is that?"

"What is what?"

"That knife, where did you get that?"

"Oh, this?" Ray pulled it from his belt and held the blade parallel to the ground. "I got it off the Bear, after he tried to kill me with it."

Sky stepped forward for a closer look, but Ray pulled it back.

"That's gold," she said.

"No, that's impossible."

"I mean it," said Sky. "The knife you're holding is made of solid gold."

"It has to be imitation."

"Then why does your arm strain to hold it up? It's heavy, isn't it?"

Ray propped his elbow against his side. "It's not that heavy. And that doesn't mean it's made of gold."

"But it is," said Sky. "I know of this knife. It's Sander's blade."

"Never heard of it."

"It was one of the sacred treasures the Celestial Monkeys left behind. It disappeared during the Autumn Revolution, along with the sword Unparried, and the scepter Rain."

"Huh," said Ray. "Julia and the other bear soldiers were the ones who led the final charge on the Temple. Perhaps the Bear was telling the truth about being her grandson."

"Ray, please listen to me. For the past fifty years, three walls have stood bare where we once displayed our three most sacred relics. To have one of those returned to us would bring a joy and relief I could not describe."

"What, this?" Ray eyed the shimmering blade. "I mean, sure, if it means that much to you, you can have it."

"Do you truly mean it?"

He held it by the blade and placed the handle into Sky's hand. "Go ahead and take it. It's the least I can do after you agreed to lend us your buggy. It's not like the knife was even mine to begin with—I just grabbed it off the Bear."

He tried to turn and walk away, but Sky took him by the hand and smiled at him until he looked at her. Her eyes sparkled. "You cannot even comprehend the happiness you have just brought my people. May the blessings of the Celestial Monkeys be upon you. They watch over you, Anteater Ray. Under their watch, you and your sister will live to return home."

"Sure," he nodded. "Now we should get going."

Chapter 29

"Are you sure this is the right way?" asked Ray.

"Sky gave us the coordinates of her route," said Jess. "We'll pass by Tusk Pack's last location."

"Is that accounting for when we stopped to hide in that cave?"

"Yes it is."

She didn't blame her brother for his anxiety. They were driving back into the heart of Wolf territory, and the dead body back in the crate did nothing to lighten the mood. They had only been driving for about an hour and had seen no wolves so far. As before, there was nothing but flat, endless desert as far as the eye could see.

"Jess."

"What?"

"Your wound is bleeding again."

"Is it really? I had that fox stitch me back up before we left."

"Clearly she didn't do a very good job. Let me take a look at it."

He stood up in his chair and grabbed the frame of the buggy for support as he reached across her chest to access her left shoulder. Jess scowled and craned her head around his protruding arm.

"What are you doing?"

"I'm trying to get a better look at your shoulder."

"I can't see the road when you reach across my face."

"There's nothing to see. It's all sand."

"Ray!"

"Just stop the car. I'll need to get out to get the first aid kit anyway."

"Fine."

She brought them to a stop, shifted the buggy out of gear, and instinctively turned the key. The hum of the motor faded away and the warm desert breeze wafted over her. She shifted her shoulder forward, only to have a sudden wave of pain radiate from the gash.

Jess did her best not to display her discomfort, playing it off as stiffness rather than agony. She gently pressed her shoulder back against the seat while Ray hopped out and rummaged through the supplies in the crate.

"Hey, where is it?" he asked.

"The first aid kit is wedged between the blankets and the food," Jess said without bothering to turn around. "I made sure to place it. I know it's there."

"The first aid kit is here, yes. There's no suture kit inside."

"What?" A jolt of pain went through her upper arm. "Ow!"

"Are you all right?"

"I'm fine. Are you sure it's not in the box?"

"All I see here is gauze, tape, and disinfectant. It's not a very large kit."

"Did we forget to put it back after I got sown up back in town?"

"I don't know, but it's not here." Ray brought the kit over to the driver side to show his sister its sparse contents. "We haven't gone too far from Beggar's Station. We could still go back and get it before we resume our search."

"No," said Jess. "Every minute we take to find Ben is a minute in which the Wolves might decide to launch an all-out attack on Beggar's Station. We're wasting enough time as it is."

Ray pulled a wad of gauze from the box. "So be it, but at least let me do what I can to patch you up with what we have."

She cringed as he pressed the fabric against the laceration and wrapped it tight. When he finished, she managed a nod and he made his way back to the crate to put away the kit. By the time he had jumped into the passenger seat, she could already see a patch of red growing in the center of the dressing. Not to draw Ray's attention to the blood, she made a final check behind her to make sure that everything was secure and then turned the key.

The buggy let out a horrible whine and both siblings cringed.

"Ugh, I had forgotten about that," said Ray. "Didn't someone from the town inspect it?"

"Come on." Jess gritted her teeth and reached over the engine hood to give it a whack. "You worked just fine when we left town."

She waited a moment and then turned the ignition again, only to hear another awful shriek. She tried again, only to hear another. And another.

Ray's fist clenched around the frame. "This is a bad time to be stranded."

"You think I don't know?"

She cranked down on the key once more, and this time the motor roared to life. As the vehicle shifted into gear, she turned to her brother.

"Good thing," he said.

"Shut up and enjoy the ride."

As they started off again, Jess found herself listening and feeling the rhythm of the buggy. She had to push harder on the accelerator to get the same thrust as before. The sound beneath the hood was louder than usual, but that could mean anything for an electric motor. Ray didn't appear to notice anything, so she did her best not to betray her suspicions.

As they rode through the desert, Jess tried to convince herself that the motor sounded the same as before. At the very least, she tried to convince herself that it was sounding better, but after a while, she couldn't really tell.

Rather curiously, there was a sliver of white on the horizon, prominent enough that Jess had to wonder if they had gone the wrong direction and arrived at the salt pan. The white turned out to be a trick of the desert sun, and shortly afterwards sundown rendered the entire landscape dark blue. From there, the drive continued on into the night. The sand beneath their tires disappeared into the darkness as they plunged into the void.

She kept the headlights on for the time being. They hadn't spotted any wolves thus far and the prospect of losing their only car to the odd boulder or ravine did not appeal to her. The ever waxing crescent of the moon provided a rough outline of the land, but she still didn't trust it to reveal any upcoming obstacles.

Around what she guessed was midnight, Ray insisted in a turn at the wheel. He was right in that she had grown sleepy, and they didn't have time to spare setting up camp, so she gave in. Jess brought them to a stop, but kept the car running as they swapped seats.

"Here you go," she said. "Just be sure that whatever you do, do not turn off the motor."

"You don't need to tell me."

She listened to the complaining buggy for an hour or so before finally drifting off to sleep. When she woke again the sun had just appeared again on the horizon and endless sand in all directions met her eyes. Her surroundings gave her pause; she recalled the hills of their final days with Tusk Pack. She had thought they would have made it closer by now.

After enduring another hour of her brother's driving, Jess claimed her next turn in the driver's seat. Although she knew not to set her expectations too high, she kept a lookout for rougher terrain in the distance. And as always, she scanned the desert for any sign of wolves.

The motor let out a horrible screech, not at all unlike the sounds it made when starting. Jess cringed, eased off the accelerator, and then slowly floored it back with a little more juice. A high pitched whirring noise remained, which gradually got quieter but never entirely went away. She turned to Ray, who thankfully had fallen sound asleep in the passenger seat.

When she turned forward again, something was on the horizon. She reached under the dashboard for the binoculars and focused on the dots in the distance. They were buggies, about a dozen of them, each at least several hundred meters apart. Although she couldn't make out any features of the buggies or wolves themselves, she knew the group was too small to be Ben's pack.

She eased the steering wheel around until the buggy veered away from the pack. She checked to make sure Ray was still asleep and then she raised the binoculars again. The distant buggies all faced her from the side. There was no sign anyone had noticed them.

Jess floored the pedal and did not let up until the pack was gone. Even then she checked behind her with the binoculars every minute for the next few kilometers.

"What is that?" asked Ray, stretching in his seat.

"Do you see something?"

"Not see, hear. The motor sounds terrible."

He was right, the buggy was squealing and shrieking even louder than before.

"It's nothing," said Jess.

She pumped the accelerator, easing off as it cried out and giving it more juice when it died down. After a minute of fighting the machine, the motor quieted back down to the standard hum. Then it became even quieter.

"No. Don't do this. Not now."

"What's wrong?" asked Ray.

She pushed the accelerator again, but the pedal gave no resistance. The motor went silent. The flat dusty ground offered little to impede the momentum of the vehicle, but gradually the speedometer dial found its way back toward zero.

"Jess, why are we stopping?"

Jess kicked the pedal as hard as she could, but nothing happened. There was nothing she could do but wait until they coasted to a complete stop.

She pulled out the key, only to insert it again and crank down on the ignition one last time. Nothing. No terrible shriek, no happy purr, not the slightest reaction from the buggy.

"Jess, did the buggy just die?"

"Not if I can help it."

She jumped out and walked around to the front. She lifted the hood, only to stare at the charred mess within. Ray stepped out to meet her.

"Well? Can you fix it?"

"This is beyond fixing. These cables are completely fried. I'm amazed they lasted as long as they did."

"Dammit Jess, we can't be stuck here! We're in the middle of the desert!"

"You think I don't know that?"

"All right then, how much farther do we still have to go?"

She cringed. "Maybe a hundred kilometers?"

"A hundred kilometers?"

"If we're lucky."

Ray sighed. "I'm sorry, Jess. It's not your fault. You're not the one who stuck us with this piece of crap buggy."

"It's not Sky's fault either," said Jess. "You make it sound like she planned this all along. She was just trying to help."

"Yes, I get it. She's a saint, all right?"

They stood there a moment, first staring at one another, then at the heap under the hood. Then Ray looked back at Jess.

"What?" she asked.

"Jess, your shoulder."

The gauze had turned a solid red and the tape was so soaked that it barely clung to her skin. In a line down her side trickled a stream of fresh blood the saturated bandage could no longer absorb.

"Oh no."

"Jess, we need to get you medical help, and I mean now."

"And what would have us do to get it? As you kindly pointed out, we're in the middle of the desert with no buggy."

Ray jumped out and walked over to her, eying the drenched gauze. He reached his hand to the wound, only to pull it back as though he feared making it worse.

"There is one thing we could do," he said. "We could fire the flare."

"To signal for help from Edward?"

"No, not for help from the Foxes. For help from the Wolves. It does send out an electronic signal, but because it first has to reach altitude, it functions as a conventional flare too. If we fire it, the Wolves will see it and come to us. If they decide not to kill us, they might help us in exchange for our copper."

"But we aren't close enough to Ben's pack yet."

"Jess, we both know Tusk Pack won't be there waiting for us. We'll just have to take our chances."

She sighed. "Right before the buggy died, I saw a pack of wolves."

"Good. So someone will see our signal."

"But it wasn't Ben's pack!"

"Maybe they would be willing to contact Ben's pack if we ask."

"It's too risky," said Jess. "Aren't you the one always telling me not to trust wolves?"

"I don't trust wolves, but you're going to bleed to death!" said Ray. "We don't have a choice!"

"Yes we do," said Jess. "We're continuing on foot."

"Jess, come back here. You've lost too much blood. You're

not thinking clearly."

"Whatever. Either stay there or follow me."

Ray resisted for a moment, but then followed. Then they walked. And walked. They walked for what must have been hours even though she had no way to tell. Every few minutes, Jess would turn around to see how far they had gotten from the buggy. As it got smaller and smaller, clouds began to roll in, blocking the sun and extinguishing every trace of blue. Just when the buggy disappeared, so did the last piece of the sky. Once again, she saw nothing but white.

"We're braving the salt for real this time," she said.

Ray ignored her.

"No buggy," said Jess. "Now we're crossing the salt pan just as people did a thousand years ago."

Something suddenly seemed odd to her. When had they crossed into the salt pan? They hadn't been heading in that direction. They weren't supposed to go in that direction if they wanted to find the Wolves. Yet here they were.

The ground crunched as she felt the salt crumble beneath her feet. She could feel the surface depress in response to her weight with each step, but when she looked down she detected no visible tracks. All she could see was a networks of cracks reaching out into billions of others.

The trek was unlike any she had undertaken. There was neither crest to climb nor valley to descend, neither trail post nor notch in a tree, not so much as a rock or twig on the ground to indicate the long march's progress. All that remained as a means to discern one space from another was the web of cracks, which grew blurrier by the minute. She knew in her mind every crack to be unique, but just as the lone snowflake disappeared into the blizzard, soon she saw no cracks. Only white.

She looked to the ground, and sure enough the cracks were gone. The floor beneath looked more smooth than grainy, more like marble than salt. When she reached down and felt it, the hard surface met her with an almost waxy sensation.

"Ray, take a look at this."

No response.

"Ray?"

She turned around, but Ray was gone.

"Ray, this isn't funny!"

"I'm rather curious, where do you think he could have gone?"

Jess spun around to lay eyes on a fox standing just a few meters away. He was an elderly fox, but lean muscles showed beneath his fur without a hint of flab.

"Mast?"

"Do you see anywhere your brother could hide? I tried to teach you about the dangers of the salt pan, but it seems you never listened. Now look at you."

"What are you doing here?"

He sighed. "I had imagined you might have been more thrilled to see your old master again. I didn't get a chance to teach you everything I knew, everything Anton knew. Yet you act like you already know all. There's more to this line of work than what you see in the sparring ring."

"What are you talking about?"

"Edward should have known that you and your brother weren't ready for a mission of this magnitude. All I see is poor planning and even poorer improvising. I see the work of children, not professionals."

"Now, now, don't be so harsh on the poor girl," said a different voice. "After all, she did succeed in her mission. She did manage to kill me."

Mast was gone, and in his place stood the Bear.

"You."

"Yes, me. I am the reason the Wolves are an issue, am I not? Your president told you to fix the problem, and you had no problem getting rid of me."

"Our mission was to observe and report."

"True, because you didn't know what the root cause of the issue was. Once you figured it out, you knew what your next mission would be. You were already in the Wolf Lands, so why waste the opportunity? You even got someone else to do the dirty work for you."

"You have done well to eliminate one of his clan," said yet another voice, "But you know it's not over. Lazarus killed me, and he won't stop until you and Ray are dead too."

"Dad."

The other anteater held out his hand. "Hello Jess."

"You're not really here, are you?"

"Probably not."

"Then why am I seeing you?"

"I wouldn't know."

"Am I dead?"

"No." A fourth voice, a voice calm and plain yet somehow still piercing, came from all around. Her father was gone, and no one took his place. "They are all dead, but you are still alive. For now."

"What's happening?"

"They're coming, Jess. If you can't stop them, it will all be over."

"Jess!"

She felt herself shaking. Two hands had her by the shoulders, jerking her back and forth until another face came into view.

"Snap out of it, Jess."

"What's happening?"

Ray stopped shaking her to give her a pat. "Are you all right? You looked really out of it."

She was back in the desert. The sky was a deep blue and the ground a bed of sand. The buggy was right there. She had barely walked ten meters.

"I'm fine," she said. "I'm just a bit dazed. Now I can believe that people went crazy here back before buggies were around."

"Who went crazy here?"

"People braving the salt."

"Jess, we've been in the desert this whole time. We're nowhere near the salt."

"Oh."

"Jess, you don't look that well."

"Figures," she said. "I've had better days."

Ray reached into her belt and pulled the flare gun from the large compartment.

"Ray, you fire that gun and there's no going back."

"I know."

"And if they come and Ben isn't with them? If they want to kill us?"

"We'll deal with them."

Jess gave a weak laugh. "Sure we will. We'll beat up the whole damn army. They're just wolves, after all."

Ray nodded. "That they are."

She gave a nod to the flare gun. "Fire it."

He took the device and held it up above his head. He paused just long enough to make Jess think he wouldn't do it. His eye twitched at the horizon, as though he were wondering where the nearest pack was, and what they had a mind to do when they set eyes on the Anteaters.

Then there was a pop, a fizzle, and a trail of smoke up into the heavens. Then there was silence. A lone red beacon drifting through the blue, and silence.

Chapter 30

"For the last time, Stewart, I'm fine."

"I just talked to the general. She didn't tell me everything, but from what I gather we're collaborating with the Bear Nation forces to watch the Tromian border on all fronts. If there's any movement, you need to get out of there."

"Stewart, don't talk to the general!" said Edward. "In the meantime, I'm just fine over here. The Bears moved me and the other distinguished guests to a more secure location. There's solid concrete behind these walls and guards behind my door at all times."

"You think that will stop the Tromians? I read the report. Guns that fire repeatedly without needing to reload? Flying vehicles that stay suspended in one spot? Who knows what else the Tromians are capable of?"

"Whatever that may be, I'll deal with it when I get back to my office. I'm the expert in military matters, not you."

"Against the Monkeys, maybe. They don't use guns."

"Guns don't concern me. They caught us by surprise last time, but now I'm wearing my liquids at all hours." Edward felt his chest, only for his hand to brush against bare fur. The jacket and leggings were hanging off the side of his chair. "Dammit."

"What is it?"

"Nothing." He grabbed the first piece of armor and put one arm through the sleeve while holding the phone in the other. "I'm leaving now for a brief talk with the Chancellor and then I'll be right back on the plane. Goodbye."

"Be careful."

Edward hung up, tossed the phone over to the couch, and finished buttoning up the liquids. There was a knock on the door.

"I'll be right out."

He stepped out of the room to join a team of bears and foxes in the hallway.

"Sir, your mask."

"I have it right here," said Edward. "I'll put it on at the first sign of trouble."

"That would not be advised. The Tromians may attack again without warning."

"There was enough warning last time. Just keep anyone with purple fur away from me and I'll be fine. Now is it time to head out or not?"

"Yes sir, the Chancellor is waiting for you."

"Good. Where's the Councillor?"

"I'm here."

The source of the voice was the one fox who was much shorter than the others. Edward hadn't recognized Tammy under the jacket that squeezed at her wrists and the mask that sagged over her face. She slouched behind a row of guards, rubbing her palm against the side of her leg.

"Councillor. How are you this morning?"

"To be honest, I've been better."

"Will you have your wits about you for the meeting? It shouldn't take long."

She shook her head. "I'm afraid I won't be joining you. To say our last meeting left me shaken would be an understatement. I still need time to recover, and until I do, I know I won't be any help to you in there."

"No bullets this time, I promise."

"Again, I must decline. I may be able to stomach days of debate on the Council floor, but fists and gunfire—well, that's your world, Mr. President, not mine."

Edward nodded. "Then get better soon."

"It will be but a day or two at most," said Tammy. "So with that, I suppose I'll see you back in the Fox Nation. I noticed the media has already hailed you as the hero who saved the Triumvirate. I'm sure that will do wonders for the Defender Party."

With that, she turned around and waved her hand for three of the fox guards to escort her from the hallway. She grabbed a metal flask from one of them before rounding the corner and disappearing from Edward's sight.

One of the remaining guards gestured toward the other end of the hall. "This way, sir."

"Lead the way," said Edward.

He squinted at the first sign of natural light as they led him from the quarters. He hadn't been in the bunker that long, but his chest loosened all the same when they climbed the staircase to the ground floor. An armored car awaited him outside the lobby.

"Is that really necessary?" he asked. "What was wrong with the limousine?"

"It's just a precaution, sir."

"Then let's make this drive quick. I have a meeting to attend and a plane to catch."

Once again, Edward found himself confined from the sunlight. The ride to the State House was smoother than he had expected; back in the war his armored vehicles had taken him over rockier terrain.

When the hatch finally opened, no sunlight poured through. He climbed out to find himself in a dimly lit parking garage, not unlike the one below his own office back in the Fox Nation.

"Is this the State House?"

"Yes. Follow me. The Chancellor is right in here."

The guard, a bear, swung open a steel door that led to a concrete corridor. He beckoned for Edward to follow, and the fox did. After a few dozen meters of dusty floors and hanging lightbulbs, they reached the Chancellor's bunker.

The chamber Edward saw before him bore none of the grungy conditions of the passageway thereto. It boasted silk rugs, hardwood furniture, paintings on the wall, almost more than anyone would expect from the modest styles of the structure above. Had it not been for the lack of windows, someone might have mistaken the underground bunker for the actual office.

A lone white horse stood in the center of the room. Oddly enough, he wasn't wearing liquids.

"Edward," he said. "It's a pleasure to see you again."

"To you as well."

"Please make yourself comfortable." He nodded at the couch.

"Thank you."

"Where is Councillor Tammy?"

"Still recovering from the previous meeting. You'll understand that it was traumatic. Where is the Vice Chancellor?"

"Meeting with the commanders of the northern regiments. I'm afraid she won't be joining us either."

"So we're just waiting for the monkeys."

"Actually, it turns out they have declined to join us as well."

"I see," said Edward. "No doubt they plan to make us wait, knowing I'm here."

"Their plane left this morning," said Pegasus. "They meant it when they said they wouldn't be here."

"Then at least I won't have to withstand more antagonism from the High Priest."

"Don't you mean the Priest of War?"

"No."

Pegasus laughed. "In truth, the High Priest is one of the wisest rulers I have ever known. In time she will come to respect you. Your presidency is young yet, but soon you'll prove to her that you're more than that old enemy general."

"Regardless, we're now down to two. Is the meeting cancelled then?"

"We're still both here, and a meeting only requires two."

"What about the input from the Monkeys?"

"We invited them to join, but they made their decision. We'll carry on without them. You can feel free speak your mind."

"I should have mentioned as soon as I walked in," Edward lowered his head, "my deepest condolences regarding your butler."

"You are very kind. Piripi was one of the finest individuals I've ever had the pleasure of working with, and he gave his life for our nation. No one could replace him."

"I regret that I only had the chance to exchange a few brief sentences with him. We will make those responsible answer for their crimes. My people stand behind you."

"Those responsible for the crime are dead," said Pegasus. "The fall from my office wasn't far, but all three Tromians managed to land on their necks. My air patrols shot down the aircraft, and again, there were no survivors, no one to question, and no one to give us any leads."

"Are you suggesting this attack was only a rogue group acting on its own?"

Pegasus shook his head. "Not even remotely."

"So you look to mainland Tromia?"

"Mr. President, a fox like you might find my nation's leniency toward the Monkeys excessive, but there is one crime for which we cannot forgive them. For thousands of years, the Temple ignored the Tromian threat, pretended they simply didn't exist. Now look at what the Tromians are capable of when we allow them to fester."

"That was back in the days of the Empire. The Monkeys can't ignore the Tromians now."

"So you'd think, but still they blame their problems on the Disgraced."

"You believe the Tromians destroyed the Ancient Circle."

"You've seen their technology."

"It was nothing that could damage one of the Five Monuments."

"We don't know that," said Pegasus. "What we do know is that our world is full of wonders we cannot explain. Tromians are not very intelligent. Had the ancient Temple recognized them as a species, they would have classified tromians as concrete operational at best. Haven't you wondered how such a people could make such advancements as we've just seen? I say they didn't make these advancements. They found them."

"Found them? Where?"

"As much as the skeptics try to deny it, there are miracles all around us. You can look to the Five Monuments, or you can look to the very liquids on your back. The Monkeys credit these miracles to the Celestial Monkeys, but whether or not their gods are real, we can't deny the power of these marvels. One source of these miracles you will find within the Temple. That's how the Quaternity united the world three thousand years ago. I'd stake anything that the Tromians have discovered another such source."

"When you say 'source,' what exactly do you mean?"

"Fountain of youth, alien artifact, tree of knowledge, take your pick. I don't know what it is, but I can see the things that come out."

"And how would you plan to fight this 'tree of knowledge'?" asked Edward.

"You're the one who waged and won two wars against the

Temple. You tell me."

"I know about the Ursidae-Tromian Conflict a few years back. Your people must have a much better idea of what we're up against. I might even suggest you already knew something about the Tromians' technology."

"If it weren't for that technology, we would have crushed them handily. We can't win this fight alone."

"So you expect my nation to fight Tromia."

"We shouldn't get ahead of ourselves," said Pegasus. "We'll continue to watch their borders and find out what we can, but when the war does come, it will come for all of us. You may see my people as isolationists, but the minute you deem it time to march on Tromia, the Bear Nation will be there to march alongside you."

Edward reached for one of the bottles on the coffee table and took a drink of water.

"You're right about the miracles," he said. "I have seen many things I cannot explain, such as an unarmored horse charging into direct gunfire and emerging without a scratch."

Pegasus smirked. "That sounds like quite a tale. I wish I'd been there to see it."

"I know I saw at least three shots going right at you."

"You must be remembering it wrong."

"I know what I saw. I feel like there's a story behind it, a story I'd like to hear."

"Maybe I'll tell you when I get to know you better. If there is any story to tell."

"All right then," said Edward. "How about your name then?"

"My name?"

"Why did you choose the name Pegasus for yourself?"

"What makes you think I named myself?"

"Did your parents pick it for you?"

"Maybe."

"It just seems like a curious name to take. I know your office comes with demanding trials and hardships, but do you see yourself as a winged horse who carries lightning bolts?"

Pegasus's eyes lit up. "You're familiar with the myth. I must say I'm impressed. I didn't expect that a general who spent years fighting the monkeys would know so much about their religion."

"Know thyself, know thy enemy, and you need not fear a

thousand battles."

"Again, a quote from Celestial Monkey mythology. There's more to you than meets the eye, Mr. President. Perhaps you and I will become good friends after all."

"You're quite good at evading my questions."

"Not in the slightest," said Pegasus. "I meant what I said. Over the last few years, I enjoyed a wholly fulfilling friendship with President Mairéad. When her term ended, I feared I would have little to relate to in the new head of state. I'm pleased to learn I was wrong."

"It pains me to admit I've taken a liking to you as well." Edward grinned. "You must visit us across the channel sometime. Say the word and I'll have Stewart plan an event."

"I would be honored. Our two nations may be in our infancy when compared to the Monkeys, but together, we make up the better two-thirds of the Triumvirate. Hope for progress in this world rests in our hands."

"And someday you will answer my questions."

"If you're lucky."

One of the fox guards tapped Edward on the shoulder and leaned down to whisper into his ear. "Mr. President, an urgent matter has come up."

"Please excuse me."

"Of course," said Pegasus.

Edward followed her over to the corner, out of earshot of the rest of the room.

"Sir, we just received word from central command. We picked up a signal on the radar."

"A signal? From where?"

"It's your two agents. They're in danger."

Chapter 31

A bump in the road jolted Brad awake. He yawned and squinted. It was light out already and the wolf at wheel seemed completely unfazed after a night of driving. Brad couldn't say the same, even as a passenger. His back hurt. His neck hurt. His ass hurt. They had been driving for days and he was sick of it.

The Bear had insisted he stay with the search, but the Bear had vanished and the search had been fruitless. He had no reason to waste his time driving in circles with the wolves and he still had no means of contacting Sonya. Their courtship was still young, and disappearing on her for a week was a terrible way to start things off. He had been gone so long, he wouldn't be surprised if Fuzz and Larry had taken the opportunity to hit on her. Those bastards.

He had had it. The Bear wasn't there to tell him to stay with the search effort. He would ask Doris to let him return to Grand Oasis, and she would let him do as he pleased.

"Doris?"

She turned face him from the front seat.

"Yes?"

"Can you spare a buggy from this pack?"

"Spare buggy? What for?"

"I need to get back to Grand Oasis. It's important."

"Brad, Sir, I don't think you want go back to Grand Oasis right now."

"Don't you start. We're paying you to do what we ask."

"But Sir, we found the Anteaters."

"We did? I don't see them. Where are they?"

"We receive radio call an hour ago. Fire Beetle Pack have them."

"Did the pack kill them?" asked Brad.

"No," said Doris. "As ordered, they await arrival of Warlord representative—me."

"Isn't that risky? What if they get away?"

"Ten pack there already. They not going anywhere. We be there within hour."

Brad sat back in his seat. This changed everything. If they already had the Anteaters, Sonya could wait another hour. Finally he would his would avenge cousin Phil.

He found it ironic that he would be present for the Anteaters' demise while the Bear would not. The Bear would be so angry to have missed out on watching it himself, but at least Brad could do him the courtesy of relaying the details. In the Bear's absence, Brad would have the final say in how the job was to be finished.

He pulled a dark cloak from the crate in the back and pulled his arms through the sleeves. He had the perfect plan. Right before he gave the final order to execute the Anteaters, he would remove the cloak and give them just enough time to realize who he was. He would whisper the words 'this is for Phil' and then it would all be over. He pulled the hood over his head.

Peering from beneath the cloak, he saw a cluster of buggies off in the distance. There were far too many of them to be a single pack. He gripped the frame as he leaned toward the door.

As soon as the buggy came to a stop, Brad jumped out onto the desert and left Doris behind. He ran toward the crowd, shoving the wolves aside to get a better look. The large wolf in the front refused to budge, so Brad got on his toes and peered over the wolf's shoulder.

There they were. Two anteaters stood in front of a buggy. Jess looked pale and barely conscious, blood dripping from a bandage on her upper arm. Ray, looking moderately healthier, had his arm around her. A column of smoke rose from under the buggy's hood, and something large wrapped in canvas sat in the crate.

"Stay back," said Jess. "We demand to speak to Wolf Ben of Tusk Pack."

"Tusk Pack?" asked one of the wolves. "I never heard of Tusk Pack."

"I heard of them," said another wolf. "They pack that defeat Black Sun Pack."

"Where are they?" asked Ray.

"How should I know? They not here."

"Can you reach them by radio?" asked Jess.

"No. You lucky we don't kill you already."

"You'll regret it if you try," said Ray.

The wolves snarled and tightened the circle around the siblings. Ray and Jess tried to back up, but there was nowhere to go.

"Make way!" It was Doris's voice.

The wolves at the edge of the circle stepped aside to make a passage for the liaison. Doris stepped through and eyed the Anteaters, her hand on the holster of her flintlock.

"Are you the one in charge here?" asked Ray.

"I am Wolf Doris, representative of Warlord," she said. "I act with his authority."

"Do you know Wolf Ben of Tusk Pack?" asked Jess.

"I know every pack and every pack leader. What you have to say about Ben?"

"We need to talk to him."

Doris shook her head. "You in no position to make demand."

"Please," said Jess. "You have to listen to me. He's the only one who will understand."

"I understand just fine," said Doris. "You are Anteater Jess and Anteater Ray. The Bear pay us great sum of money if we eliminate you."

She removed her gun and leveled it at the Anteaters.

"With the seal of Warlord, contract is fulfilled."

Brad grabbed his hood and prepared to step forward.

"Wait!" said Ray.

"What?" asked Doris.

"Don't shoot. You won't get any money for us."

"What you mean?"

"I'll show you."

He reached into the crate and hoisted the cumbersome object in canvas over his head. He unbuckled the straps and tossed it at his feet, where it unraveled to reveal the contents.

Brad felt sick. It was the Bear, or what was left of him. He could see bullet holes on his leg and side, and flies buzzed around his lifeless eyes.

"He's dead!" said Ray. "You'll get no money from him."

An uproar erupted among the wolves. Some of them just growled or snapped their teeth, but one of them leapt toward the siblings.

Jess still looked as though she could barely move, but she barely had to. She turned her body and placed her fist between herself and the wolf. The brainless beast ran face first into her knuckles, knocking himself out.

Doris fired her flintlock into the sky. "Enough!"

The packs fell quiet, but they didn't back away. Doris kneeled down to inspect the Bear's body.

"What you doing?" asked one of the wolves.

"It him," said Doris. "This is the Bear."

"Yes, we all see," said the other wolf. "We needed his money. Now he dead. No one rob us like that and live."

"Stand down." Doris stood up and faced the packs. She waited until she had silence before she continued. "Warlord have me work closely with Bear. I learn all about him. He have no respect for friends or allies and he fight without honor. He follow legacy of evil Great Bear."

The wolves eyed her. "So what we do?"

Brad cringed and took a deep breath. What was Doris doing?

"We wolves are poorer without the Bear," said Doris, "but the world better off without him. So we move out."

"You're letting us go?" asked Ray.

"Yes. I suggest you go now and never return to Wolf Lands."

He took one look at his barely conscious sister, and then back at the wolves.

"You all still want to make some money?" He removed a bag of coppers from his belt. "Who here has a first aid kit with a suture set?"

The wolves met him with blank stares.

"Never mind. What about your fastest buggy and a radio? I have three times what it's worth."

As the wolves stepped forward with offers, Brad tried to shove his way past the heavy wolf in front, but the wolf blocked him yet again.

"I need to speak to Doris," said Brad. "Even if the Bear's dead, I have money. I can pay for you to finish the job."

"Shut up." The wolf elbowed him in the gut.

Brad fell to the sand, clutching his stomach in pain. The wolves didn't have the decency to give him any space, but they finally backed away when Doris barked another command. By the time he stood back up, the Anteaters were driving off in their newly purchased buggy.

"Dammit!"

He tried to kick a nearby pebble, but wound up only hitting a wad of sand.

"Brad," said Doris, "we return to Grand Oasis now. You coming or you want stay alone in desert?"

"Screw you," he said.

"Contract void now," she said. "We under no obligation to help you. I suggest you be polite if want to return at all."

"Fine, I know," said Brad. "Just give me a minute. Please."

"All right."

He stood there and watched the Anteaters ride off toward the horizon. He had come so close. How would he enact justice now without the help of the Bear?

The Bear's body still lay on the ground next to the broken buggy. Surely the wolves weren't just going to leave him to rot. Brad could at least provide his friend with a proper burial if nothing else.

"Excuse me."

A male wolf approached him. Behind him was a cluster of buggies with wolves still behind the wheels, as though they had just arrived while most of the packs prepared to depart.

"What do you want?"

"I just get here. What happened?"

"What happened? We had the Anteaters and Doris just let them go."

"Is Jess all right?"

"Jess?"

"Anteater Jess. Is she alive?"

"She didn't look all that well, but she's alive. Why do you care? Who are you?"

"My name Wolf Ben."

"Oh," said Brad. "Jess was asking about you. She wanted your help."

He nodded. "Then I was too late. I hoped to see her again."
"Whatever," said Brad. "I'm done here."

Chapter 32

She opened her eyes to find herself in a dark place with flashing red lights. She felt the ground beneath her bump up and down and shift from side to side.

"Where am I?" She tried to sit up.

"Whoa, calm down," said Ray. "Take it easy. You shouldn't get up just yet."

"I feel all right."

"Well, I should hope so," said a different voice. "I stitched up your wound and gave you a blood transfusion. Given your youth and strength it probably wasn't even necessary, but we had our instructions to give you only the best treatment."

Jess rubbed her eyes. "We were with a wolf army."

"That was about five hours ago," said Ray. "The Fox Nation detected our flare and dispatched rescue units. One of them picked us up shortly after we reached the salt pan. We're in an armored carrier heading back to the Fox Nation. We're safe."

"Really, I feel fine. I want to sit up."

She felt a hand on her back as she lifted herself up.

"Slowly, if you must," said the other voice.

Ray sat on the troop bench next to a fox with a red cross on her belt. Jess was on a hospital bed. They were indeed in the interior of what she recognized as an armored personnel carrier. Her brother took her hand.

"You're looking better," he said. "This is Doctor Quinn. She's been patching you up."

Her eyes fell to the bandages around her brother's wrist. Ray was quick to follow her gaze.

"I only had a few scratches from our run in with the Bear," he said. "Don't worry about me. We're all more concerned about you."

"I'll need to check your pressure again," said the doctor, "but you seem to be responding well to the transfusion."

Jess looked at the floor to see a tangle of bloody tubes.

"Thank you for saving me."

"No need to thank me. It's my job."

"How did you even have anteater blood on hand?"

The doctor smiled. "The army is nothing if not resourceful. Now hold out your arm."

The fox wrapped the band around her arm and tightened it. As she did, Jess looked to her wounded shoulder, now held together with a new clean line of stitches.

"She did a good job with the suture, didn't she?" asked Ray. "I bet that feels much better than having a wolf sew it up."

"You mean Ben?"

"Yes, Ben."

She moved her arm back and forth. "Really it feels about the same." The doctor scowled. "No insult intended."

"Be that as it may," said the fox, "all things considered, you're in excellent condition. You'll be better with a little rest and recuperation."

"Of course she'll be fine," said Ray. "She took my advice. She knows to always to the hit in the shoulder."

"That's right." Jess chuckled. "It's better than in the neck."

Ray turned to the doctor. "If you're no longer needed here, would you mind giving my sister and me some time alone? We've just been though quite a bit."

"Of course." She stood up and walked over to the door leading to the driver's area. "We still have at least another five hours on the road. Get some sleep if you can."

"Don't disturb us until we get there, if possible."

"As you wish. I'll be in the passenger seat if you need me."

The metal door slammed shut behind her and the siblings were alone.

"See?" asked Ray. "I told you I'd get us back safely."

"Ha. We're not back yet."

"We made the right call to fire that flare."

"Eh, we don't know that. Maybe we would have found Ben."

"And maybe not."

"Whatever," said Jess.

"Do you remember punching that wolf?" asked Ray.

"When?"

"Right after we showed them the Bear's body. Not too long before you passed out."

She laughed. "Did I really?"

"You recall nothing?"

"Only vaguely. Wow, that's one for the record books."

"I'm proud of you."

Jess squeezed her brother's hand and he squeezed hers back. Her hospital bed rattled as the car lurched to a stop. Ray looked around.

"What gives?"

"We can't be there already, can we?" asked Jess.

"Maybe we're just stopping for gas."

The latch unbolted and the door swung open.

"Dammit," said Ray. "Did you not hear me when I said to give us a moment?"

"Is that any way to speak to your Commander-in-Chief?"

"Edward!"

The tall fox was dressed from head to toe in liquids, his old military belt tighter around his waist than it used to be.

"How are my favorite agents doing?"

Ray ran over and gave Edward an enormous hug, which the fox returned.

"It's great to see you, Edward," said Jess. "I'd hug you too, but you know." She gestured to the hospital bed.

Edward patted her on the back. "I'm just glad to see you all right."

"What's with the liquids?" asked Ray.

"Right, I suppose you haven't heard the news. Well, you will soon enough."

"Edward, about the mission."

"Don't worry about that right now. I'll read about it in your report."

"Still," said Jess, "you must be wondering how we managed to piss off that many wolves."

He shrugged. "The thought might have crossed my mind."

"The Bear was behind it."

"Bear Theo?"

"He's the grandson of the Great Bear. He paid the Warlord of the Wolves to have us killed."

"And where is Theo now?"

"He's dead."

Edward nodded. "I see."

"We'll explain everything in our report," said Ray.

"And I look forward to reading it."

In spite of everything, Edward couldn't help but grin at seeing the siblings side by side.

"So anyway," he said, "You wouldn't believe the week I've just had."

Chapter 33

"Are you sure you want to get out here? We're in the middle of nowhere."

"I'm sure," said Sky. "This is definitely the place."

She sat in the passenger seat of a truck, which had just reached the end of a dirt road in the desert. The driver, a grossly overweight bear, looked around with a frown.

"Normally I'd say 'suit yourself' and let you go, but really, this place is deserted. I can't in good conscience drop you off where you'll die of thirst."

Sky pointed toward the horizon. "A few kilometers in that direction are the Sand Monoliths. That's where I'm headed."

"Oh, shoot! Because you're a priest, right? I didn't drive onto the sacred grounds, did I?"

"No, you're fine."

"That's a relief. I can't believe I forgot about this place. It's so far from any major cities."

"Here, I have a few coppers for your next power cell recharge."

"Keep them, I insist. Goodness knows I could use some favor with the gods."

"Then once more, I thank you for your kindness."

"The pleasure is all mine." The driver bowed his head. "May, uh, the blessings of the Celestial Monkeys be upon you."

Sky returned the bow and then stepped out to let her feet once again touch hot sand. She started walking, putting some distance behind her before the truck left and kicked up a cloud of dust.

This was it. In a few hours she'd be at the doorstep of her first assignment, walking the same halls the Celestial Monkeys had tread upon eons ago. She rehearsed the customary greeting for the Grand Master, along with her opening prayer. She was nearly a week late, but Sky wasn't scared. Just before she had left Beggar's Station, word had arrived in town that the anteaters she had helped had made it home safely. The Celestial Monkeys had smiled upon her.

Despite the heat of the day, she felt a chill run through her body. A figure stood on a nearby hill, a few hundred meters in her current direction. From where she stood, it looked like a monkey, although taller and skinnier than most monkeys she knew.

"Hello!" she said.

The figure turned to her for a moment, then jumped away and disappeared behind the hill.

"Wait!"

Sky ran toward the hill, but it was farther away than it looked. It proved to be taller than it looked too. She panted as she reached the top and looked around, but the mysterious figure was gone. There didn't appear to be anywhere to hide, nothing but desert as far as she could see. She looked off in the direction of the Monoliths.

"Huh," she said. "I thought I'd be able to see it by now."

Even, so she couldn't help but laugh to herself. She had come thousands of kilometers to be here. What were a few more?

She reached into her belt and pulled out the sacred dagger. She looked at her reflection in the golden blade, saw her freshly shaven skin and tuft of hair atop her head. She was a priest, a loyal servant of the Celestial Monkeys, who, mysterious as they were, always had a plan for her and a plan for the world. She felt her mark of honor and the stump where her tail used to be. The stump hurt no more.

And with that, she continued toward the horizon, and the midday sun shone more brightly than Sky had ever seen before.

www.ingramcontent.com/pod-product-compliance
Lightning Source LLC
Chambersburg PA
CBHW071141170626
46809CB00002B/718
9780998334905